ASGARD PARK

By

RONALD SIMONAR

EVENTHOR

TO ANNA WHO MADE IT POSSIBLE.

I ASK FOR A HEARING | OF ALL THE HOLY RACES
GREATER AND LESSER | KINSMAN OF HEIMDALLR.

VÖLUSPÁ

Revised second edition.
ISBN 978-91-987452-7-6

TABLE OF CONTENTS

Book 1 - Shequere Avxhiu

Book 2 – Birger Wallenberg

Book 3 – Burton Crane

Book 4 - Heimdallr

Book 1, Shequere Avxhiu

Chapter 1

ACROSS THE SLEEPY BOULEVARD from the Hotel Dajti, a sagging prewar hotel built by Mussolini, two young girls passed the time of day in the shade. They sat on the cool surface of stone that topped a concrete parapet circling the small park. It was the perfect resting place. Behind them lay a tree-lined expanse of wilted grass.

One of them was no more than a kid, dressed up to show she was not, in American jeans and a black sweatshirt. In the summer of 1991, this was not a typical outfit in Albania. The older girl was in her late teens and wore a faded cotton dress with traditional patterns.

Traffic was sparse at midday in Tirana. A few trucks rumbled down the road with growling gearboxes, spewing plumes of exhaust. Under the palms outside a hotel entrance among the straggle of well-waxed cars loitered the hangers-on. They were a blend of fixers, pimps and honest people looking for a break.

The sun beat down with intensity that kept foreigners holed up inside the hotel within easy reach of the only public bar of the communist republic.

Outside, the handshakes were many and conversations went on forever. The fixers had nothing to sell. They were conduits of contacts within a hidebound government, one year after the abandoned one-party state. They were mediators between officials who could deliver nothing but block everything.

Inside the hotel, under the discreet eye of the Sigurimi, the Albanian secret police, officially disbanded in the recent reshuffle, the only currency was dollars. It allowed access to a threadbare restaurant and poorly stocked bar. Down the hall at the far end, the hotel offered the city's only long-distance telephone open to the public, and in working order.

Within the hotel entrance there was a tiny shop that offered a handful of western products for currency. Few locals had the means or courage to enter. They were proud people who could afford nothing. Albanian women of repute were not welcome in The Hotel Dajti. In a nation of traditional values, chaste women knew their place. The only women in sight outside were the two young girls shooting the breeze on the other side of the boulevard.

"You must be careful", said the older girl in Albanian to the Kid, "the foreigners promise you anything, job or visa to their country. Afterward they forget. You have no rights with foreigners."

This was no daunting prospect to the Kid, who frowned and tossed a handful of straws over her shoulder. "For one so old, you know so little, Avxhiu. Foreigners pay in dollars. The Sigurimi has agreed that I can work in there. I have to pay them but maybe I will meet someone later who can get me a visa."

Shequere Avxhiu knew the matter was out of her hands. When the Kid was a baby, her parents had been unable to keep her. The father was a traitor who had spat on the statue of Hoxha. Avxhiu's mother had tended their neighbor's youngest, but the task soon became her daughters.

Now Rakipe Hallidri was the Kid, half-grown and wild with men. That's how she earned her English nickname. Avxhiu knew that her protégé would never get a husband.

"Albanian boys won't marry you if they hear, Rakipe, there is already talk. Everybody knows what goes on in the Dajti Hotel."

"What do I care? Albanian boys are stupid and dirty and unsophisticated."

"Unsophisticated?"

"They don't know how to treat a woman. They are louts. They don't wash and they don't dance. They have no manners, and they know nothing about the world. They are jealous bullies. They lock you in the house. Is that a life? What if I like to fuck foreigners? They know how to treat a woman. Why should I care about Albanian boys?"

"Don't be angry," the older one said softly, and put out a hand, "don't you want kids and a family?" They had this conversation often; too often.

"Come on, Shequere, what home can I get in this dump? Do I want a mean husband without money who drinks all day? How would he get an apartment?"

The older girl did not complain. She lived in a photo studio where her husband hung himself from a sewer pipe in the ceiling last fall. There had been nobody to take over his job, so she did. But the commissions for photographic work from the Sigurimi dried up. Now it was closed.

"Rakipe, you already got a room in Tirana, and you are young and single."

"Yeah, a stupid laundry room with a filthy joint toilet. It's always clogged, and the water never comes. I had to suck the cock of that committee secretary for every tile in that bloody room. There was no heat this winter," the Kid smiled, "the one good thing about the place."

"The cold was?"

"Yeah, it was so cold the bastard wouldn't take off his trousers. He found a warm room for another girl and stopped coming."

Her older companion gave a squeal of merriment and slapped the Kid's shoulder.

"You are impossible!"

"Oh, Shequere, you should see the rooms in the Hotel Dajti. They are warm in winter and there are large beds with clean covers and hot water in every bathroom and the toilets always flush and they are spotless and clean."

"Hot water? You are always boasting."

"Come in and I will show you."

"I am not going into that place!"

"It's another world, Shequere. I can buy anything in there, and you are even sexier than I."

It was an uncommon compliment, and the older girl blushed. She worried that in a short time her scruffy protégé had become stylish, with painted nails and a face that looked almost foreign. The bluish tattoo on the back of her hand gave her away. Foreign women were not that wild.

The Kid had bought western clothes for the first dollars she got at the Dajti, jeans and sweater and a short black leather coat from France. The Kid wanted to enjoy life. Maybe she thought it was almost over. In this, Avxhiu knew better.

"I will find another husband, Rakipe, and have children."

Her resolution was an honest expression but her natural optimism had little foundation in reality. As a widow she was not a virgin, and hardly eligible for a good marriage. Her mother had secretly prayed to God, during the Hoxha years. She had told her that God would save her from evil. In this her mother had been wrong.

"Come in with me, Shequere, and I'll buy you shampoo. It is soap, only a hundred times softer than soap, and it smells like perfume. Can you imagine?"

"Go and buy me this soap. I will wait for you here. Then maybe I'll believe you."

"You promise?"

"Well, at least I will believe you better."

"A deal," said the Kid in English. They shook on it.

She watched the Kid prance across the boulevard in her Italian shoes with high heels. It made Avxhiu proud. She has the bottom of a kid, she thought.

Chapter 2

HARDLY WAS THE KID out of sight before a young man walked across the street.

"How are you, Avxhiu?"

"I am fine, and how are you and your family?" She kept the conversation carefully within the rules of conduct.

"I have a proposition for you, Avxhiu. We can make money together. American money. And later I can get you a visa to Italy. It is little work and loads of fun."

Her brother Spiro and the Kid said that living was easier in Italy. She had no great confidence in their judgment. They believed everything they heard.

"You keep your filthy proposition, Skender Krasnigi, or I tell my brother you asked me to whore for you."

"I only wanted to help, Avxhiu. I heard you were not doing well."

"You should not believe everything you hear."

"You are attractive for a widow. Why not use it while you can?" He shook his head and ambled back to his cronies.

It was always like this. The men she attracted wanted up her skirts or to use her for money. Few husbands would accept that she spoke English. It was for the elite. She had learned English from her late husband. Emir had owned four English novels. They came from his academic father who sat in the Politburo until recently. Emir had taught her to read all four novels, every word, and to pronounce most of them correctly.

The Kid came prancing back across the boulevard. She carried a paper bag. The men gave catcalls and made dirty gestures. The Kid handed her a pink plastic bottle with a lovely round picture. It was a young foreign woman with long blond hair and a halo of flowers.

Best Apple Shampoo. The label made Shequere suspicious. She knew 'best' and 'apple'. "This is for drinking, she complained."

"Zote, how silly you are! Open the bottle. I would not taste it. It is soap but it smells like perfume."

Carefully she screwed off the cap. The fragrance was overwhelming. Its freshness shook her to her core. She had never experienced anything like it.

"Wow!"

"When you use it to wash with, you smell like that. Your lover will want to smell you all over." The Kid gave the older girl a knowing nudge with the elbow.

"Thank you for the shampoo." She embraced her friend. "All right, tell me what the foreigner told you."

This sudden trust caught the Kid a bit off guard. "Well, I don't believe all they say. They boast a lot. I can tell when they are boasting, I'm not stupid."

"So, tell me."

"Yesterday I fucked my first American. Ugh, he was old, but I think he is rich. His father was Albanian, so he's not really American. He wants to change Albania, so it is more like America. He was stupid that way."

"So, what is it like in America?"

"In America they have democracy, and everybody gets money to spend."

"I got Leks but there is nothing to buy."

"That is not the same, they get dollars, and the shops are open for everybody and full of goods."

"What goods, milk and bread?"

"All kinds!"

"Meat and vegetables?"

"You don't get it, Avxhiu: everything! Good coffee and soap and toilet paper and Coca Cola and whiskey and chocolates and cars."

"Don't be silly! How can they buy cars in shops?"

"He said there are big shops full of cars; new shiny cars that nobody sat in. People can go in with dollars and they can buy any car they want to and drive away."

"And you believed this?"

"Maybe he was boasting about the cars." "Cars in shops, I ask you."

"He said cars had telephones in them to use when driving."

"Silly, he'd run out of cable before he got halfway across town."

The Kid sulked a minute for missing the obvious, then brightened. "Anyway, he wasn't a real American, was he? Leonora Bocaj has been to Greece with her family. She says it is better there; plenty of food. They had no foreign money so they could not stay. Her father could not get paid work."

"Then it is the same. If you have dollars, you can buy everything."

"I get dollars from the foreigners. I can go to America. I'm going to live in a house with an electric stove and a hot shower and television. I can show you. There are Italian television sets in the Dajti. One is in color. The picture is not good but there are women dancers!" The Kid lifted her eyes to heaven.

Avxhiu fought the temptation. It was hard because her independence masked a childlike admiration of all things foreign. She admired the self-assured ways of the foreigners. They came and went as they pleased. She had a different relation to them. She almost belonged to them, having mastered their language.

She brightened when she saw the old battered Italian car of her youngest brother roll up, the only one of her rural relatives who made a good living. Spiro helped her out all the time. Her older brothers envied him, but they were burned-out drunkards who faced the same old rut, their brains spoiled by bad liquor.

Spiro had worked hard for what he'd gained. He told her little. The state had imprisoned him for burglarizing the wrong house. Avxhiu did not hold it against him. Without him she would have starved this winter. She had no illusions. Her molars had begun to spoil, the first tangible sign of the decay ahead.

Her brother walked round the car to inspect it. People stole what they could get their hands on. The wing mirrors and the chrome were already gone, and so too the sign that said Fiat. There was nothing left to pilfer from the outside of the car but everything under the hood was in working order. There were excellent mechanics in Albania. They could do wonders with modern machines and Spiro knew many of them. He always had petrol for the car.

Shequere stood up and greeted her brother fondly. He was a few years older, of medium height and slim strong built, and he wore modern clothes.

"I got guts for you!" Spiro put down a rusty bucket on the sidewalk. The handle was a piece of hemp, and the top was covered with cloth. Her brother had contacts in the slaughterhouses outside Kavaja. They traded him guts for Italian cigarettes at fair prices. Shequere felt the hunger stir from its slumber.

"Clean it well. If the electricity is off, wait. Cook it well before you eat it."

As if he had to tell her. Avxhiu lifted the cloth and recoiled from the rancid sour smell.

"This is not fresh. I must cook it at once."

"Stinks worse than an unwashed cock," said the Kid and made a face. She was getting used to better fare, invited by foreigners to eat at the Dajti since her deal with the Sigurimi last week.

"It's bad out in the countryside, sister. Next time I must take friends with guns. There are bands all over. They have no respect. He waved at the car. Someone had scratched a curse 'JA QIFSKA NANON' into the matt green paint with a nail, right across the hood. Spiro put his hand on his sister's shoulder.

"Cousin Fatos asked to tell you he has repaired Emir's motorcycle. It is running again. He will bring it. Pay him nothing. That is between us. Keep the bike inside and cover it. They are stealing everything now."

From his breast pocket he fished out a batch of cards and handed one to each girl. "This is my calling card. It is in English!"

"SPIRO SHITUNI" Director, Skanderbeg Enterprises Ltd. Rruga Siri Kodra 206 Tel:355 42 273 60 Tirana - Albania leave message!

Avxhiu didn't recognize any words from her old English novels except 'leave message' but she knew that directors run state companies and Skanderbeg was the famous national hero who ousted the armies of the Ottoman Empire. She played her curiosity deftly.

"What is this enterprises?"

"My company! Foreigners do business with enterprises. I call mine Skanderbeg Enterprises. Keep the cards!"

Avxhiu was proud of her youngest brother.

"The foreigners all got cards," said the Kid, "some have colored cards. They give them away."

"I need an important favor from you, sister. A powerful businessman is coming to Albania from Germany this week; to meet influential men on private business. They asked me to find an interpreter who does not report to the Sigurimi. I know nobody else who can be trusted and speaks English. He will pay you well in dollars."

The suddenness of the offer shocked Avxhiu, but, of course, she was no informant. There was recognition in that.

"There is nothing else, Spiro? This man will want nothing else from your sister, other than English?"

"Trust your brother! He will want nothing from you but English!"

She didn't know how far she could trust her brother in such matters. His release from camp last year was part of the general amnesty and his group thrived despite the times. Some of her neighbors called them petty criminals. Some said they distributed for an Italian smuggling network. Tongues always wagged whenever anybody made good. She shrugged and thought of faraway places where life was simple.

Chapter 3

IN THE SHADE ACROSS from the Dajti Hotel, Avxhiu made up her mind. "All right!" she told her brother in English with a stately air. She would translate for this German foreigner. Happy to do her brother a favor, she wanted more details, but Spiro had spotted a man coming out of the hotel. Her brother nodded at the Kid.

"This is the man I told you about."

Spiro Shituni left them to cross the limpid boulevard in the sunlight.

Avxhiu saw him shake hands with a tall old foreigner on the hotel steps.

"Who is this foreigner?" She asked the Kid.

"A rich foreign businessman: maybe he wants to fuck a young girl. Spiro is helping them out because the old man didn't want anything to do with the girls in the hotel."

"But you work in the Dajti?"

"He doesn't know that. Some of the tourists think the Sigurimi will spy on them and blackmail them."

"Do they?"

"Spy sure, but I don't think they blackmail. They have always spied on people. Spiro says they have nothing else to do. They like to watch."

"That is disgusting! Where will you take this man?"

"Spiro will sort it out," the Kid's voice was wistful. "I wish they paid me for talking, like you, "especially the older ones." Avxhiu smiled, Rakipe was thinking of the businessman from Germany she was to translate for.

Spiro guided the tall foreigner out of the afternoon furnace to the shade of a tree. Between fifty and sixty, he wore a dark suit with tiny white stripes. Avxhiu had never seen a suit that fitted a man so well. Wearing a spotless white shirt and colorful silk tie, the man was perfectly superior and sure of himself as only foreigners and State directors could be.

They stood up to greet this new visitor to their poor country, and her brother introduced him to the Kid. The man had fine soft hands, and the strange cuffs on his shirtsleeves were joined by a gold link. And he had a big gold watch.

It was the first time Avxhiu had met a foreigner up close. She would have to talk to him, since neither Spiro nor the Kid had any English to speak of. This made her uneasy. She stood away from the covered rusty bucket of smelly guts and placed her newly won bottle of shampoo in front of her. He could see she was no peasant.

The foreigner turned to her.

"And this lovely creature is?" His voice was mellow and clear. The words he expected none of them to grasp rang in her ears. They were the first words spoken to her by a native of this great tongue. To her amazement, she understood, and her natural assurance trickled back.

"Shequere Avxhiu, nice to meet you, yes please, sir."

"Ah, what a wonderful surprise, you speak English. I have been here ten days and you are the first woman I can talk to," his hand was large and strong, and he did not let go of hers, "not counting the Sigurimi spies."

"Thank you, sir!" She was not sure why she was thanking him. "Could I invite you over for a drink at the Dajti? The heat is unbelievable out here." She withdrew her hand sharply and he immediately let go. He was well mannered. There were drops of perspiration on his chin.

"No thank you please, sir. I am younger sister for Spiro. I am good girl!"

"I am sorry. I meant no disrespect. You are a beautiful young woman. I understood your brother wanted to introduce me to someone. I didn't know who. I made a mistake. You must forgive me."

"I forgive you very much, sir."

Charles Grenville was Canadian. The director of a profitable mining company, he was long married with four grown daughters, all of them older than this nymph. What a striking young woman; unpainted, in a simple cotton dress; Eve in a Garden of Eden cursed by the ideologies of misguided men. Her apparent innocence went well with the delicious craving that flushed through his body. Grenville was thrilled by a lust so long dormant. In his married life he seldom cheated on a wife whom he quietly loved. Aside from the odd lapse in fidelity, he prided himself in being a man of unassailable virtue. It was his strength in the real world. This was not the real world. Maybe he had one more experience coming.

"Would you possibly have dinner with me tonight at the Dajti? with your brother of course. This is a lonely place, mademoiselle!"

"Talk slow please. You pay dinner for all people, yes?" "Of course, I will!"

"I ask brother and girlfriend, sir."

As the teenager spoke rapidly to the others, Charles Grenville tried not to stare.

"My brother ask if you want Rakipe to come, yes?"

The brother was probably a pimp for the Sigurimi, and the kid was too young; her youth so insistent that it shone through the layers of cheap cosmetics, put on with a bricklayer's trowel. He was wary of accepting that offer on so many levels. It put him in a bind.

"She is your friend, is she?"

"Avxhiu best girlfriend, yes."

"Well, as your friend she is welcome to join us."

This was a problem that would be easily solved with a twenty-dollar bill after dinner. In this hermetically sealed nation, there seemed less need to hold his every move against the mirror of middle-class morality.

"We say all right to dinner. We thank you very much so. You have card, please, sir?"

Grenville pulled out his leather wallet and handed her an embossed card. She glanced up at him in wonder and their eyes met. Looking back at the card, she started to blush uncontrollably.

That blush made old Charles Grenville's day.

"Shall we make it six o'clock? I will await you by the entrance." He wiped the sweat from his eyes and lips, and tasted salt in his mouth.

The others wanted cards too. Grenville handed them out. He felt safe with his budding decadence. It had caught him unawares. The paparazzi on the Riviera would not snoop around here, even if they could. Visas were hard to get outside the country. The tourists here were expatriates with families on the inside to bribe officials to obtain their papers. Others who cleared the hurdles were gritty pros bred in a shady flora and unburdened by ethical baggage. This was no place for tenderfoots.

Pressed by the economic collapse, the government was desperately seeking foreign capital and new technology. They wanted to capitalize on 20 million tons of chromite reserves in the mountains to the north; a vital source of currency. But what should have been a profitable visit was being sabotaged by corrupted officials. The ideas of their government on equity financing were more obsolete than their mining and smelting techniques. The State had no intention of sharing the profits with anybody.

He felt overdressed and out of place. The unpleasant odor from a covered bucket to the side troubled him. He gave the three youngsters a spirited smile. He knew it was a perfect smile, but it felt like an echo from some parallel universe; he didn't know if it got through. Wooing this magnificent young woman felt more real than government intrigues but the problem was the same. The secret police would be in the way. They had already executed hundreds of Central Committee members. The body count of ordinary citizens was anybody's guess.

It would take a few days for the Lehman Brothers in New York to turn down the proposed equity venture. Winning this girl was a thrilling thought. Doing it with the Sigurimi looking over his shoulder was not.

Book 1, Shequere Avxhiu

Chapter 4

ON THE STEPS OF THE Hotel Dajti, it didn't pass Charles Grenville unnoticed that Shequere Avxhiu had mixed feelings about entering. The three of them had arrived in her brother's car at six. With the promise of evening coolness, a few youngsters were already milling about the park. As he greeted the girl profusely on the steps where everyone could see, he noted their spiteful eyes on her back.

He found her on virgin ground inside, and wearing the same cotton dress, probably her best. How easy it would be to dazzle this girl with quality clothes. None were available. The scruffy setting and threadbare carpets, the dull seedy upholstery, the chipped crockery, and mismatching cutlery insulted his senses.

The Kid, with her easy puppyish ways, was out to claim her price from the start. Grenville felt awkward to be the sexual target of one so gracelessly minor. With bird in hand, instead of indulging, he found himself for the first time in his life trying to renege on a deal.

As the evening wore on, the restaurant became a noisy place. The privacy of the table was tested by broad-faced Balkan men in various stages of sobriety, claiming to be friends of the family. They all wished to meet the rich foreigner and tell him, through Avxhiu's halting version, about their ambitions, their profitable empires and how they all had hated Hoxha. It became a religious ritual. They bided their time, waited, and watched for an opening at his table. They scurried up to kiss the cardinal's hand, to confirm an alliance, like backward boys of a favorite family. And Avxhiu loved being at the center; eyes gleaming on translating their homage.

Throughout the Dajti dinner, Grenville, trained in the steel-trap subtleties essential to a wealthy Canadian mining director, skillfully cast his nets for the older girl. With the studied air of an afterthought, he offered her a temporary position as an interpreter. The salary would be fifty dollars a day. He had meant to say a hundred but held back. Not that he was infected by a grudging hand; offering too much would signal hidden motives. Perhaps fifty dollars a day was a small fortune in this wretched place.

It was in fact such a princely sum that nobody put his offer down to professional needs, except one young woman infatuated with a newfound skill. It went against every grain in her body to question the source from which such blessings flowed. The dark suspicious look of her brother was nonetheless duly noted by Grenville.

A country with Muslim undertones hid the trade, but sleek young buttocks came a dime a dozen in this place. The Kid had a gross body language that repulsed him, if not as much as her sensuality attracted. The older girl filled him with more abstract longing. He had not even brushed against her. It astounded him to find a dormant feeling so vividly alive.

"What is chromite, please, sir?"

"It is a mineral vital to the production of stainless steel." "What is mineral, sir?"

He saw that any sensible answer to that mixed up enough ingredients to trigger several follow-ups.

"A special metal found in rocks, like iron."

He saw another question forming and made a preemptive strike. He would love to soak her sponge but all in good time.

"Look here, Avxhiu, I need someone to step in when official interpreters are unavailable. I don't need you to translate de jure or turgid official texts but rather to ease my contacts with people; small talk, like now."

Familiar with the many charming gaps in her English, Grenville had no intention of actually using her linguistic services. Many officials he dealt with spoke halting English or used State interpreters. If she agreed, he could wine and woo her for days. If nothing came of it, he would be richer for the experience.

Having eaten voluptuously, Shequere Avxhiu had become the slightest bit tipsy. Albanians delighted in drinking your health. The schnapps was strong. She had hardly touched it, but her forever-blushing face beamed. It was a fine job offer, and she conferred with her drunken brother.

"If Avxhiu take job, I must take little time to interpret for Spiro business friend, yes please?"

It turned out that the girl needed some uncertain time off to translate for a visiting German businessman. It was a provision easily granted. Smiling his assent, he noted how awestruck she was by her bargaining power; how smoothly this was going. His crush on her did nothing to change the cynicism that came with age. That girl would be defeated by any complex text. He raised a tumbler to toast their association and felt the Kid's hand slip up his thigh to crudely massage his crotch under the stained tablecloth.

It made him lose what lust he had felt towards that little pixie. For a moment he wished he was back in the real world.

Chapter 5

THE SMELL OF DEVELOPER and fixer still clung to what passed for Avxhiu's home. Charles Grenville found himself sitting in a run-down crumbling cubicle that once upon a time had doubled as photo-studio and apartment.

The days had gone by in a heady blur. Grenville had loved her company, but the young woman had ended their agreement in the face of his attempts to win her. To let her go without compensation was cruel. Succeeding in eluding his Sigurimi shadows, he had tracked her down to this run-down rut. Sitting on her single, rickety chair, staring at bare walls painted blue in the early days of Hoxha, he still wanted her. It was no longer a physical urge. Was he compromising her? Having a foreign man in her home at night might brand her.

"I am leaving tomorrow on the flight to Rome."

His eyes wandered a rusty iron pipe along the flaking ceiling to seek out marks of the rope where the husband of this raven-haired child had hung himself. There was no reason to prolong his stay. Her dreams of a better life had no tangible connection with reality. Dreams of the good life rarely did. He would make one last pitch.

"Sweet Avxhiu", he said carefully, "accept my offer. I will set you up in a private apartment in Paris."

"I have apartment", she said making a flippant gesture with her slender hand, and pride he did not understand.

"Avxhiu, a good apartment in Paris costs a million dollars or more. Hoxha studied there. He could not afford it. You love books. I will buy you books to read. You'll have a good apartment, the best food in the world, fine clothes, money in your pocket. Everything you dreamt of."

"And old man in my bed."

Grenville understood that the first tiny cracks were showing in her defenses; that she was angry and needed to fight an unwanted temptation.

With her back to him, she was boiling water on a one-ring stove. He could no longer let her run the slack. He played the ace up his sleeve.

"If you like, Avxhiu, you can take the Kid with you. The two of you will love Paris. The Kid wants to go. I asked her and she said yes. I don't want her, but you need a companion. I can get both of you a visa and we can fly out together. Don't stay behind, alone."

"I'm not alone. I have brother Spiro!"

Grenville got up and crossed the floor. Being tall, he towered over this fine creature in her flat worn shoes. A slim white neck above a flowered cotton dress smelled of shampoo. Carefully he reached out and touched her waist from behind with both hands. Sensing her resistance, he made it a fatherly touch.

"Sweet Avxhiu, your brother has asked me to get him a job in Canada."

"Can you do this, please?"

"Yes, of course, a well-paid job because he is your brother; and for you I will do anything!"

"I don't fuck foreigners," she said to say something.

Grenville smiled. She must have picked up the phrase from the Kid whom he fucked on that first night. There was no escaping that. A deal was a deal. He had walked brother and sister out into the warm summer night. Waving them off, he had taken the Kid to his room. Since then, it was a frantic race between age and days ebbing towards departure, doubtless with the Sigurimi watching. The Kid was a force of nature with no boundaries, an exhilarating and occasionally uplifting experience. Her persistence exhausted him. The smell of her slim adolescent body after a bath, her childlike looks with the cosmetics gone. The way she moved around a room like a half-grown. She was none of that when pleasing him. He had never thought anyone could go so far to please, even for money. What an odd discovery after so many righteous decades.

Grenville was not much for gossip. He had listened to boardroom discussions on forbidden pleasures. For many colleagues, it was humdrum routine. He was the bigger fool for it. But Avxhiu was no model short-shifted by falling demand, looking for a sugar daddy to keep her in designer clothes and sustain exclusive habits. She was no fading flower clinging to an agent's scrapbook. It was enormously pleasing.

Grenville thought of Helene, his beloved wife, formerly Miss Kimberley. It was an oddly impersonal thought of a woman with whom he had shared a life. He had discovered a boardroom joke he would never tell; life sucks if you are married to a woman who doesn't. And he reflected about his Grace the Archbishop, his lifelong friend. It evoked no remorse. On the contrary, if the Lord saw fit to smite him with the supreme sentence for this spell of unprotected carousing, he could abstain from the world and nurture a precious memory. Not that he was religious; he went through the motions with friends and family. Even the thought of his sweet granddaughter stirred no guilt: Laura was years older than the child who had fondled his private parts, trying patiently to work the miracle of life, and painfully succeeding at times. They would all think him a dirty old man if they knew, but for a few days he had been a happy one.

The heart of his problem was that Avxhiu had proved too wise and chaste to succumb to his machinations. In a way her steadfastness pleased him above all else. No vice president would keep a downtown flat with her installed as a prop for a rainy night. He tried to fuse the memory of the Kid's slim body onto the memory of another face, another smile. A composite secret assembled from the Kid's limbs and Avxhiu's noble face. There was no contradiction in this, he felt. Two ideals fused into one; the earthly lover who greedily nestles in your darkest dreams, and the image of unattainable innocence.

"I am sincere, sweet Avxhiu. If you come with me, you will never want for anything."

"If Grenville good man, please go away, but first I give coffee, yes."

He left her by the little stove that was her pride and returned to sit heavily on the wobbly chair.

"We drink coffee together, yes please." She bowed as she handed him a small, cracked cup of black boiled coffee.

"You wouldn't have sugar and milk?"

He saw that deep blush again, close to tears. No, of course not; how could she have sugar and milk?

"You drink Avxhiu coffee?"

"All right, sweetheart."

The wretched coffee was like something scraped off a new asphalt road. He toasted his secret love in this nauseating brew. There was this certain gleam in her eye; dark and mystical eyes that twinkled of sweet-natured perfection; eyes to occupy his secret memory.

"Sweet Avxhiu."

He studied her face in the barren light from the single naked bulb in the ceiling. She studied him back through dark pools of beauty. A strange silence had descended on him. He wanted to say something but did not know what. A terrible pain had spiked his stomach. He saw a star swim in her unearthly eyes and dared not breathe. It seemed that his entire sensory system was drowning in a sea of pain. But his eyes enjoyed her face.

In the end, all that remained was the sparkle in her eye, a reflection of a barren bulb. It swam in his secret sea of fading light until the last twinkle died.

Avxhiu dared not sit on the bed for fear that he might come and sit beside her. She disliked him intensely, his velvet arrogance. His unwillingness to listen, a trait he hid behind an attentive ear. Making him coffee: a gift from Spiro, she was unsure how much sleeping medicine to put in. She needed to calm a lovesick man, not put him to sleep, and she was not going to let him make love to her. Spiro kept his drops in a can in the corner among the photo chemicals. The Kid had told her Spiro used them to drug people to rob them. What did Rakipe know? Spiro was always pulling her leg. The electricity was on, and she hoped it would last. The lamp had expired last time she used it. She was out of oil and did not wish to sit in the dark with a foreigner. The neighbors were suspicious enough. If he tried to have his way, she would not dare call out. They would not believe her.

And why was she even thinking about his lurid offer? It was Spiro and the Kid. Accepting, she could give them a future, but she recoiled from her part in that future; from the idea of kissing these thin colorless lips.

Memories of recklessly careening down potholed roads together on her husband's bike with freedom on their faces, scattering flocks of chicken were different. In the mountains, they spent time off the road to make love. She ached for the feeling that life was going somewhere. Was this man her rope?

Avxhiu watched him go to sleep on that small chair. The incisive eyes grew soft in his pale, friendless face. This caused the first stirrings of panic. His pensive stare had nothing of its usual directness. The foreigner might think she planned to rob him.

"Maybe I go to Paris, Mr. Grenville, if Kid comes. Please no sleep here, sir."

He did not close his eyes. The grand old head edged out of balance to the left; in the direction that he combed his thin well-groomed hair. Avxhiu thought he was going to be sick. She reached out deftly and relieved him of the coffee cup. With two cups on her cupboard, this was the better one. If he was going to throw up, it would be a mess: the water was not on.

He didn't. Instead, he gently toppled over and tumbled onto the floor, slamming his head into its chipped bricks. His chin took the impact, but he did not make a sound. She knew it must have hurt. With the coffee cup in her hand, she was too slow to prevent it. His mouth was open in an ugly scowl, a familiar snarl of dim-witted pain and apprehensive distrust. Alarmed, she found it unsettling on the face of a rich foreigner.

"Mr. Grenville, you the winner. Maybe I go to Paris in your bed like Madame Bovary." It was in one of her books.

In spite of her eloquence, the man on the floor was unmoved by this tactical surrender. Grenville had lost all interest in matters of the flesh. Avxhiu knew that this was not a healthy way to greet a conquest. She put out her hand to nudge a chest that no longer heaved. She bent down to put her ear to an open mouth. It offered no material temptations. This was all wrong.

It was how she felt when she found Emir hanging from the pipe in the corner, the familiar shock of suspended disbelief. This man was dead. Raising herself from the floor she stood motionless for a long time and stared at the distinguished foreigner who was no longer promising anybody a way out.

A little later, into her maze of thoughts there came a familiar sound associated with joy. It was the sound of a motorcycle. She fought to fit it into this calamity. The knock on the door brought her to her senses. Her cousin Fatos had come to return Emir's motorcycle; as good as new, Spiro said. He would want coffee or a drink if she had any to offer. To send him away was rude after all his labors with the bike. She must not let him in. Allegations of promiscuity are better than accusations of murder. Shaking off the cotton dress, she stepped out of it and grabbed the bed sheet to drape over her shoulders, as she stepped outside. She took care that her cousin did not see the body on the floor as she whispered to him that she had a man in her bed. "Sigurimi," she added for good measure, "come with the bike tomorrow and I will have something good for you."

Had Spiro lied about the sleeping drops? The Sigurimi had closed the prison camps, but people said prisons were no better, particularly for women. She studied the pipe in the ceiling, but her courage betrayed her.

Besides, the Sigurimi had impounded the rope.

Chapter 6

IT WAS NIGHT IN Tirana. Avxhiu waited outside the house where her brother had his apartment until Spiro returned to get more stuff to sell. When she told him about the dead foreigner, he was furious at her for using his medicine drops. Nobody would believe that his sister poisoned and killed a foreigner on her initiative, using his poison. Otherwise, he took it like a rock.

"Little sister, if you want a man to live, you use no more than two or three drops," he confided.

She was relieved that Spiro Shituni did not abandon his favorite sister. More important, he knew what to do. The two of them walked back to the store. The foreigner was dead all right, on the floor where she left him.

"Serves him right, trying to screw my little sister."

Rakipe must have told him he wanted to, Avxhiu thought dejectedly. She had not dared. Her brother was unfazed by the tragedy and went briskly about his business. He removed the chemical bottles from the chipped white enameled tray on the kitchen table and placed it on the floor by the body. Then Spiro went through Grenville's pockets and put his personal stuff in the tray, the one Emir used for developing photos in.

In went the keys, the pens, the passport, and tablets. As he rifled through a wallet, her brother looked happier with his task.

"Nine hundred and twenty dollars!"

"He was to pay me two hundred dollars for my second week as interpreter, I got two hundred for the first," Avxhiu hastened to point out.

"Good shoes and expensive clothes." Spiro started to remove the clothes.

"What are you doing? don't take off his clothes. What will people think?" Then it occurred to her that this was no longer of primary interest. Her brother slipped the gold watch off Grenville's wrist and put it on his own. The fine band of gold was a little wide. He smiled broadly and started to remove the belt and trousers. Two golden cufflinks echoed in the tray.

"We can sell this. We got to pay the Sigurimi to look the other way. I don't think this is enough!"

Her brother was right; they had only themselves to think of. They had to survive.

"He had a computer briefcase," she said quickly, "I saw him use it; IBM PS/2 L40Sx," she quoted from memory. The old man had put it by the bed.

Spiro weighed the laptop in his hand. He lifted the lid to study the keyboard and the screen.

"It is used to play games with. I will give this to a friend in the Sigurimi. I don't think they care that you killed the foreigner, but they need somebody to blame. He was after our mining industry. I am told that the Sigurimi wants to share the mines with our Italian friends."

Relieved at the prospect of salvaging some future, she started to help Spiro. She pulled at the shirt while he rolled the body over. The old foreigner was heavy, but the shirt came off. They both saw the broad beige belt. It was of thin cloth and wound around his waist above the shorts that her brother would take off later out of respect for her.

"Rakipe told me he had this belt. He never let it out of his sight," said Spiro. His voice was hoarse. In confusion, Avxhiu was affronted that he spoke to the Kid about her affairs with men. The Kid was family.

"Rakipe thought he kept money in it."

The back of Spiro's mind was buzzing. His fingers had unhooked the elastic belt. He felt nimbly for the paper inside. It didn't feel like money, more like bits of wood. There were two compartments with a zipper on top. His nervous fingers unzipped one; it was more money than he had ever seen, big new bills, thousands; tens of thousands. In the end, it wasn't the manslaughter that got to him, or the awful smell of a corpse that had begun to soil its shorts. It was the money. Swiftly he folded the belt and tucked it under his own.

"I don't think we need to worry about the Sigurimi. The money in there is enough."

He had never seen anything like it. It was a fortune. It was his ticket abroad. He could set up his bar in Greece, or a restaurant in Italy, with Albanian girls on the side, taking the Kid along for starters. Their days of poverty were over.

Everybody pissed on the poor man. Spiro chuckled; the foreign bastard had bribed his way around and lived like a king. He had paid extra for the Kid to go behind the back of the Dajti, as if the Sigurimi did not know. The man was wise not to use a bank; but the nerve, to carry all this money around.

As her brother rolled the foreigner's body into the blanket from the bed and dragged him up into it, Avxhiu hoped wretchedly that the smell would wash. It struck her that the honorable Charles Grenville had achieved the task he had set out for – to lie naked in her bed. She failed to see humor in it, much as did Grenville. Scared of staying behind with a corpse, she followed her brother with the loot to Spiro's apartment. From there they walked over to the embassy street where Spiro kept his car. He had a deal with the guards who watched the street. She saw them smoking in the dark. It was a good arrangement, with vandalism on the increase. They drove to the Hoxha museum that would soon be turned into what foreigners called a disco, a dancing place. Spiro had a deal to take care of their liquor deliveries. Leaving her in the car, he returned with a couple of trusted friends. They were rough men, a little drunk; not the sort to be around for a young woman at night. They squeezed into the small car behind her. And with speed and routine that amazed her, they left her alone by an empty bed.

When Avxhiu woke, the dismal prospects besieged her. Thoughts of Albanian prisons were never taken lightly. For days she had eaten voluptuously at the foreigner's expense. Back in the old rut with nothing but subhuman existence; the blame was hers. It would be unwise to spend the two hundred dollars of American money that she kept in her sock. It would cause suspicion. If only she had let Grenville take her out of the country and put her up in Paris where she could have left him. He had not been a violent man. He would have let her go.

When the electricity came on in the late afternoon, she cooked the latest batch of guts her brother brought, hoping the power would last for it to cook properly. She was proud of her one plate stove. It was a wedding gift from the Avxhiu family. They were well connected in the party. With the luxury of an electric stove there was no need to scrounge for wood.

Most of the trees in the city had disappeared last winter, after the government stopped handing out coal. Even the motorcycle was a gift from his family, property of the Geophysical Department of State. It had been Emir's to do with as he pleased. Avxhiu decided to send word to her cousin Fatos; to keep the bike for a while. After repairing the machine, it would please him to do so.

Later that morning in the breadline at the State bakery, she felt exposed. There was talk of the police looking for a missing foreigner. Had her neighbors seen something? She got half bread for her ration slip. It had slipped her mind last night to reclaim the dollars that the foreigner owed her. There was enough in that belt for her brother to pay both her wages for that second week, and the Sigurimi. They were selling sardines in one of the State stores and she waited two hours to buy a tin. After days of luxury, it was tough to focus on basic survival. The best thing about her overcooked meals at the Dajti, ladled onto the plates in tasteless brown sauce, was that there was always enough; all you could eat.

In need of someone to confide in, she went to visit the Kid. She'd be asleep after her night at the Dajti. The Kid was the only other person she could trust. They had both worked for the foreigner, each in their way. They could give one another an alibi if needed.

In the cramped gangway between the toilet and the old laundry room at her door, she heard the excited sounds of lovemaking. The Kid had a customer. Avxhiu retired to the shade outside the house. After a while, when nobody came out, she went into the hallway and listened by the door. There was talk, and she recognized the voice of her brother. She pounded on the door. There was panic inside, whispers and goings-on, and she realized that her brother would be afraid it might be the police, because of last night.

"It is Avxhiu!"

After a while the door opened. Her brother was tucking his shirt into his trousers. He obviously felt none of her letdown.

"Shame on you! How long had this been going on?"

The Kid, half clothed, was happy as a lark. It did not bother her a bit. "Shame on you Spiro, she is family."

"No, she isn't, Avxhiu, you are my sister, she's not." "How long has this been going on?"

"Come one, little sister, it's none of your business!"

The Kid chimed in, "don't be angry Avxhiu; it's been years, since I was twelve or something. Spiro asked me not to tell you." She crossed the room to get a cigarette. "I heard you killed old Charlie last night. You should have taken him into your bed instead. He could buy visas for all of us."

Now it was Spiro's turn to be angry. "Don't say that. My little sister is no whore!"

"And I am?"

"Sure, you are. You are the best whore in Tirana," and now all three of them laughed. Perhaps it wasn't so bad after all. They could still be a family, just different.

"Spiro is taking me with him to Greece to live and work. You can come too," the Kid beamed.

"Is this true, Spiro?"

"Yes, I was going to tell you this afternoon. We will leave a week after the German businessman comes, the man you are to translate for. Will you come with us?"

"The money from the foreigner, was it enough?"

"Most of it goes to the Sigurimi. They also think we should leave the country. I had money saved."

"The foreigner owed me two hundred dollars. Will you pay me, Spiro?"

"Yes, all right."

"Then I'll go with you to Greece!"

They all embraced, and Avxhiu discovered in mild panic that the smell of love still clung to the pair of them. "Do you think the police will find out that Grenville came to my house last night?"

"I doubt it. The man trusted nobody. He asked the Kid for the address and walked from the Dajti. The Sigurimi lost him. So how can the police know? Maybe somebody robbed him and buried him. He had only himself to blame. Maybe he left the country. If somebody finds out that he visited you, say that he left after one cup of coffee. You are a widow. You did not want a foreigner in your home at night. The police will understand."

"You paid the police?"

"The Sigurimi; and if the police start to bother you, they will know who is boss," her brother smiled at her. "Foreigners are so stupid," he added.

Avxhiu had the uneasy feeling that foreigners were not stupid. And there were too many turncoats in her country. A bribe only got you a breathing space.

She wished they were already in Greece.

Chapter 7

SHEQUERE AVXHIU HAD FOR the second time in her life washed her body with Best Apple Shampoo, a gift from the Kid. She used it as perfume and had most of it left. Wet and fresh smelling, she stepped out of the small wooden barrel she used for washing and dishing. The soapy trail of water across the brick-laid floor avoided the spot where a Canadian mining director made his peace with the world. Putting on a clean well-worn dress, she tucked her American money into the white stocking.

As the days passed, her fear settled. Her brother Spiro had been right about the police. They came to ask about the rich foreigner who had disappeared, but their hearts were not in it. What did they care for a foreigner who wished to profit from the Albanian people? Was she not an honest widow, an interpreter? They accepted her coffee and were grateful for a drink of Skenderbeu Konjak, a bottle she had bought for this eventuality. Any spirit would have done but Avxhiu had a proud heart. Besides, the police knew that Skenderbeu Konjak was impossible to get on the free market. It showed she had contacts. She had paid ten dollars to Emir's family for the bottle; a hefty price. The family was clinging on. They had a new member of parliament. They were all liberals now. The police had chosen to believe her.

The trip to Greece, with Spiro and the Kid, was drawing closer. Today she would translate for another foreigner. She had promised Spiro. The man was important to his business. Her brother had offered her service as an interpreter to show his importance. But could he guarantee that this new foreigner behaved?

Spiro came to pick her up. They drove in his car to the Ndermarrja Kartografike Company. The foreigner had set up office in the state printing house, a concrete complex on the outskirts of the city, surrounded by high walls. A straggle of farmers had gathered at the side of the road to barter scruffy sheep and chickens. In the yard outside the whitish building, a few trucks stood parked, and a couple of private cars.

They went up to the second floor where she sat on a bench and waited. Spiro knew everybody. He was laughing, but he was nervous, she could tell.

She realized how important the foreigner was when she recognized a minister being led into his provisional office for an audience. People like that did not go out of their way to meet foreigners, not unless there was a lot of money involved.

There was also a member of parliament. Avxhiu knew that these people spoke English. She was not needed yet. The effeminate concierge of the Hotel Dajti slipped into the office. That man had his nose in everything. The Kid had told her that he organized the girls at the Dajti, and that he was a cruel man.

The foreigner kept them waiting for hours. It was evening and everybody had gone when the man who guarded his door signaled to Spiro. They talked briefly and Spiro came over.

"Go in now, little sister!"

"And you!"

"No, I have an errand."

"You leave your little sister alone with a strange man at night?"

"Don't fuss, Avxhiu, go and do your work. He will not lay a finger on you. And don't ask him to pay." This was about the tenth time Spiro stressed the point. "Tomorrow you interpret for him at our Camorra meeting in Lushnja. Then he pays in American dollars. Go in now!"

The room was large and stifling in spite of windows thrown open to the barely cooler evening air. The foreigner, Helmut Mayer, was neither old nor young. Broad and handsome, his hair was almost golden. It was fool's gold because there was something unsettling about him. He was clearly bothered by the sweltering heat, fumbling with a large typewriter. The sullen atmosphere made her tense. She noticed a healing three-fingered scratch on his chin, no doubt a woman. He did not acknowledge her presence. It was a form of slight she knew well.

At long last, he pointed to a chair. "You are to translate this agreement into Albanian, - when I am finished." His English was different, but she understood and took heart from that. This was how important officials put people in their place. This foreigner was a disappointment, but he was a forbidding man. He rose a few times. She noted he was tall and well built. By the window, he poured red wine out of a foreign bottle and drank it from a long-stemmed glass like the ones they had at the Dajti. Then he turned on the desk lamp and continued writing without offering her anything.

She felt in over her head. Spiro had said he was German; did he write bad English? Were there words in his document she had never seen? She waited and watched the man type. Her confidence faded with the light.

Helmut Mayer was aware of the friction with the Italian Camorra. The Italian infusion of aid had reached over one hundred million dollars. The Italians wanted the biggest cut. Last March, the government signed a 500-million-dollar oil prospecting contract with the German Denimex and the European Union was also throwing taxpayers' money into the pot. It was becoming a big bone of contention. The Albanian Camorra must sever its ties to the Naples organization. He had put down on paper a firm agreement on procedures for funneling aid and western reconstruction funds into their hands. Now that this European country was about to enter the democratic fold, massive funds would be forthcoming.

As he battled with the antiquated typewriter with its old keyboard, silently cursing missing characters and illegible smears, his mind drifted. The Berlin folder was a serious blow. It was a list of former STASI agents on the inside track in the West; people who would yield to pressure. The loss of the list was not a problem. Culling the names from the original sources was easy. The problem was that, in hands of the BND in Bonn, they were worse than worthless. The information could be used against his people. It was a stroke of luck that the woman had given the general her name. It was on the shortlist of visa applicants to the former East Germany; the last list before the fall; people to arrest on their next visit. It allowed him to catch up with her the same night, to get her exactly where he wanted her, on the stove, ready to talk.

The woman had died on him. It had never happened before. It had slipped out of his hands. He had not found the file and had to direct the leadership to prepare new files for all the names, branding the former agents as traitors instead of collaborators. It could be useful if accusations became public. The leadership had the equipment, the paper, and the stamps to make it stick. To play that hand would pose several delicate problems.

He stroked his chin and stared at the teenager. What a sullen race this was. The scratch was healing. It was careless to leave his genetic prints in that woman, even under her nails, but they did not have his DNA profile. Interpol would have his prints on record but not his identity. He had left no prints. Ans as the thought formed in his mind, it struck him with terrifying clarity. The tumbler. He never removed the tumbler. He had forgotten because the woman died on him.

Helmut Mayer had come far in a short time. The Eastern Block was ripe for entrepreneurs. The fall of the Curtain had left many comrades in trouble;

some in misery. It was a matter of survival to tie organizations together as a shelter against the changing tide.

He finished typing up the text. Despite the missing characters and the smears, it was legible. The girl was a supposed to be a top translator, but he didn't trust these people. Mayer had seen his share of incompetence, learned to swim in it; but never like this. He handed her the two pages of typewritten text and fixed his eyes on her.

"I want this translated word for word, meaning for meaning. You can change nothing. If there is any doubt, you ask me. Do not guess!"

He placed her at the desk to work in the light and watched her read the agreement. She was sweet, in a plain sort of way. Her innocence held no appeal. The irritation rose in him on seeing her problems. Was this the idiot offspring of some committee member?

Avxhiu was close to panic. The text was packed with words she had never seen; she gained no insight into its meaning. The words she recognized were out of context: the text went on and on about financing regional development through limited joint companies and ventures with hidden stock options for prospective investors who arranged third-party equity capital. None of it made any sense.

She started to ask but backed away. The German was not the least helpful. He was angry and agitated, not at all like Grenville. She soldiered on to introduce a grain of sense into the mess, hopeful that he would not notice the difference. But the foreigner was not stupid. What he did unnerved her. When she had finished, he retrieved his text and told her to translate her Albanian version back into English. Verbatim, he said; whatever that meant.

There was nothing to do. She bit her lip, threw down her pencil, and lowered her head, flushed with shame, listening to him rave about her people. That she might be in physical danger occurred to her first when he went out into the hall and said something to the guard watching the door. There was nobody else in the hallway. The German locked the door to prevent her from leaving.

"Please to be polite, thank you sir. My brother Spiro Shituni not like men speak bad to sister, please sir."

"That punk is your brother? This is a family affair?" The foreigner laughed in a disgusted tone. Avxhiu did not know what a punk was, but relaxed. He knew her brother.

Mayer abruptly changed subject. "Comrade, do they have an electric stove in this printing house? The sort you cook food on?"

The foreigner smiled at her for the first time, his flat eyes full of wonder. The man had wanted to put the fear into her. Pleased that his attention had drifted from her bungled translation, Avxhiu smiled for the first time.

"Yes, I think so. You cook, sir?"

Their eyes met.

"I'm more of a barbeque man but a stove will do fine. Will you join me?"

It was at this precise moment, she later recalled, that it happened; the dull eyes gazing into hers began to lose focus. They stared right through her as a bewildered look passed over his face. A horrible expression took over, asphyxiating panic. The contours of his face harked to some unspeakable terror.

"Nein! Mein Gott! Nein!"

The wineglass with the long stem dropped from his hand and broke with a tinkle on the concrete floor. Avxhiu recalled the cup she had so deftly removed from Charles Grenville as he died. The unassailable struck her: she was again in the presence of death.

So clear and awesome was its presence in the sultry air that she felt its breath on the back of her neck. She jumped as a rash of gooseflesh rippled across her skin. There was something in the room. So overwhelming was this feeling that she peeled her eyes from Mayer's face to look around; fully expecting the grim reaper behind her. There was nobody.

Avxhiu steadied herself. The foreigner had locked the door but there was a bodyguard and others who could help. Important buildings were never left unprotected. She would get the key from his pocket.

Scared out of her wits, she fixed her eyes back on the German. He had started to scream, gurgling as he fought for breath. It was a losing battle. His eyes turned up and inwards, horribly white, his body stiffened in wooden convulsion, inexplicably hanging upright, about to take a dive.

And then Mayer died.

She knew. The German was no longer with her. He was dead.

As she waited for him to fall, there was nothing to be done. Strangely, he hung upright like a corpse, defying the laws of nature; and again, stronger than before, an overwhelming presence filled the room.

For years her mother had prayed to God in the privacy of her bed. Her grandmother had grown up in Italy and she had passed her faith on to her mother, who had taught her daughter to pray; to save her soul, if not her life.

Always in silence under Horxha, or you could end up in the camps.

Her religion had had cost her life when they found her grandmothers Greek icon.

"Our father, who art in Heaven . . ."

Chapter 8

"HALLOWED BE THY NAME . . ."

Avxhiu hesitated as the inexplicable stopped her short. The German had come back to life. The whites of his open eyes begun to turn in their sockets; the blue pupils came down slowly. The death tremble in his limbs fell away. He took a deep breath as if nothing had passed.

As Avxhiu's alarm spiraled out of control, somewhere deep within, confusion fought a rearguard battle. This was not the same man. His eyes were the same blue, but they were no longer flat. They shone with sparkling luminosity, and they looked at her for the first time with strength and directness.

"Don't be afraid, Shequere. I used a default program. You are in no danger."

"Default program?"

"A back door from the early days of evolution. Can you keep a secret?"

"Yes!" Her voice broke. The tension made her weak.

"I bypassed the authentication of his will. It is a symmetric backdoor that allows a god to enter and take control of the design. I am trespassing. The back door is there for Heimdallr to monitor the system."

She realized he was making fun of her for the bungled translation, using words like that. But the tone was so humorously tongue in cheek that her fear started to subside. It lasted the briefest of moments before she realized he spoke Albanian. Now she understood nothing.

Again, he moved to put her mind at rest. "I was putting you to a test, Shequere. I was less than polite. I wanted to see if you could cope. You have much to learn but that is not a problem at your age. Not with your mind."

He extended a hand, and she took it. For a moment they became one. Her heart stood still, then skipped a beat, as she quickly withdrew her hand.

"Mayer no need translator, please sir?" She reacted to her own words. She was still speaking English, unable to keep the disappointment out of her voice.

"No but let that remain between us. Nobody else must know. This is our secret. Will you be my interpreter in Lushnja?"

"Yes, thank you, Mr. Mayer."

But she knew it was something else he wanted; didn't try to hide it either.

"You arouse feelings in me, Shequere."

He reached out and touched her chin. It shook her. She wondered what was wrong with her. This was a man to her liking, one who knew what he wanted and went for it. They both knew what he wanted.

"Become my wife, Shequere."

"Mr. Mayer, you are the second foreigner I have met. The first offered me an apartment in Paris and told me I could have books and clothes and more food than I could eat. Are all foreigners like this?" He laughed with his bright new attractive voice.

"Grenville wanted you in Paris to warm his bed for his entertainment. I want you to study. I want you in Paris to bear my child."

"You are very forward. I do not speak any French. How could I study in Paris?"

She wanted to tell him that she had read a French book in English, Madame Bovary, when it struck her that this foreigner was exceedingly well informed about her past. How did he know about Charles Grenville and what the old man wanted with her?

"I would enter you into the best art schools in Paris. I have this feeling you could paint. You would learn your trade with the best teachers, in a warm studio of your own, with canvas and paint more than you can use, and a nanny to tend to our child. That is what I would give you: a happy life in exchange for a child."

His words washed a shock through her. Nobody knew this but Emir, and he was dead. Emir's family knew but they did not believe she could paint because she had shamed them. His family had entered her into the Tirana Academy of art. Her eyes filled up. She had made the mistake of painting a gipsy. It led to immediate dismissal. This chapter was closed in her mind. Not even Emir had known of her pencil drawings at home. Not even Spiro; and now this.

"Study painting in Paris and I will support you!"

She tried to find her voice. "Why do you think I can paint?"

"You are artistic. It is a feeling for one I love. Am I wrong?"

"No, you are a fine man."

They talked, and she felt silly, laughing at his wit a little too loud, moving to his responses with exaggerated gestures, her manner too brash. Almost despite herself, she was sending out signals, her awareness on a different plane. Not that she expected this to go anywhere; but she enjoyed it, besotted as she was with the man. Her rushed breath snapped to the quickness in the sultry air, riding this wave of unfamiliar exhilaration, waiting for it to break. Joy like this had not been in her for ages.

She checked herself abruptly. "Avxhiu will go now. This is not proper."

The foreigner was far too kind about it. He unlocked the room, and talked briefly to the guard, then alone and against her protests, walked her home over unpaved roads eaten by erosion and traffic. He walked her through the warm Balkan night, across empty crossings and silent bypasses, with neither streetlights nor stars to guide him, but somehow, he knew the way.

There was no place for fear in her emotions. She was a vessel filled with a different passion. In this dark city where evil men went about mugging people in daylight, she felt no pause. The wind in electric wires whispered of mystical events. Their laughter broke into slivers in the balmy air, a sound foreign to this city, unwelcome as a curse from a church pulpit.

They were halfway home when she saw a man sidle out of a building site in front of a ramshackle two-story house. The abode was someone's dream built into a nightmare on a vacant lot, brick by stolen brick. The rotting mortar had gaping cracks between bricks and wood. The finished part was falling apart faster than any progress could reclaim. The stranger tripped over rubble on the lot, a piece of trash skittered onto the road. He was wearing a thick duffle coat. Avxhiu came down to earth in a flash. She recalled the German's gold watch. It was too late to hide. If this was a mugger, she hoped he was not violent. He would not expect to find American money on her. Keenly she felt the small bundle in her sock against the ankle.

Avxhiu's alarm proved well founded: the man held a handgun by his side. The German was leading her by the arm. She had enjoyed the sure grip a little too much. It didn't falter. The stranger stood in the road grinning with a half-toothed smile through days of stubble, aiming his gun at Mayer. There was no mistaking his elation, good clothes, gold watch, solid new shoes. He had hauled a foreigner all right.

"Money, mister," he said, and made a sound suggesting a shot, as if he was clearing his throat. Avxhiu had seen the gun her escort wore strapped to his body. Verbally, she attacked the mugger.

"Why do you do this, scum? Ja Quifska Nanon! You are a shame to all of us. This is worse than Africa."

The curse was not fit for a woman. On realizing that her companion understood, Avxhiu blushed intensely. The mugger grinned even wider.

"Money, mister. Clock mister!" Pchacch....

Strangely, the foreigner had lost none of his good spirits. He replied in Albanian. "Step aside, Shpetim Grezda, let me pass. I have no wish to hurt you."

This bewildered the man. "You know me?" He spoke in a dialect from the north. "Do I know you?"

"If you did, you would think twice pointing your gun at me."

"Give me your money and your watch or I'll shoot you and defile your woman."

A flurry of fear went up her chest. It was the feeling from earlier, a feeling of a presence in an empty room, a shadow dancing in a dark empty road with nobody there.

The man must have felt it too. He made a startled move and spun around, then back. It was nothing, but somehow his confidence was fraying. She saw apprehension as he fought to keep his courage. The gold watch glittered in the half dark; the price to end all prices. And then the bewildered man in the road bowed his head and started to cry in silent despair. "Please forgive me. My family is hungry. I did not know what to do!" His voice broke, his cocky bearing gone. Tears kept coming into the stubble of weathered cheeks. "Forgive me. I didn't know what to do."

Avxhiu was moved. The man was an idiot. A poor sot stuck with a feeble mind.

"Go in peace, Shpetim Grezda," said the German as he slipped off his heavy gold watch and handed it to the wretched man, "keep this to remember me by."

Against his will, the man received the gift; violent fear raged behind his eyes.

"Wear it with pride!"

Avxhiu would never forget the look in that face. Her heart grew warm for the German against the sharp claws of jealousy. It was hard to see an expensive watch handed to the first antisocial half-wit that crossed their path.

"You shouldn't have," she stopped, shamed by a thought of her own watch with its plastic strap and chipped glass, and its knack of telling the wrong time.

"Noblesse oblige; I had to pay. Shpetim could have killed you and complicated our friendship."

"He is a highway mugger."

"All the same."

When they came to her store, she asked Mayer inside, aware that she had lost her footing. She could not care less. There was Skenderbeu Konjak to welcome him with.

Then she showed him the pencil drawings. They were at the bottom of the box along with the light sensitive paper that the studio no longer had use for. She had exposed the paper to light so many times that it had lost all its senses, much as she had.

"These are the lines of a young master," he said, and he didn't say more because her mouth was on his. What she wanted was more tangible than praise.

Chapter 9

AVXHIU WAS WAFTED INTO consciousness by the sounds of late morning. Beside her, the German slept peacefully on the sagging bed, large feet protruding from under her old yellow cover. If there ever was a dawning of a new age, this was it. Waking up was easy.

She squirmed with the delight of a new hot day, so different in its familiarity. The same old sun played with the empty glass jars that held her onion plants in winter. They split the morning sunlight across the flaking window and soaked the mildew on the tattered lace curtain with color. The sun had worked diligently to erase the fine print of communism from old brown newspapers used to soften the advances of winter through the warped window frame. Faded news from a fading era.

Avxhiu was happy. Her hour in the shade was at hand; with the second man in her life. Young, she told herself with no great hesitation; powerful; a perfect lover; and a foreigner. There could be no doubt, that he was deeply fond of her. His tenacity in the night was a revelation, and his ability to sweep her into mindless pleasure. His will seemed greater than his body. The memory of his death and resurrection was profoundly disturbing, but her strange misinterpretations would not stand in the way of the future.

Propping herself up on an elbow, she smelled his skin, the ghost of last night's wine on his breath. She blew the light, feathery hair on his chest, so different from Emir's black bristles. All the time she smiled. She had found a most wonderful man. Her future had taken an amazing turn.

She listened to his breathing as the neighborhood came alive. Now they had something to gossip about. Gently she stroked his sleeping loins, warm with the morning. And again, almost despairingly, she felt him stir to life, filling up her hand. This was not natural. Then, giggling like the young girl she was, she slipped off the lumpy bed to escape his immediate growing attention.

There was not much she could offer a foreigner. The biscuits she kept for important guests had grown old and tasteless. The coffee was bad. But what did that matter to a man in love? Coffee could be had at Hotel Dajti. Avxhiu tried to imagine the day, the meeting near Lushnja where she would translate for her man, the center of attention, then another evening and another night.

When he woke, he was surly. For a moment she feared that the rude German had returned, but he hadn't. These were the effects of a misused body, the aftermath of conjugal fatigue and run-down juices. The edge to him made her nervous. After taking two cups of raw coffee, he began to resemble her new man. He snooped about the store but found little of interest except the sledgehammer that Emir had stolen from the bus depot when he was repairing the bike. Mayer weighed the heavy hammer in his hand and Avxhiu immediately made him a gift of it. It was just a square heavy block of chipped iron with a short wooden shaft, grimy after years of useful service. From his gratitude she inferred that life in the West was not all it was cracked up to be. She didn't care. It was a good sledgehammer. This was her man, and she was proud to have contributed.

"You have a fine place here, Shequere, but you will go to Paris to study painting and carry my daughter. Never let any shadow fall on her."

His severity bewildered her.

"We will be going to Paris, Mayer," she said softly, "and we will both take care of our child."

She had cooked him the couple of eggs, but they were both bad, and he couldn't stomach them. She would keep them for later. It was a frustrating on a happy occasion.

"I won't be going to Paris, Shequere. I will be there with you in spirit only."

His words took the wind out of her. It was a ruse, his promise of a new life. In a blink of an eye, the horizon clouded up.

"You will not be going to Paris with Avxhiu?"

"Understand, Shequere, I value you enough to make you my wife, but I cannot come."

What conceit, what diabolic cunning! He came after her, all thunder and lightning, plucked her bare and was off to a new conquest. She bit her lip for believing him.

"The watchman will see to your future."

His solemnity and dark eloquence confused her, and she wanted none of his band of criminals.

"I tell you this, Helmut Mayer: the widow of Emir Avxhiu can make her own way. I don't need the help of your henchman. I wanted you to take care of me. That is why I gave myself to you. You got what you came for."

To hide her trembling hands, she tried to water the plants in the blazing window, but her nervousness made her drop the cup she had saved from Grenville. It went to pieces on the floor. Why had he pulled the ground from under her? Why did he seem so much more than a man to her? Avxhiu Shequere was full of bad forebodings.

"Do not refuse the life I offer you, wife."

"I slept with you. That does not make me your wife. I was no virgin." She cast a severe glimpse at the three-finger scratch across his face.

"The woman who marked you had more courage than I."

Helmut Mayer brought his hand slowly to his chin.

"Yes, she did, but Helmut Mayer didn't figure on me."

"Why do you taunt me? You are Helmut Mayer."

"Not really."

"Why can't you come with me to Paris?" Watching her from the window, she saw his look of a caring husband. The powerful emotional bond confused her.

"Because today, this body dies."

"What are you saying!"

"Today you are twice a widow. This body will rot in the ground, and nobody will grieve for it."

Avxhiu would, but she could hardly tell him that. He was taking leave of her. There was no budging him. Her hour in the shade was over before it begun. She would go to Greece with her brother.

"We must go," he said, "to the meeting in Lushnja. The friends of Helmut Mayer are waiting, important men."

"Yes," she said.

The outcome of that meeting was important for Spiro's future. For here, there was nobody else to rely on.

Chapter 10

"ENTERTAINING FOREIGNERS IN YOUR bed now," Avxhiu heard the woman mutter, as she and Mayer stepped outside. The housewife from upstairs gave them a malicious look; the story suited her well enough.

The family upstairs wanted to take over Avxhiu's store for the stepson and his wife. Her husband was the trainer of the Tirana soccer team, a well-connected communist who had traveled abroad. People like that stopped at nothing. Forever dropping dirty suggestions, he'd keep trying to get his hands on both her, and her apartment. The coach was afraid of Spiro, but that did not stop his wife from slandering her. Avxhiu ignored her and they walked downtown where a car waited with his foreign driver.

The drive to Lushnja was oddly silent except for occasional sharp exchanges between him and his driver in a language she did not understand. Mayer had wrapped her gift in paper, reverently handling the sledgehammer. He appreciated her gift, and she did so want to salvage his love or friendship.

"Is your chauffeur German, Mr. Mayer?"

She felt funny addressing her lover so formally in English. She hoped she sounded sophisticated, exchanging a fleeting look with the eyes in the rearview mirror.

"His name is Konrad Muller, a German intelligence agent, like your Sigurimi with a twist, a NATO spy."

The car swerved slightly on the road. The perspiring driver exchanged another furtive look with her in the mirror. Avxhiu bartered away her pride and put her hand out to Mayer. Last night, he was hugely dear to her. In the back seat, her foreigner embraced her. A kiss and a promise of another night, and things were good again.

Breathless, they settled back, she flushed and red in the face, avoiding the eyes of the driver as the Mercedes came down into a sun-drenched valley. They were a good distance from the nearest town. She spotted a tiny square house, a bleak provisory beer pub, a birrari by a dusty road, their destination.

It was not for the drinks, because the soupy brew offered in such places was not refreshing for refined western palates.

Four walls of white, flaking concrete; a door showed the front. One small window perched high on its side. That was it. Men milling about outside, waiting. A few run-down types: footmen and errand boys, a handful of gorillas to apply the pressure, and a couple of costumes with brains, a microcosm of Albanian gangland.

Avxhiu's European husband was unfazed by the lean men with closely cropped hair, and bristly sharp-edged faces. They came from both sides of the barbed wire with distrust in dark stoic eyes, their visions gnarled by prison labor. They expected no friends. To them the world was a different marketplace.

Avxhiu stepped out to greet her brother and to present her lover to this unsympathetic flock. She did so with mixed emotions. Mayer shook hands as he cradled the wrapped-up sledgehammer in his left. His gesture took her mind back to last night, the cause of his gratitude, and Shequere Avxhiu flushed in the hot sun.

Her brother gave the names as Helmut Mayer greeted the costumes. Avxhiu noticed that Spiro was proud of her.

"Avxhiu good translator, yes?"

Her brother had rehearsed the foreign words. She knew they had no meaning to him. He looked up at Mayer, inviting praise.

"Shequere Avxhiu is an excellent translator and a dear friend," said Mayer, who now spoke only English.

Avxhiu did not translate but blushed all the more when some of the costumes nodded. They got the gist. The young hot pride swelled in her. Her brother seemed somehow to know that the foreigner had spent the night in her bed. It was in his eyes. That it pleased him caught her by surprise. He was always protective. Spiro was working his way to the top, and his little sister was sleeping with the foreign boss. It pained her.

"As a measure of the spirit of our agreement, I want no guns in the house. Let us leave our weapons outside." Mayer pulled his gun from the holster and said a few words to his driver who drove off on some errand.

As Avxhiu proudly translated, the costumes nodded. They were many and they had no need of guns. Their knives were sharp enough. This foreigner was a strange comrade: some security. Several guns were handed to lackeys awhile the costumes and their gorillas stepped inside, leaving the lower castes outside in the dust of the tireless sun.

It took a while to adjust to the dark interior. It was a shell of a house; four walls, a single room. A green wooden table served as a bar. Three cases of warm western beer stood among the green recycled glass bottles, full to their broad necks with dull, faintly golden liquid, the standard Albanian fair. There were some small tables with checkered cloths, so dirty and spotted that it was hard to distinguish a color.

The German locked and bolted the door from the inside. Avxhiu, with undue apprehension, fought the feeling that the meeting was about to go wrong. Why did this foreigner always prove so unsettling?

As the only woman in the place, she helped put out the spirits on Spiro's instruction. It was always so: her people liked to greet their guests with salutes of strong plum brandy. This would be no exception. But it was not to be. The beast inside Helmut Mayer had other designs.

"I want to present to the head of the Albanian Camorra a special gift."

Avxhiu put away a bottle of plum brandy and translated to the gathering of roughly twelve. A wiry man, his hair combed back in slick European style, rose to accept the token. Avxhiu became uncertain when she saw Mayer unwrap the sledgehammer. This was not a good gift between powerful men. Perhaps it was symbolic. He spoke English.

"I present you with this hammer. It may not look like much, but it is the harbinger of death to my enemies and a shield for my friends."

Seeking eloquence, Avxhiu grappled for the right words. She had no idea what a harbinger was, although the leader was nodding at Helmut Mayer. He too understood symbolic gestures.

Shequere Avxhiu was still looking for the right words when the sledgehammer swung through the air. In a wide arc it accelerated to lightning speed to meet its resistance on the top of that slickly combed head. Avxhiu watched without a thought how the heavy hammer penetrated in line with the shoulders.

After this, it didn't seem relevant to couch words of friendship to a man whose head had received its message, cracked like eggshell as this harbinger sank through the tissues of his gratitude. Brain, blood and spinal fluid spattered walls and tables and filled glasses held to toast a momentous friendship.

Then, yanking the heavy hammer towards him, the man's body followed, to be flung down and aside as another arc whined through the air. Avxhiu stood with her mouth half open, her lips still aching from the frantic tumble in the car. Now she closed them to spit out blood as the man on her right caught the sledge on the side of his head.

Flecked with the warm glue of human tissue, a fountain of panic rose in her and her compatriots. There was no time to think. She could swear that the sledgehammer was singing as it slammed into another head. First reactions are instinctive: get out of harm's way. They are seldom wise when panic spreads in a crowded place, but certainly natural. There was a struggle as men shuffled and fell over one another, over chairs and upturned tables, away from the center of danger. And all the while the hammer kept falling. The walls were streaked, the slippery floor treacherous.

These men were no strangers to slaughter. Those still living found their bearings soon enough. Their knives were drawn; one man fumbled for a hidden pistol. A shot rang out, and another, as the hammer sang.

A blade buried itself in the stomach that Avxhiu had so delicately stroked this morning. A gleaming edge slashed across the grinning face she had caressed, changing its contours. The berserker took it like a maddened bull. The only way out of this ring was death. Mayer waded into the flying knives, the hammer coming down left and right. Bodies crumpled into broken glass. Plum brandy and blood mingled on the tiles in a potent heathen brew.

It was a swansong, an orgy of death. The clamor dwindled with the numbers, the screams for aid an enigma to the men outside. They pounded the door from outside, as the mayhem inside tapered off. A shadow passed the small window high on the wall. Someone tried to peek into the half-dusk. Shooting their way in was not a choice. The unarmed foreigner was alone. They wondered what was going on but lacked the authority to intervene. Half a century of indecision had put its mark on the criminals as well as the rest.

Avxhiu had taken refuge behind the bar. She stood like a pillar of salt, with her brother holding her arm. And as the last man met his fate in the far corner and fell into that bed of carnage, Spiro Shituni made a dash for the bolted door. With terrifying speed, the flayed hulk of her bleeding lover was on her brother, her sledgehammer singing through the air.

Where it came from, she never knew, but her scream was sharper and more unyielding than any razor that cut him.

"Not my brother!" For the first time the heavy hammer missed its target.

Her lover's wrath was done.

Helmut Mayer looked only at Avxhiu, his disfigured face a jumble of cuts. His tall frame was oozing blood, draining away the juice of life; a drumming heart discharged the last goblets from his barrel of claret, held up by limitless will.

He stared at her for that one moment. Was he smiling? It was impossible to tell. He collected his body for one last effort, forcing out a wheezing sound from his punctured lungs.

"Wallenberg," he croaked.

Shequere Avxhiu, caught in emotional limbo, could not understand what he was telling her. She wanted to plead but her voice caught.

And then, from one second to the next, her new husband was no longer there: all that remained was a falling mass that obeyed only the call of the Earth.

Her German lover was dead.

Book 2, Birger Wallenberg

Chapter 1

"WHY WOULD THEY PICK me for their mysterious Institute, Roos?"

Far below, the darkening sky was swallowing the North Atlantic. Soothed by the distant din of the airplane motors, Birger Wallenberg relaxed in the embrace of his generous airplane seat, stowing the Asgard Park dossier back into his briefcase.

Beside him on the night flight from Stockholm to New York; his childhood friend Roos raised the footstool for a nap.

Birger Wallenberg had sought the Directorship of Asgard Park to humor his mother, who claimed to have a friend on the Midgard board, the vast hospital conglomerate that controlled the Asgard Park Institute. He had not expected to be appointed. Even now, he wasn't quite persuaded.

"I can't see a laid-back lunatic asylum in upstate New York as something to write home about." Roos sighed. "The Midgard Group has a top-notch board. I guess they thought you were qualified. I've never heard of Asgard Park."

Roos was the Deputy Executive Director for Finance and Accounting for the Nobel Foundation. And he was right; nobody he knew had heard of it, except his mother Caroline.

"They agreed to fund a team of researchers around my ideas of the mind brain. How could I turn them down?"

"I'm sure your mother had a hand in it. Look, I need to rest; you should see my schedule in New York."

As Birger drifted into sleep, he knew that whatever reasons had swayed the Midgard board, Asgard Park was a perfect fit for his scholarly ambitions.

Never a heavy dreamer, he embraced a comfortable dream.

It was an oddly clear vision of chatting with a professor. The man was trying to sell him a less than levelheaded idea, offering him the chance to utilize a remote probe that let a psychotherapist access a patient's mind.

The professor raved about the benefit to psychiatry; to see what a patient saw; to feel what he felt, to think what he thought. It was the stuff dreams were made of. The professor's erudite voice coached him to enter a distant host.

Suddenly, his body was that of an exhausted woman in a hotel bed where he lost almost all sense of himself. It was uncanny. As a passive observer, he thought the thoughts of this woman. He looked out through her eyes, in the warm yellow light from the bedside lamp. She took comfort in the old snapshot, the fine rugged features of her long-dead lover. An accident had claimed his life seven years ago with their affair barely out of the starting gate. She had no idea at the time that she was pregnant. Bill never got to know his daughter.

Amelia was asleep. A hotel room provided no sense of security for a six-year-old. Not after a day like this. She stroked her skinny back, thin like a bird's and turned over the well-thumbed photo. On the back, with a blunt pencil, smudged by years of fingering, Bill had scribbled words of love that were no longer legible. She knew the awkward text by heart.

Smudged too was the New York number to call if something cropped up: his death, as turned out at the time. She had called the number once, days after he went missing. A man promised to call back, but never did. Certain that Bill had dumped her, she had moved. Later, with the pregnancy to deal with, she pushed on with her studies. It was months before a New York attorney tracked her down to a cramped student flat to tell her of the accident that took his life. That she was mentioned in Bill's testament had changed her life. As a theoretical physicist, she knew the odds against that.

She eased her head against the unfamiliar headrest and sipped her Macallan. Strong spirits were not her everyday fare, but this was no ordinary day. Her nerves needed calming. Going over old memories, blunted by time, was soothing, like having old friends for dinner. She eased Amelia's arm under the covers. It felt absurd to hide in a Manhattan hotel, minutes from home. The first whiff of danger had come to her in the privacy of her own spacious bathroom, twelve stories above a rain-sodden Central Park as she spilled white dust on her gray skirt.

"Did Jack make the toilet dirty?"

She had given no reply to her daughter's question but a flutter of mirth had chipped at her gloom, her halfhearted laughter faltering. The child did not grasp the brittle sound of despair. Her mind did the math: ten million at least; the street price for the drugs she was destroying. With trembling fingers, she had dumped the last of it into the toilet and flushed till there was no trace, carefully wiping the seat clean. The brief role of Jack as her live-in lover was over, having confessed to holding two suitcases of crack cocaine for a man called Eric Schaeffer Spears. It had slipped his mind to tell her that, which in retrospect was understandable.

The Scotch clawed at her insides like a purring cat, relaxing her in the hotel bed. She wondered if Bill's old crony was still there, all these years later. She felt an urge to call the old number, an odd feeling after seven years. Why did she need to talk about this calamity? She drew doodles on the stationery as she dialed, easing her fear, glancing furtively around the room.

"How can I help you?"

It came flooding back, the same crisp greeting without introduction. That is why she could not recall a name. He never gave it. The voice was familiar. For a moment she thought of hanging up. She had nothing to say to this man. But the Scotch found her voice.

"Good evening, sir. I don't know your name. We talked on the phone seven years back about a common friend," she hesitated, "Bill Rayman."

"Miss Kirkpatrick?"

"My God, you remember." She felt incredulous, relief inflating her reaction.

"Time passes. What can I do for you?"

Margaret sipped her whisky. The question was blunt. This was not a man for small talk.

"I just wanted to hear a friendly voice."

A sliver of irony slipped out, buried in the words. She had nothing to say to this man. It made it easier to tell him everything. She tried not to sound too vague as she plodded on.

"A friend of mine, Jack Gradidge, hid ten million worth of crack cocaine in my apartment, forty bags, I think. I flushed the lot down the toilet. Now I think somebody is trying to find me. It is not the police."

The same calm silence.

"Half the rats in New York must be high." Why did she find this amusing? He clearly did not. It was not.

This is the whisky talking, she thought. There was no other explanation for this conversation. "They think I stole the stuff. Well, I bolted, didn't I? Remarkable what fear does for your condition." She was rambling. "I am sorry to bother you; we've been hiding in this hotel room."

He laughed her most sparkling New York laughter. "You are my last friendly ear."

She knew that this scatterbrained broadside would scare him off but the gruff attitude and silence that bordered on rudeness upset her.

"Which hotel is that?"

Her story had not alarmed him one bit. Listening to the timbre of his voice, doodling as she was, attentive to the atmosphere, she drew a blank. Perhaps it was the way in which it did not alarm him that struck her. And there was this something else. Or was it in her mind; a sudden new dimension, a hum of urgency that was almost spooky.

"What?"

"Where are you staying, which hotel?"

"I am thinking about leaving town for a couple of weeks", she objected reluctantly, holding on to her precious secret, "there is no need to involve you in this." The idea had suddenly surfaced that this stranger might try to take advantage of her circumstances. It was a wholesome New York reaction. She was coming to her senses.

"Are you armed?"

"Good heavens, no!"

"Did you register under your own name?"

The fear flashed through her again. How careless. She was a novice at flying under the radar.

"Did the desk know there were two of you? Is that your daughter with you? Did they know that?"

The man turned the screw with every question. "Yes, yes, yes!" Jesus Christ, they had it all. A few calls and they would run her to earth.

"Would these be the men of Eric Schaeffer Spears?" This stunned her. Something was deadly wrong.

"How do you know about Spears?" She breathed into the handle. "My god, who are you anyway?"

The man brushed her off. "Let me sleep on this, Miss. Just sit tight where you are."

The phone went dead in her hand. She almost sobbed into it. This time the brush-off had a nasty twist. How did Bill's old friend know a Mob kingpin called Spears?

She flung down the scribbled stationery in anger over her weakness and poured another shot of malt whisky. Her choices were between getting hysterical or pissed. The seething anger warmed her, or was it the Scotch? Neither dampened the fear.

At precisely that moment another implication exploded dimly in her brain; first in a hazy way, unraveling with all kinds of potent ramifications. As a sleepwalker on the edge of the abyss, she reached for the stationery. It was there among the doodles. It was not imagination: the scribbled word this man had no way of knowing.

"Daughter?"

Her hand fell to her side and clawed at the bedspread as she searched mindlessly for a connection, trying to clear her head. There was none.

"Is that your daughter with you?"

This man had no way of knowing she had a daughter. She had called him seven years back., unaware she was with a child; much less that it was a daughter. Never talked to him again, until now.

She jumped out of bed and started to dress.

There was a soft sound as the door opened. For a second, she stood in surprise at the dressing table before her mind accepted that the two heavyset men who entered her room were probably here on an errand for Eric Schaeffer Spears. They had secured the room before she grasped what was going on.

A powerful slap to the side of the head sent her reeling into the wall. For a moment, it all seemed inconsequential. Thick hands hauled her up. A bull of a man slipped handcuffs on behind her back and spun her around to pin her head against the wall. His gloved left choked her by the throat in a stranglehold that allowed no sound. She tried to focus. Disembodied thoughts of Amelia brought her back. Out of the dimly red corner of an eye, she saw golden hair on a pillow. A man held a wad over Amelia's mouth, chloroform.

"You, good-looking; you think this a way out?" The man holding her shook his head slowly to tell her no. She had put on her gray two-piece Calvin Klein, the plain skirt as straight as her hips allowed. His grin was telling her that taking down a classy dame who had only overdosed on etiquette was a cinch. She would be a far cry from his usual fare of Bronx junkies, brought up on a steady diet of abuse.

"Me, I'd take your kid anytime."

She tried to challenge him with disgust, but her eyes could not hold it. She panicked. His lack of refinement had no bearing on the situation.

"All I want is forty keys."

The big man hit her on the mouth with his gloved fist. Her lips broke and a tooth gave way. He punched her eyebrows; pummeled her with a tradesman's attention, cracking her nose with a gloved right, pinning her to the wall with his left. Somehow, he took care not to knock her cold, then spun her to the dressing mirror to a horrible mess that gagged back half-blinded through tears, choking on blood and teeth.

"Try snorting Mr. Spears's nose candy through that fucking mushroom." The man pushed the punched-up nose with his gloved finger and choked off her attempts to speak. She felt woozy, fighting to hold on.

"You watch us take turns with Goldilocks here. When we can't get it up no more, we take her with us in a couple of plastic bags." The man must have thought she had the general idea.

"I think you better tell us where you stashed..."

The hotel phone broke the spell. The baby-sitter, now searching the room, gave a signal and the bully reacted like a trained dog. The man in charge put it on speaker.

"Room 504!"

"Miss Kirkpatrick, please."

"She stepped out. Can I take a message?"

"Would you tell her that the state attorney has been delayed; fifteen minutes at most."

"Sure, thanks!"

"We move them out." The man in charge threw a towel to his understudy who wiped the blood from his gloves, then wrapped her grisly face in it. She had called no state attorney. She fought to see as a third man from the hallway picked up Amelia. The numb pain told her that this was the end. The vertigo made her sick. The elevator opened with a soft bell to a luxurious lounge with a beige carpet. From behind her, the man in charge led her forcibly ahead. The gloved bully, who had molested her, strode in front, blocking her toweled face from public scrutiny.

They walked without sound, followed by the thug with her daughter. There was no point in trying to run without Amelia. She vomited inside her towel. Drops of blood and puke spilled on the carpet. They were moving too fast. There was no time. The lounge opened to a small lobby with glass display cases of ancient jewelry.

Her heart, racing for life, thumped her chest half to breaking point. She must save the child. She would go for it.

"Help me, somebody!"

Her tongue was rubber, the voice muffled by the towel, pushed at breakneck speed into the lobby.

"They are kidnapping us," she blurted.

In moments they would be out of there. The words came out as a slur. Her tongue was numb and there were strange gaps in her mouth. She was spilling saliva and blood. No one would hear her.

But somehow it was all wrong. As her plea left her broken lips, she sensed the strangeness of it. Her words did not drown, they filled the air. They fluttered about the lobby like so many panicked doves in an empty cathedral.

Two heavily armed men in pale blue hospital overalls stood watching them from behind the desk.

"Shit!"

Her escort came to an abrupt halt. The gloved one in front had his gun out. The deafening gunshot jolted one of the men by the desk. In spite of lethargy, Margaret instinctively cringed as the gloved man came down sprawling to the sound of rapid-fire bursts that played to a more muffled tune. She whipped her head around, unraveling the towel, spattering blood and puke on her escort, almost blacking out by the effort. Her daughter's keeper lay by the elevator, oozing blood from his neck onto the carpet. Amelia was gone.

"You guys back off while you can." The angry voice of her escort came from behind her; the man in charge used her as a shield in his grip.

"Tell Schaeffer that the child is protected. We will set up a meeting about the drug matter," said a voice from the desk.

Her feet could no longer carry her weight. Her escort let her slip. She reached for the floor to ease onto her back. Her vision undulated in a red haze. The man above her studied faces. Through the pain it dawned on her; the man would have mugshots to sift through. Spears would turn the city upside down to find these men, her rescuers, whoever they were.

"And who the fuck are you?"

"Just deliver the message!"

"The child is protected. What the fuck does that mean? A story like that gets you killed."

"Then make sure you tell it."

Like a cornered bull, drowning in the red of her eyes, the man in charge shook his neck to clear his head.

"Sure, Mr. Spears will be in touch!"

The mother closed her eyes, and it all went away, as Birger Wallenberg woke up from the first brilliant dream in his life, thirty thousand feet above sea level.

The beating! It was so real that his hand came to his face in panic. Nothing was broken. The pain was gone. But how strange the radiant awareness. Every detail was etched into his mind.

Book 2, Birger Wallenberg

Chapter 2

THUS, ON A DISMAL rainy Thursday morning in late June 1991, Dr Wallenberg passed through customs at Kennedy Airport. In the arrival hall, a card caught his attention. The Asgard Park Institute had rolled out the red carpet and sent a car to whisk its new Director upstate.

The driver deposited his luggage in the polished black boot of an armored limousine with easy efficiency. Impassive eyes noted everything but his passenger. Not a word was spoken. From a privileged life, Wallenberg knew the sort. The driver carried no insignia, and nor did the limo; most likely a hired car, driven by a professional bodyguard for the New York glitterati. Although relieved to escape the transport hassle, Wallenberg made a mental note of the unwarranted expense. With him at the helm, the Institute would put its funds to better use.

They crossed Canal Street into SOHO. The relaxing ride offered him a reflective moment as the streets drifted by in a silent aquarium beyond green-tinted glass. He looked out through his thirty-four-year-old reflection: the issue of a single mother, not the scion of a wealthy family; unrelated to the famous Wallenberg family of Sweden. His mother had earned her vast fortune as a tireless captain of hi-tech industries. By her skillful machinations he was already a wealthy man.

The driver kept a remarkably even pace up a congested Broadway, past the Bronx and into suburban Westchester County. Rural areas with estates took over. The harshness of the city fell away. He felt his spirits coming up. The day had started wet and gray but as the sogginess eased, the fog remained. They passed a far gatepost. The shape of a guard cradling a shotgun against the milky background reminded Wallenberg of grouse hunting in the marches. He gave a private smile in the back.

He had arrived in America.

Ahead, on the extensive grounds of a private estate, the white Victorian building emerged out of the fog, at first detached from the modern addition that would house his new labs. He stepped out of the car to the refreshing smell of waterlogged soil and walked briskly across the drive into the airy hall, leaving his bags to the driver. The mist dampened the sound of well-shod feet on gravel.

At the top of a grand staircase, an orderly ushered him into the offices of Dr George Kennan, his acting caretaker and chief psychiatrist. The tall, dignified man cut short a phone conversation with a bleak smile.

"Dr Wallenberg, welcome to Asgard Park. Unfortunately, we have a small problem. I better fill you in. The press is likely to hunt you down; as our new Director."

"What is the problem?"

"A schizophrenic male, Haakon Beale, left the Sidekick Suite last night. We have learned that he killed two men in a Manhattan hotel lobby, allegedly."

The contours of the room sharpened in the shock of recognition. Wallenberg paused, breathed hard, grunted a question to win time, and waited for his mind to clear.

"The Sidekick Suite?"

"Our ground-floor exit ward. There was no breakout."

It was a bizarre coincidence. He had better come to his senses. "Is the Institute at fault?"

"Two of our senior psychiatrists are reviewing the case. Beale's recovery was considered stable. He may have failed to take his medication. It is a routine matter."

Wallenberg knew what happened with crystal clarity: more than was proper or rational. His experience on the plane had bordered on the mentally unbalanced. The flux made it difficult to keep his attention focused. He had to fight premonitions of danger in a storm of emotions.

"Does the name Dr Margaret Kirkpatrick mean anything to you?" he asked, hoping against hope. He must not bungle his first crisis. The silent gaze of his chief psychiatrist was hard to fathom. To tell him that he had experienced that incident firsthand would be neither wise nor well received within these walls.

"She is a well-known scientist, and her six-year-old daughter was in the hotel room while they brutalized her."

"That's what I heard," he said to put it right.

"It has always been the hallmark of our directors."

"What?"

"To be well informed!"

Wallenberg held the mask. To be found deceitful on your first day at the helm was not a good start.

"Asgard Park will offer the woman free care until she can fend for herself."

Wallenberg grimaced at his chief psychiatrist. This was not he beginning he had hoped for.

The questions piled on the fault lines in his mind. Was he having a nervous breakdown? The Institute that had seemed such a perfect vehicle for all his ambitions was already weighing on his sanity.

In downtown New York, rain had reclaimed the city. During his ride through the leaden grayness, Wallenberg's uneasiness grew. Something was not right. Not in him and not at the Institute. He had better come to his senses.

At the large hospital, he felt immediately at home, another doctor with a picture tag. He was unaware that an urgent fax had reached the hospital's administration from the Midgard Group that controlled it. The orders, followed up by phone calls, were to make all efforts to aid the visitor. An impressed hospital Director waited to guide him through the labyrinth.

There was an army of cops all over the drab hallways on Beale's floor. Wallenberg found two detectives at the window of a small private room that had seen better days. Beale slept fitfully after routine surgery. He recognized the man from the hotel lobby and felt violated on doing so.

Turned out that the detectives were well acquainted with the Asgard Park Institute for the Criminally Insane.

Got papers on this guy?"

"This is his psychiatric evaluation," handing it over. "Our patient has no history of violence. A girlfriend got word to him by phone last night. He may have been trying to catch up with her when he walked into this mess."

"Kirkpatrick's his old flame," the lieutenant skimmed the file."

"There goes your theory." The middle-aged lieutenant of detectives glanced at his partner, unable to hide his pleasure, and Wallenberg discovered that his breath lent devastating weight to his words. The man could keep criminals off the streets by walking them. "The dead Sicilians worked for a guy called the Jew," said the lieutenant. "They call him Eric Schaeffer Spears. Probably not his name. "

"Eric Schaeffer Spears does not sound Italian to me." Wallenberg spoke without thinking. The name that came from inside a woman's mind was surely a delusion. They did not pick up on it. It had to be common knowledge.

"Think your patient got caught in the cross-fire. Haakon Beale don't sound greaseball to me."

Wallenberg gave a slight shrug.

The junior partner looked frustrated. "The perps who rescued her herded the hotel staff into a linen closet. Too neat for a schizo."

Book 2, Birger Wallenberg

Chapter 3

THE WOMAN HAD A two-room suite on the more modern eleventh floor. There were cops outside her door too. Gaining access as her psychoanalyst, tired eyes studied him from the bed. She had taken a pounding and he knew every blow by heart. Ugly multicolored swellings crept into the bloodshot mass of her eyes, and she had difficulty talking.

"Bill Rayman, Amelia's father - died before she was born. I just phoned the number he gave me. Unlisted Asgard Park number. My lawyer traced it. They came to save Amelia. Why? Please help me."

Her strength was wearing thin. Her sluggishness made her speech hard to decipher. She reached for a white shoulder bag on the bedside table, streaked with brown. He had no recall of a shoulder bag. Fishing about inside, she came up with an old snapshot of a young man, with faded writing on the back. He knew the awkward words by heart: by her heart. She thrust it at him with the pad.

"Bill told me to call this number if I ever needed urgent help."

He decided to put his own madness to the test.

"They let the Italian that beat you up go. With a message," he whispered. She looked up into his eyes, her mind clear as crystal, working out the implications. There was no way he could have guessed. Nobody knew the message but Eric Schaeffer Spears, who got it, and whoever sent it.

"Tell Schaeffer, the child is protected, he whispered."

She looked at him steadily, as if trying to fathom his motives. He put her at ease. "I cannot have this incident damage the reputation of my Institute. If you claim amnesia, my experts will back you up. You remember nothing. No harm will come to you or Amelia. Do you understand what I am saying?"

She nodded slowly, confused.

"I will have you transferred upstate to Asgard Park. We have the proper staff to deal with post-traumatic stress. You get some rest." He patted her hand warmly, sharing in her confusion. Margaret Kirkpatrick closed her bloodshot eyes and fell asleep.

The case was creating interest. CNN took it worldwide. Kirkpatrick was a respected physicist who had recently launched a hotly debated explanation of the variations in spatial heat found by the COBE satellite. The story was a godsend during a dry spell in news; a physicist finds ten million worth of cocaine stashed in her Park Avenue apartment and flushes the lot down the toilet.

The Institute was off the hook. A mental patient rescued a child. Nobody made any reference to Asgard Park, but the questions piled on the fault lines in his mind. Was he having a nervous breakdown? The Institute that had seemed such a perfect vehicle for all his ambitions was already weighing on his sanity.

Walking out of the New York hospital, Wallenberg strode aimlessly into the afternoon bustle, assaulted by the cacophony of city sounds. Halfhearted spatters of tepid rain played the streets. They felt like another New York aggravation flung in his face. He could not escape the paranoid feeling.

On a June day like this, the young wives in Falsterbo Sweden, across the strait from Copenhagen, would be ambling down to the finest sand in Europe, miles of white powdered beaches, with baskets in hands, trailed by bare-bottomed toddlers. He needed a walk to clear his mind. He missed the silent woods and the empty marshes. He even missed Bobby, his mother's golden retriever.

Entering his private rooms at Asgard Park, he found them furnished with emphasis on the tedious. They came with a library of gloom that perfectly fitted his frame of mind. A quick inspection confirmed that tomes of outdated psychiatry had little to offer but a vague smell of decay. He missed the airy pleasures of his modern apartment in the university town of Lund in Sweden.

Asgard Park served as a temporary shelter to some of the world's most violent mental patients, brought to this unknown asylum to have their cases studied by resident specialists. Was he brought here as a resident or a patient?

Later that night, Dr Kennan treated him to dinner in the rustic old dining room and introduced him to senior staff. As the discussions ebbed and flowed, everybody had a learned pitch to the new Director. Academic feathers are easily ruffled. Having come prepared for the odd dose of petty jealousy from the top staff, he found none. He decided to keep his deferential chief occupied with the daily chores of the asylum. It would afford himself leeway in the delicate task of gathering his team around his own ideas.

Gradually, the discussions on the nuts and bolts of day-to-day research brought home the scale of his task. It would take a miracle to turn this seedy place into the sophisticated outfit he envisaged. He looked forward to quiet nights of solitary study. It would, he decided, be a happy time.

After dinner, Dr. Kennan gave him an early evening tour of the floors reserved for his new laboratories, currently an empty shell. Some of the older labs were fully staffed at this late hour. Many of the temporary residents were here on grants and intended to make full use of their time. The intensity was infectious. The new Director passed through too many doors and saw too many faces to commit them to memory.

In the coolness of the ground floor autopsy suite, he studied a recently removed brain and spinal cord. These served in a catalog of tests, partly in the study of the illness that had brought down the patient, and partly as reference in larger studies on differentiation in neural morphology. Wallenberg had to tear himself away.

The maximum-security block took up an entire modern wing except for the ground floor ward, commonly called the Sidekick Suite. Many of the maximum-security cells were modern apartments, with exclusive furniture and paintings. His paltry quarters paled in comparison. It was the second time it surfaced: why was the Institute spending money on perks that had no bearing on its research?

Later that night, in his private rooms, he pored over personnel files and administration charts. The codes supplied by Dr Kennan gave him unlimited access to the in-house databank with vast tracts of information. He was appalled to find nothing but half-hatched plans for his new labs. Correspondence with potential researchers had yielded no takers. The Midgard board had led him to believe that the groundwork was in place. At his disposal were the empty shells of the labs, and the required funds to build his team, but that was all. It was a nasty surprise, but only a temporary setback.

It was night, and the rain had abated. With a certain enthusiasm he put on the parka and donned the Wellington boots he had bought for the purpose. To clear his head, he slipped down the empty backstairs and went happily scouting the unlit grounds in the drizzle.

On his way back, the dark bulk of the west-wing showed a few spots of light on the upper residential levels. Wallenberg was trying to locate his rooms when the lights came on in the autopsy suite next to the morgue, where the hammered glass prevented inspection. It would be the cleaning detail. As he passed the outer door to the hallway, he put security to the test. The unlocked door opened to his hand. It was a serious breach.

Wallenberg entered the dark hall next to the row of pathology laboratories. It was an odd sensation to sneak around these unfamiliar quarters in the dark. Only the round and powerful surgical lights were on. Somebody was here, he could tell. Somebody was waiting; he felt it like an old certainty trickling up from a deep core.

An autopsy table, with glittering stainless-steel faucets where draining channels stood out in the brilliant light from above. The tools and the cutting utensils waited on the sidelines for a body to carve up. The cool, clean water in the spigots waited for dark fluids to wash away, heavy tools, fine scalpels with cold blades. A drop of condensation fell sparkling through the light and made a hollow sound. The smell of formalin was overwhelming. Suction tubes writhed on the edge of his vision like snakes. It was cool in here.

Wallenberg waited for something to happen. He was aware that fear had invaded him. As he tried for calm, he heard movement and started to turn.

Then something else happened, that he had never experienced before. An icy calm descended on his mind. The fear fell from him and there was no longer any confusion. His vision became calm and his control unshakable. He turned.

It was nothing to worry about. Another man stepped out of the shadows into the light. Not the kind you want to meet alone across an autopsy table after midnight with a scalpel in his hand, but the armor of Wallenberg's new stoicism was unyielding.

The middle-aged man in a white coat did not carry the compulsory photo tag. The open front showed a fine tweed jacket and Tattersall checkered shirt. His demanding eyes looked the young man over. Wallenberg countered in the same manner.

"May I ask what you are doing here?" It was the older man who spoke, in a firm, strangely disinterested voice. There was no hostility in him, as if he already knew the answer; he had seen what he had come for.

"I am Birger Wallenberg, the new Director. The outer door was unlocked. This is a sensitive area. I insist on an explanation. I take it you are member of staff. Where is your name tag?"

The man lifted the solid scalpel with its fluted handle and looked into its perfect mirror, then replaced it unhurriedly on the stainless table tray. Strong well-tended hands, no wedding ring.

"Dr Wallenberg. I would have startled a lesser man, sneaking up like that. I like that strength in a man. I am Karl." It was clear that the scholarly voice was used to public speaking; it sounded familiar. The man gave a smile but not a hand.

"I am one of your certified pathologists. I saw the lights come on down here. I found the door unlocked – and your nametag?"

Had they met at a conference? He was a fine specimen of humanity, and likeable. The high and attractive face would be hard to forget. Wallenberg was confused; there was something about him.

I came to warn you. I brought you to Asgard Park for a purpose that is not to your liking. This is your chance to walk away; to keep command of your life."

'Keep command of his life?' If the man was jockeying for position, this was a bloody strange way to do it.

"You are the chosen one. If you stay, you must give up part of your mind to represent the great god Heimdallr. His vanguard will enter your mind and seek to anchor at the bridge of Bifröst. After the god enters, there is no turning back. Your life will never be the same. His is a molecule of great potency. His tasks are special, and his powers, such as they are."

"You are not a member of my staff, are you?"

"That would be debatable, I am Dr Karl Leamas, the former Director, the old director. Age and circumstance have rendered me a liability." The erudite voice sounded amused. "Take a word of advice; embrace his spirit. Do not fight the losing battle."

"Doctor Karl Leamas who built this Institution? I have read about you, well, what little there is."

"Public exposure is not beneficial to our task."

Wallenberg sighed, uniformly disgusted with himself and his chief security officer. It was seriously slipshod to allow a patient to pinch the keys to pathology. He tried to approach this rationally, but his mind wasn't in it. The Midgard board had told him that the former Director had stepped down for reasons of health, not that he suffered from mental delusions.

"Our task?" Wallenberg stumbled to play along.

"Heimdallr has many sentries, but the watchman will be yours alone, like it was mine for almost half a century. You can enter all minds. You have discovered no more than a sliver of this ability."

It struck him suddenly. It was the Professor from his dream on the plane, the one who invited him to enter the mind of a female scientist.

"Ah, you have recognized me from you dream, Birger."

"Yes, it is troubling, but I am honored to meet you."

Shaken, Wallenberg held back until the old scholar had locked up. His mind had been calming, writing it off as stress. Now his heart was racing again. On the gravel outside, he waved goodnight, as the former director headed for the Sidekick entrance.

It was highly improbable that Dr Karl Leamas belonged in an exit ward for fully recovered patients.

Chapter 4

WALLENBERG GAINED INSTANT ACCESS to the file of Karl Leamas with his computer code. The patient was a Doctor of Medicine and an accredited psychologist. His career spanned decades, mostly in administration, at the helm of the greatest institutions of his time, but that was before the gods got to him.

Karl Leamas had taken a shining to the heathen gods of the Nordic tribes. He believed in divine atomic intelligence, a whole flora of them. The gods within he called them and eventually his ideas became an obsession that started to affect his work. Being a lifeguard by the human gene pool was a nice thought, but a typical delusion. He was the chosen watchman; the vessel of Heimdallr, the god in Nordic mythology credited with social order on Earth, the one who guarded the rainbow bridge that joined the worlds.

With his formidable intelligence in no way impaired, Dr Leamas had set out to protect the humans he considered to be the handiwork of the greater gods. His task was to allow their divine experiments to reach fruition. Even this obsession was harmless enough, until the killings started. Not that he murdered anyone in person, but the good doctor would stop at nothing to protect the chosen children. He had induced patients to do his bidding, and that meddling became his undoing. His wealth allowed him to interfere. Wallenberg looked up in sudden apprehension. Why had he not been told? The former Director was a dangerous patient. The omission could only be premeditated. It never occurred to him that he could be in physical danger.

As he pottered around the tiny kitchenette, hating the taste of instant coffee, he missed his Italian espresso machine. The full weight of his first day was upon him. What had brought him here were his own plans to indulge in cutting-edge research. The whole thing was sham. The realization that his former director might wield influence at Asgard Park was devastating, given yesterday's indication that the institute was being used as cover for secret activities.

Wallenberg looked around him and felt a sudden kinship with the archaic volumes of outdated psychiatry hovering in despondent silence on the sidelines. He gave up on the coffee. The malt whisky he had bought at Copenhagen airport had aged with better character than these books. This apartment was not the haunt of a hip bachelor, although a stuffed wingback chair under a reading lamp received him contentedly enough. Its green knotted fabric made him feel like somebody's granny. Freud would have felt at home here. It had a footstool and a lamp.

Slowly, he settled to immerse himself in the problems of the man he met earlier in the autopsy suit. The idea that evolution had a helping hand was not new. The Bible Belt here was still on a warpath against a bearded Devil named Darwin.

Adding to the daftness of Karl Leamas was the argument that a child fathered by anyone possessed by a god was to be protected by the watchman until the individual design could be evaluated. Was this true for female deities, he wondered? Or were they less keen? Virgin births are tricky, and Dr Leamas was not forthcoming on the subject.

After a hot refreshing shower in an old-fashioned white tub behind a flowery shower curtain, he put on a favorite robe, refreshed his drink, and burrowed back into an engaging story.

Leamas was not selling salvation or protection in this life unless you were chosen. His gods were not omnipotent. They lacked the allure of the Old Testament; unable to rain fire or unleash plagues. In this, Wallenberg noted, the Bible Belt had a better candidate. Was there a market for inadequate gods?

Was Heimdallr the controlman at the end of the production line, monitoring the chosen products. Markets are preceded by older models, and older folks care little for innovations that render them redundant while strange kids have a harder time of growing up before they reach their potential. Can you blame a designer for seeking to protect his patent? Was Karl's delusion about quality control? The god who settled social order among was able to monitor every human being through streamed observations on the fly.

Wallenberg stopped reading. It was too neat. The file was clearly doctored. The text was not a serious analysis of a mental condition. It was an account of a privately held conviction. This was the work of his predecessor. Did Karl still have that level of access? It was a frightening thought.

This late, it was early morning in Sweden. Wallenberg called his mother to tell her about the crises of his first day. Mom was a serious student of Viking mythology. She had often talked to him about the great Nordic god

Heimdallr, her favorite god. Catarine laughed off his troubles. He would master his new home soon enough. She was on business in Berlin. They agreed he would fly back next week to meet. He had some unfinished business in Lund. He'd wait to tell her of the broken promises by the Midgard board. Wallenberg hung up wondering if he had had sounded drunk.

It was time to shape up. His predecessor was not the only patient in his care, and there was excellent science underway at Asgard Park. As the new Director, he owed it to the Midgard board to get to the bottom of this mess. Members of his staff and perhaps some of their patients were involved. Were they dealing drugs?

It was his duty to ask the Federal Bureau in the State of New York to go undercover and look behind the scenes at Asgard Park.

The next few days passed quickly at Asgard Park. Low-key scholarly discussions mingled with heated rows, trailing non-stop through endless meetings. Wallenberg had no time for reflection. I two days, he would take a week off to relax back home in Sweden. After that, his calendar was booked solid.

The relations with law enforcement agencies were excellent. He had accepted a few undercover federal agents on the prowl, keeping a low profile. They expected feelers from Eric Schaeffer Spears. Not a whisper of implication had touched the Institute. It was an ideal state of affairs.

Book 2, Birger Wallenberg

Chapter 5

THE DAYS PASSED QUICKLY at Asgard Park. Low-key scholarly discussions mingled with heated rows, trailing non-stop through endless meetings. Wallenberg had no time for reflection. Only matters of urgency reached his desk; his calendar was booked solid. Distinguished visitors waited impatiently in the anteroom. His scientists were rare examples of a threatened species whose egocentric environment was required for their survival.

Stalking the corridors to check procedures; followed to the letter, he picked an authoritarian bearing. The relations with law enforcement agencies were excellent. He had undercover federal agents on the prowl, keeping a low profile. They expected feelers from Eric Schaeffer Spears. Not a whisper of implication had touched the Institute. It was an ideal state of affairs.

If only it were.

This fine afternoon, Wallenberg had managed to squeeze an important interview into his schedule. An orderly brought coffee with cream on a tray. How he loved this splendid setting; an airy Victorian room sparsely decorated in fine taste with delicate color balances under lofty ceilings and heavy cornices.

He had spent an hour this morning reviewing the contract stipulations between the Institute and the Estate of Dr Karl Leamas. The good doctor had built Asgard Park. Its terms made it impossible to get rid of the patient. Wallenberg could not so much as move him to new quarters without an army of lawyers descending on his office with ironclad veto rights. The power to impose his will on this place stopped squarely at the threshold of that lavish apartment.

Karl was not on medication. Drugs had no bearing on his predicament. The patient made sure he would never receive shock therapy or medication to dull his deranged mind. That was in some ways wise; care in too many mental institutions consisted of tranquilizers and heavy medication. The Asgard Park charter made sure that the Institute would not become a dungeon for the psychotic. Nobody touched Karl at Asgard Park without a nod from his Estate and by inference the patient himself.

The tall windows faced west, and he opened the balcony doors to let in the afternoon air. There was no denying that the man had built this great center of learning for all the well-publicized reasons. The patient journal he read on his first night had been heavily doctored. Staff with lower clearance saw a stripped-down official version where there was no mention of protected children. Officially, the patient suffered from paranoid schizophrenia.

Dr Karl Leamas would find the airy room ideal, having designed the setting himself. It soothed abrasive nerves and introduced notes of harmony into troubled minds while the analyst probed. Wallenberg was not sure what to make of the man. Religion rarely bothered with details of paranoia. They left it to the Devil to lighten the path. Only Leamas claimed contact with the watchman. His wealthy friends used influence on his behalf, but that sounded like any aspiring church. With the god, fully installed, Karl Leamas knew all minds, and could simply signal his wants to the executive arm of his empire to mediate in any conflict.

What version of Dr Leamas were industry leader's privy to? Did they discuss Heimdallr over rabbit loins and wild baby asparagus? Did they know that when a progeny with the right genes mated with a roving god, it enhanced the design? There was no way to tell. With decades at the helm of several mental institutions, his predecessor had a finger in many pies. He exercised real influence, subversive or otherwise, and had done so for decades.

Wallenberg sighed as breeze moved the curtains. There was an understated sense of beauty about this place. It breathed comfort. The meadows were freckled by sunlight. Oaks planted a century ago by a forgotten industrialist were mementos of a different time. He tried to assume their stoic trance, as he pushed the buzzer.

The soundproof door softly opened and closed, and he turned to ask the orderlies to release the patient. He wanted them on equal terms. He need not have bothered. Dr Leamas was alone and relaxed, with the comfortable patina of his gathering years.

"Of course, you are sane version," Wallenberg offered with a smile.

They sat facing each other in the upholstered chairs by the window, the prisoner of a warped mind and his sane keeper; even odds that anyone could pick the patient.

"Coffee with cream?"

He poured the coffee. The perfect grind was another of his small victories in this place.

"Well, young Birger, good coffee. I am told that you brook no opposition in reforming Asgard Park. We are all proud of you; but resisting Heimdallr is not a good idea."

"Karl, you are neither paranoid nor schizoid."

"There is no objective biological test for schizophrenia. My inability to tell the internal from the external renders me untouchable. True, when I was a young man, I too had ambitions and ideas, just like you, with decades invested in education. Intellectual snobbery was important to me at the time."

"And Heimdallr cured you?"

Karl rose and moved to a small table decked with porcelain and loaded with snacks: petite sandwiches, and English cakes. He smelled the newly baked scones and smiled at Wallenberg.

"You have outdone yourself. Yes, soon I shall have nothing but intellectual snobbery. I am losing touch with the god. We are in crisis."

They sat in silence and enjoyed the coffee, looking out on the tended gardens. The sun on the meadows infiltrated the spaces under the lofty ceilings and bathed them in buttercream off the walls.

"So, you are losing contact? Does that mean you are no longer reading minds around the world?"

"Did you know that Tim Berners-Lee at CERN, The European Laboratory for Particle Physics in Geneva, has proposed a web of nodes to store hypertext pages to be viewed by browsers on a network, a world-wide web? His Gopher protocol sets up a hierarchy of stored information on remote university computer terminals, connecting a net of scientific websites, each accessed as a file system with a text menu interface searchable by key words. Can't you see the parallel to Heimdallr?"

"Heimdallr crawling minds around the world? My friend Roos tells me McCahill is trying to codify the Gopher's menu-based hypermedia into uniform resource locators or URLs as he calls them. He has a team looking to navigate information resources on a network. The idea is to let a text search engine crawl open files on a world-wide web. I'm sure McCahill will be pleased to hear about the god."

"No need to be flippant, Birger. This is intelligent design at its best. It shows us that the gods are taking our capacity to the collective human level. We are already investing heavily."

"Meaning what?"

"Our knowledge of what is brewing in the minds of men gives the Midgard Group an edge in investment strategy."

"Wouldn't that be insider trading?"

Dr Leamas put away his cup and helped himself to another scone. "Take your friend Roos. His appointment to the Nobel Foundation was backed by some of my friends, eminent folks who advise the young man. Is that a conspiracy?"

"You know Roos?"

"Don't you love the ethereal calm of this room?"

Off guard, Wallenberg conceded; an antique rug covered the warm parquet. The marble fireplace under a mirror had none of the usual paraphernalia. It sat in isolated splendor.

"Have you Gophered my mind?"

"I should not enter the mind of my successor once he or she is chosen."

Wallenberg sipped his lukewarm coffee, full of flavor. The answer lets him off the hook, he would not be called upon to prove his ability. When he thought about his vision earlier, it came to him in the guise of a digital mental camera that stored its stash by a secret algorithm.

"Yes," Leamas told him.

"Yes what?"

"Digital mental camera that stores image and sound by a secret algorithm."

"I was just thinking that."

"I know; it comes with the package."

"You are a scary person."

"You don't know the half of it."

"Tell me about Bill Rayman."

"Who fathered Margaret's daughter, Amelia?"

"Yes, I have discovered that Asgard Park got saddled with a bogus inheritance claim after his death."

"You have been digging, young Birger!"

The orderly entered the room with a tray. There was a pitcher of cooled juice, a humidor, and an ashtray.

"You don't mind, do you?" Karl selected a Churchill sized cigar from the humidor and smelled it at length. Wallenberg pushed on.

"The funds came from the Skuld Insurance group. Paid as a fraudulent claim against Asgard Park. Wallenberg fished a paper from his breast pocket. "I tracked down the release slip, co-signed Karl Leamas."

"Yes, these new models must be protected until the market can test or assess their limitations."

"I don't need divine reasons to help a child."

Leamas sighed wistfully and looked out across the peaceful meadows, enjoying the scent of his unlit cigar. A horse grazed into view.

"What of your vision, Birger? Dr Kennan tells me that you were well informed. Was it clear?"

"I can recall every blow she took that night, and her every thought. You are a psychiatrist, Karl, you can appreciate my misery."

"Delighted to hear that; his scouts are in position. My advice is that you consent sooner rather than later. You are on the fence. That is not a good place to be. I am losing my ability. His armies have begun to transfer."

Dr Leamas used a small guillotine cutter for a precise cut and studied the cigar cap carefully.

"You must understand that we have operators from all walks of life on an array of associated payrolls who know nothing of Heimdallr. We rely on a handful of trusted people at the helm of the executive branches, worldwide. Fortunately, if the lower ranks smell a rat, they usually expect it to be their own."

Birger watched his predecessor light the cigar, a man scratching an itch. The room was a fitting backdrop for the indulgence.

"The hand that wields the sword must remain hidden."

"This is my problem, Karl; schizophrenics do not hide from the world; much less tell others to do so."

"So true, that is the forte of our cunning homo normalis. Allow Heimdallr to enter your mind, to anchor at the bridge of Bifröst. His forces are gathering in you. Grant him access. Take on the rest of his powers."

Wallenberg watched him gently puff. The room was airy enough to appreciate the mild aroma of secondary smoke.

"Tell you the truth, right now, intellectual snobbery seems a much safer harbor."

Karl Leamas slapped the upholstered arm with the flat of his hand and chuckled as he rose; leaving his cigar almost intact to die in the ashtray.

"You do take life too seriously, dear boy.

Karl had given a warm smile as he left, but Wallenberg knew that his grand delusions were deadly serious, and his power to reach out was undiminished. He certainly seemed to have the Midgard board in his pocket. That made his situation here untenable.

Book 2, Birger Wallenberg

Chapter 6

THAT NIGHT IN HIS private rooms, Wallenberg brooded over his dilemma. Booked out of Kennedy in the morning, he had cleared his calendar over the Fourth of July holidays to visit his mother. Dr George Kennan, his chief psychiatrist had gracefully accepted the extra workload.

On his newly installed television set, the kind family men of the LAPD could not stop beating Rodney King on a looped amateur video. He put the poor man out of his misery and went to bed.

Sleep came, and with it came a dream of a woman. Ready for sleep, he wanted to go with the firm skin and long limbs he found there. He wanted this dream, and tried not to spurn it, allowing it to run its course, lulled deeper into it; didn't become afraid of losing control until it was too late. Trying to pull back, his self-consciousness fell away into a brilliant awareness as it turned ugly, and he had pulled the four-plate stove from the wall as far as it would go. After he had poured the vegetable oil on the plates and slid her naked body face-down onto it.

He secured her hands and feet with tightly drawn steel wire to each corner wheel of the stove, resting her breasts and stomach firmly on the plates. The woman was waking up with panic-stricken tugs. He checked the tape that secured the glass tumbler in her mouth. She would make no sound. He talked gently to her about his urgent need for facts about the STASI dossier she had stolen, pouring oil between her buttocks. Watching it trickle down the rounded cleft marked by the white of an absent bikini, he got excited about it. He had done this before. In fury, angry that she had scratched his face, approaching the ecstasy of ejaculation; he reached down and turned on all four plates of the stove, and rode her over the finish line. His groans of pleasure escorted silent arching agitations of unbearable pain. He emptied his charge into her bowels with the sizzling smell of fried meat flirting with his nostrils. He did not withdraw but laid himself comfortably to rest on her body, pressing it onto the hot plates. She, like him, went limp, her last resistance broken. His power over this woman was complete. When she came to, she would give him what he wanted for the blessing of death.

Gasping at reality, Wallenberg woke drenched in his sweat-entangled sheets. The lack of empathy remained singularly clear. There was no comfort in the sexual part; the bare thought stuck in his throat like a hook. It was an evil vision all through, ashes in his mouth.

On the professional side, there was a minimal chance of this crime being real. With a house full of the criminally insane, he could speak with some authority on that. The clarity gave him the shivers; the brutal ecstasy fed by memories. He was an inert observer in the mind of a perpetrator. There was no sense of self. The burn-marked knuckle had appeared normal enough to his eyes.

Who was he and who was his victim? The STASI dossier the man sought to recover came out of a spy novel. Did he read something like this recently? There was never time. The ill-famed East German Ministry for State Security, the STASI had been recently shut down, their vaults of dossiers sealed.

At long last he fell back asleep and woke shortly thereafter with a splitting headache to a bright summer morning. As he shaved, he promised himself never again to take counsel from a mental patient. And never to give in to his longings unless he knew what they were. Coming to this place to study unstable minds; back on safer ground in Europe, he'd better take a hard look into his own sanity.

Book 2, Birger Wallenberg

Chapter 7

BACK IN SWEDEN, FOR the holidays, Birger studied the sky through the kitchen window of his apartment in Lund, the old Swedish university town. It was a windy but increasingly sunny Sunday morning; the brooding clouds of a passing storm fading in the east. Reassuring shafts of sunlight were stalking the strait towards Falsterbo. On the Danish side, the sun had already claimed the day.

His sojourn at Asgard Park had upset him. Paranoia was not a good thing in an administrator. He looked forward to a short respite in this gentler world that would get him back on solid footing after the wringer of New York.

In the calm of hindsight, he had made astounding errors of judgment. He had failed to grasp the influence of Karl Leamas who had not relinquished his grip on his vast network of friends in high places. Was the reputation of Asgard Park worth his own budding reputation as a scientist? By withholding information from the police, he had invited disaster at every turn. Was his future served by a web of lies and omissions?

Arriving last night from New York, he had gone to bed early and alone. His mother was not taking calls. It was time to enjoy his brief vacation. The old gang would be curious about the Institute.

He treated himself to a solid breakfast at the nearby Grand Hotel and read the papers. The skirmishes in Bosnia had a familiar ring, as did a bomb blast at Kings Cross. Sixty massacred in a Soviet enclave was not really news and neither was the harassment of Russian immigrants in Lithuania.

In an Albanian countryside café, a German tourist had struck eleven men dead with a sledgehammer. Wallenberg put aside the papers to greet Roos, who joined him for breakfast. He enjoyed smoked salmon with poached eggs as his friend tucked into steroids. They discussed the possibility of a joint climb later in the summer. Roos was an avid mountaineer, and Wallenberg loved being back in the old rut.

On the southbound motorway from Malmoe, red gabled farms passed as the sun chased the last clouds from the sky. In the spring he had traded in his Porsche, his third in a row, for a tamer Saab. It was his way of shedding the fickle skin of youth. Or was it to assume a mantle of repute? He must use the time to pick his mother's brain and seek the backing of her contacts on the Midgard board.

Ten minutes later he was in the old part of the small, picturesque village of Falsterbo. The freshness in the air after a passing thunderstorm had brought fragrance out of the damp earth. Luxury cars occupied every nook and cranny on the narrow winding street, many with Swiss number plates. Youngsters in rumpled clothes were enjoying each other's company, all part of growing nature and its pungent smells, the kids giving a party.

There was no response to his mother's doorbell; the congenial thuds of tennis balls connecting with racket strings carried through the scented air. It was his favorite sport. At one time he had trained with the pros. His mother's Mercedes was in the driveway. He groped for the keys on the doorstep.

The faint familiar odor in the hall did not belong there. It took him a moment to grasp its significance. A gush of fear erupted. Alarm rushed through his veins. The scent darkened in the hallway as he entered; the soft sweet noxious air of it. It was the smell of death.

He didn't realize how strong it was until he almost gagged. With nothing in his head but pounding fear, he ran through the villa, bracing for a shock. It took him moments to grasp that the smell was strongest in the hall where he entered. In the same instant, his mind lost its way in another mental spasm: the kitchen. His putrid evil vision.

He tried to take stock of himself. He was a doctor. Death was no stranger, but the kitchen. He clutched wildly after the clinical distance he conjured up at the autopsy table. He was unable to assume that vacuum shroud of indifference. His mother had been his companion for over thirty years. She was the only person he loved.

In his vision, as the perpetrator left the scene, he left the door ajar. Now, pressing a handkerchief over his mouth, he reached to push open the kitchen door. It was ajar. From somewhere in his mind there came an almost audible snap as the complicated controls shifted. They entered him into the hands of a more primal module, buried within humankind's first forgotten knots of gray, a command center shorn of feeling, stripped of the mercies that hampered survival through impossible ages. It was the center that sent mammals creeping out of the primeval slime to be rewarded with brains that made the center itself redundant util now. Birger entered that old outpost of intelligence. It remembered its maker.

A cold calm descended on him.

He pushed open the door. A naked body lay draped, stomach down, over the four-plate electric stove, pulled from the wall as far as it came. A thin steel wire secured the wrists and ankles to the four wheels. In the struggle the wire had cut through the skin and disappeared. The plates had fried the flesh. Elsewhere, the bloated, mottled blue skin showed deep cuts and bruises. Body fluids had seeped to the floor, its dryness adding to the stench, but with days had past, that odor had been replaced by another.

Birger threw open the window before he checked the face, the taped mouth. The strong tape was wound around her head in circles, under her chin and across the top. The circumstances were clear; they had been etched into his mind for days; the brilliant awareness that came to him at Asgard Park. It had arrived through the eyes and the mind of a stranger who did not know his mother.

He left her untouched and stumbled out onto the garden terrace where the atomic freeze-frame silence in his mind gave way incomprehension. He threw up, gasping to regain his breath to the far-off voices of happy youths.

The arm of the law on the Falsterbo peninsula was not long. The single duty officer had fathered a child and exercised his choice by Swedish law to take paid parental leave. His bicycle gathered cobwebs for the summer. With no replacement to watch this sleepy community, the call went to the nearby village Vellinge. Their squad car reached Falsterbo in fifteen minutes.

The two good-natured officers, family men with scant experience of murder, backed out of the house in panic and started to cordon off the property. They soon ran out of reflective ribbon and spent time speaking on the police radio. The cavalry, with a retinue of experts, was on its way from Malmoe.

A bestial murder, in an exclusive neighborhood, had all the ingredients to titillate a bored public. But it was the victim's name that sent an army of reporters scrambling for their cars. Catarine Wallenberg. A merry-go-round lurched into gear at the excited crackle from the police radio. At the center, as always, was his late mother, engulfed in a vortex of human action, and in the calm eye of a media storm where time had stopped. She who had been the spear of a new breed of career women, powerful and rich, the most unlikely person to be found in her kitchen tied to an Electrolux stove.

Inspector Larson was an informal man with a studied lack of respect, culled from years of digging through other people's dirty laundry. Birger felt a vague dislike for the man on a deckchair on his mother's terrace. He was relieved that the preliminaries were over. They had felt like an out of body experience.

What he dreamt at Asgard Park was real, and that was impossible. Having witnessed Mother's death, scared him like nothing ever had, but that wakeup call was preserved for him alone. Was he mentally prepared to approach his terrible situation? He tried to focus on reality; to get the rest of the formalities over. He breathed deeply a couple of times to shepherd his balance.

"Did your mother have close male friends?"

"I know nothing of her male friends, except that she had them. Mother was 47 years old. She remained single after father died. She had no time to keep a husband."

"No special friend in Berlin?"

"Not that I know. You will hear that she had a sweet tooth for men. It would not surprise me if they were young. They never concerned me."

Wallenberg tried to steady his voice. The inspector shifted on the edge of the deckchair and eyed him with practiced sympathy.

"Any known enemies?"

"Not enemies like that. Mother built her private investment company into an industrial empire. That takes grit. She was hard as nails. Fair, but hard. I'm sure she nailed a few to the cross. They were the kind of enemies who brought unflattering oil portraits to her birthday bashes, or orchids which she hated."

A helicopter passed overhead, and he ignored it.

"Not one of ours," said the inspector, and squinted at the sky, "probably the press. You want to finish this inside?"

Birger shook his head, wanting it over with.

"No financial problems?"

"Mother was a careful investor."

"And your financial standing, Doctor?"

"I have money of my own, Inspector, more than will last me a lifetime. Mother invested wisely on my behalf."

Gripped with a sudden impatience, he rose, and the Inspector followed his example.

"Can we confirm your whereabouts for the last week?"

"My days are back-to-back meetings. I run Asgard Park, a research institute in New York. Hundreds of the most honest people you will never meet can vouch for every minute of my time, several Nobel laureates among them." He hesitated. "When can you have the sperm residue DNA analyzed?"

"We use a British lab. There is a waiting period of a month or so."

Birger shrugged it off; in the shadow of this horror, he could not summon anger over petty quibbles. Nothing was won by objecting to official complacency at the lowest level. He could pick up the phone and override the queue in a minute and have a chartered plane whisk the parcel over. What he really needed was to get away from here.

He needed to brace against the psychological fright, patch up his shattered feelings. His pleasant existence was permanently distorted. The severe implications would not wait for him to find balance. Rationality must be his guide. There had to be a way to revise his mental disturbance without lapsing into delusions.

"Is there is anything I can do to speed things up," he asked distractedly.

"Thanks, but they don't much like arm-twisting."

Back in his Lund apartment, Birger Wallenberg resisted the urge for a drink to settle the splintered thoughts. He tried to override his anguish by checking in with his mother's many directors, one after the other. Nothing shed any light on the calamity.

His mind darted back to bygone times when mother and son walked the slopes of an Icelandic glacier valley, dwarfed by a vast theater of silence. The moments in life that were granted with the least grudge crowded you when the time for thanksgiving had passed.

The recognition that both of his visions were true was unworkable. That darker awareness. He had witnessed the deed. His mother had been a stranger to the man's eyes. The clarity made him shudder. How do you treat a sound mind?

Tomorrow would be a madhouse of condolences, of shocked friends and associates with business deals dead in the water. It would be worse than the asylum he had left for tranquility at home. It pained him to dwell on his measly problems with Mother in a morgue. She who had sat with a sick child and fed him broth, while her business minions stalked downstairs; moving her headquarters home, rather than have a nanny care for her son.

Birger also knew he had to get into her private safe before the investigators did. The police would be watching her house, perhaps his apartment. They needed the overtime. He must save Mother whatever embarrassment her bedroom safe held. It was the least he could do. He suspected that the police would leak every tidbit they came across, all in the name of transparency.

In dark clothes and a leather jacket, he took the back stairs to the garden. The Harley was a gift from Mother. Birger pushed the heavy bike across the backyard into a side street. With the helmet on, he did not look the like a director of a renowned Institute, not even the heir to a vast fortune.

It was the end of term with students milling about in the summer night. Was he running away from his mental troubles? He was more worried of what lurked in his mind than anything he'd find in Mother's safe. For all the shadows weighing on his senses, there was only one source of relief to lighten his mind; Asgard Park with all its dark mysteries was a world away.

Dark visor down, aiming for the motorway, he tore past the bulky cathedral in Lund, taking the motorway to Falsterbo.

Chapter 8

ON THE EMPTY MOTORWAY to Falsterbo, Wallenberg kept to the speed limit. Half an hour later, he parked the bike at the edge of the boardwalk to the empty beach. Walking the broad strip of soft sand in the moonlight, he found the familiarity of lapping waves consoling. He had stayed out here untold nights, and never alone.

From the sand dunes below his family home, he spotted a police car up front. For ten minutes he stood under the canopy of trees by the back gate, in the shadow of a full moon. Slipping across the back garden he used his key. The police were not expecting a beach landing. They had left the garage unsealed and turned off the security control panel in the hall. As he passes through the gym, he picked up an old tennis bag, eyes adjusting to the darkness.

A strongbox is only as safe as its disguise. What you can carry into a house, you can carry out. Wallenberg ignored the Chubb in the corner. The real safe, in her bedroom, was in plain view. It was the lower half of the wood-burning stove in the middle of the room. No burglar would check for a built-in safe below its ashtray. It opened with the remote to her satellite disk. He had no trouble recalling the code, using the matching letters.

He punched in the word 'Heimdallr' and pushed the exit button. There was a sound of cylinders drawing back. The safe was small, for private things. Aside from money, there were several ledgers and a small pile of dossiers and heavy-duty clasp envelopes. He moved all its contents into her windowless walk-in closet and put on the light to sort it out. Each clasped envelope held a passport, credit cards, driving license, and a mixed array of documents. The passports had assorted State emblems. He shook his head in wonder as he dropped the lot into the training bag.

The small photo album went in next to last. Looking hurriedly through the pictures; it was worse than he feared It shook him up badly. At the bottom of the pile from the safe, there was a sealed yellowed envelope, addressed to him in Mother's hand. It had clearly been there for a while.

He cut the light in the walk-in closet and returned the currency stacks and company-related dossiers to the safe. As he walked down to the waterfront, it was close to four o'clock. Faint light edging into the sky. The Harley took him to Lund in less than twenty minutes, full throttle.

Getting sparkling water from the fridge, the condoms on the bottom shelf told him; it had been a long time. In the bedroom, after a shower, he made a fire in the round floor to ceiling tiled fireplace. With an acrid smell, the forged documents made the transition from evidence to rumpled knots of plastic. He flipped through files of long-term strategies and tried to get his head around it. One dossier had hundreds of pages listing people and their positions in West German companies, providing details of collusion with the East German secret police. She had jotted 'STASI informers' on the cover, which freaked him out. It was the file the man in his vision had been looking for; and never retrieved. Here were all his grade papers from first year at school up to his doctor's degree; another dear topic of Mother's. Why had he taken that?

Then there were the pictures. In some his mother was a younger, more beautiful creature. In some she was naked, as her obsession would have it. She was a member of the nudist colony in Skanör, something he did not appreciate as a teenager. The naked flesh did not bother him. The photos were all decent. They could be favorite snaps of any spirited woman, trophies fit for a coffee table.

The presence of Dr Karl Leamas, as a young man was impossible to accept on so many levels. And there was plump little Birger, no more than four, between his mother and Leamas. She had written a caption: 'With Karl and his apprentice in Lausanne, 1963.' The word apprentice leaped out at him. Why had she lied when he told her about meeting Karl Leamas in the autopsy suit; if not overtly, certainly by omission? She gave nothing away.

In another snap, Leamas and a teenage boy were holding his hands on either side. The caption read: 'Karl with Birger and Keltenbrunner in Lausanne, 1963.' Dr Leamas had somehow turned his mother to his crazy schemes. Neither of them had seen fit to acknowledge the other. Karl had lectured him on the purpose of a secret thread. His highly rational mother took it seriously.

As he leafed through her papers, another truth became apparent; her ties to the Midgard Group were far deeper than a friend on the board. His mother was one of its five major shareholders. Talk about job security. The web of secrecy, lies and false document was genuine enough.

He kept her letter to the last, a reverent occasion. She was speaking to him from beyond the boundaries of death. It was a rambling note, written in her perfunctory style to prepare him for a different kind of shock.

'My Son!

When you read this letter, I am dead. Do not grieve, I had a full life. If you by now understand that you have been chosen to serve more demanding masters, no words are needed. If not, I ask that you immediately contact Dr Karl Leamas of Asgard Park in New York. He heads the organization you have been chosen to lead in the fullness of time. As I write this, he is the Institute Director. Do not take his position at face value. As the conduit of Heimdallr, Karl has influence beyond your imagination. All my investments and those of the Midgard Group rest on his insights. Let him give you guidance in your coming ascendancy.

I serve Heimdallr, one of the few hundred Vanir chosen for his network. Most are by necessity closer to the centers of operational power. They have the highest positions in law enforcement, in intelligence agencies and national security. Often, these organizations cannot be swayed in time to prevent spontaneous events. We use backups of private soldiers. As a last resort, criminal elements are pushed into service. The aim of Heimdallr is not to change society. That is the domain of human evolution. As a student of psychiatry, you find my confession painful. The learned texts will tell you to assume the worst.

When you were younger, I amused you with stories of the Old Nordic gods and their preoccupation with us humans. It was not a topic suited for a teenager, so I let the seed rest. Now I call you to a hearing of all the holy races, greater and lesser kinsman of Heimdallr. Accept the god who created humankind. Do not take Viking interpretation literally. How could they grasp what still eludes science?

The gods still cross the bridge that joins gods and humans, the bridge of Bifröst that is guarded by Heimdallr. Do not look for it in the sky. It is hidden in the quantum field. As a Vanir, my son, do not fail me in your cardinal test.

Mother'

For a while he sat in front of the fireplace, trying to take aboard this revelation. This was not an easy letter. As his visions, there had been things in her life she could not explain; that was upsetting enough. He was well aware of the thin line dividing psychosomatic visions from reality, but nothing could induce observations that dovetailed with reality across vast distances on the fly.

What was she telling him, that she had taken Karl's advice on financial investment? He could not fault the outcome. Many had found his mother eccentric and secretive, but she believed what she wrote. It did not make her delusional, just naïve, which did not sound like his mother at all.

Unconsciously, his toes made happy with the pile of an antique silk Qom in front of his fireplace: it was his foreplay rug.

His mother had kept a diary of sorts, page after page. It occurred to him that these thoughts were meant for him. For a psychoanalyst, it was so absorbing that he almost forgot that this was his mother speaking.

"Karl's age has become a problem. He tells me we are often flying blind and out of contact with the watchman. The transfer of Heimdallr is at hand. Should I try to make it less of a confrontation? I know how stubborn Birger can be. He is off to New York to take over Asgard Park. We all hope for a smooth transition."

"Birger called. Karl has made his intentions clear. They are wasting no time. He told me that Birger had connected because he knew about a New York incident that took place yesterday. I could not bring myself to upset him more on his first day. I am off to Berlin to pick up that STASI file. It's a minor matter, so, I'll be back in time.

Birger put down her diary. As a student, he had never questioned the basic assumptions of human existence. He respected the parameters of natural laws and social rules. There was never time to question reality? Why clutter up a comfortable existence? Maybe a Porsche on your eighteenth birthday did that? Every winter, for as long as he could remember, he went skiing in the Alps and mountain climbing in summers. Mow, he was all out of time.

Catarine Wallenberg was buried in the Falsterbo cemetery on July 10th, 1991. The ceremony was graced with spring sunshine, and the old church of St Gertrud's was packed. The royal family had sent the old prince.

Distinguished in dark cloth, Birger drifted among the mourners.

Out of reach, beyond the cemetery, a large contingent of a motorcycle gang looked nothing like his mother's usual entourage.

They kept to the side and showed respect.

Chapter 9

AT ASGARD PARK IN Westchester County, another day began gray and wet. As Fourth of July wore on, the tone grew lighter, but the fog lingered, possessive as a mother tucking in her child.

In the office of Chief Psychiatrist, Dr George Kennan, was preparing for the next meeting of the grant committee. With his Director in Sweden over the holidays, he would tend to the matter. His Chief Security Officer, John Matson, entered after a casual knock.

"Eric Schaeffer Spears is coming down the drive; four men in one car, no appointment."

"I'll deal with Andrea Fassati. No need to inform Dr Leamas, he sent me his file this morning."

"What about the Federal agents?"

"Give them a lecture. And treat our visitors with due respect. This is a reputable institution."

George Kennan ignored Matson's grin, pleased that Wallenberg was not back to deal with this impromptu visit, so soon after his mother's death.

Ten minutes later there was a knock on his door and Matson ushered in a dapper man of uncertain middle age. Well-dressed without flair, he introduced himself as Andrea Fassati with a limp handshake, and beckoned his two bulky bodyguards back into the anteroom to watch over a prim secretary.

"This is a private conversation, doctor, wouldn't you agree?"

"Yes, Mr. Spears. Can I offer you coffee or tea? My secretary will see to your men."

"I am Andrea Fassati. Why do you call me Spears?"

"A Freudian slip," Kennan gave the New York Jew an apologizing smile, "won't happen again."

"You would not be setting me up for a federal sting, doctor, wearing a wire? What is this place anyway?"

"Our charter is to broaden understanding of the human mind," George Kennan ventured to explain. "Recent developments in information processing have highlighted the need for a unified theory of the mind-brain. The aim is to splice classic psychology to the advanced neurosciences."

Seeing the faraway look in the man's impatient eyes, Kennan cut himself short. "There has been some progress."

"Yeah, but what's the place fronting? What is your real business? And what is your beef with me?"

There was a harsh undertone to the soft voice.

"We have no disagreement with you, Mr. Fassati. You did agree to the compensation we offered."

"Yes, but nothing fits. This is my problem. Nobody wants to touch your outfit. The authorities respect you. That kind of respect requires deep pockets. Are we not in the same business?"

"We are not. This is a center of learning. The drugs we prescribe are rarely appreciated by the recipients."

"Best setup I've seen. I respect competence, but with my best men in the morgue, I want answers."

"Mr. Fassati, our remuneration came with the condition that you back off."

"Twenty keys are not the end of the world."

"I wouldn't tell that to a judge," said Dr Kennan.

"You promise to pay and then insult my intelligence. I think you are holding the woman here. I can blow your cover wide open; think about that."

Dr Kennan put away his pen with a dejected shrug.

"My advice is not to threaten us, Mr. Fassati."

As a Sicilian by descent, and a tactician with a keen sense of the pitfalls of his particular trade, Fassati knew that he was regarded as a strange bedfellow for the gangs of New York. Nobody denied he was an asset. He took pride in playing hardball with professional distance.

Careful and pedantic, he had eked out his game with infinite care, expecting all the desperate moves and hedging his bloody bets. Now, he felt cornered and compromised, his position uncertain. The families were falling over one another, ordering him to back off. It was a maddening itch. He had to know.

He was about to press that point when Dr Kennan handed a thick folder of computer printouts across the table. His eyes flicked at the pages and back to the doctor several times before the text took hold. He sunk in the comfortable chair.

He read carefully, turning the pages with a studied lack of expression; only the eyes betrayed him with a feverish sheen reflecting the printout. The outlines of all his racketeering arrangements in the State of New York, the families, the names and dates, princes and pretenders, the legitimate companies, the funds and scams, the import and distribution networks; the whole bloody business.

The details on his own outfit were so accurate that they brought drops of involuntary sweat trickling down his neck. What got him were the deals within his faction, done behind his back. His captains had their hands in the till. Episodes came into focus. If knowledge was power, this was pure power.

Fassati turned the last page and tore his eyes away. It was the end of the line. They could indict him on the spot. They had the details to sink the ship. His Italian friends were no better off. Nobody could contain this. The scope was enormous. It would take years to restore, and he'd not be around to do it.

He hated the feeling; like a kid; an unknown beast had moved underneath his bed. There was nothing he could do. The government did not need to offer a deal. He was unable to speak. Why had they waited? The printout went back decades, and they had interfered. The beast had moved when he disturbed its privacy. No wonder the other families were warning him off.

Gingerly he assumed the mantle of a plodding clerk as he probed for something to salvage. But he had nothing to offer. His hoarse voice caught.

"What do you want?"

"Our earlier agreement would have been a better deal, Mr. Fassati."

"I understand that now."

"If I chose to withhold this information, you stand deeply indebted. We keep our secrets well; but there is a catch."

"There always is."

"I am glad you see it that way. On rare occasions you may get a call asking for your cooperation. At such a time you will do our bidding with all means at your disposal. Drag your feet for an hour and you will be dead within that hour. There is no appeal."

The calm ferocity was convincing. Still Andrea Fassati tried to salvage more.

"And in return for these favors, would it be possible to receive information from your sources? The scope of your investigation . . ."

"There will be no contact. A call may reach you when you are an old man, or perhaps not at all. Until then we look the other way. That is the deal."

"I accept." This shrink had connections up his sleeve that Andrea did not desire to test

"Good. We want your involuntary association to be as smooth as possible. Should we ever call for your help, we will of course repay the costs accrued." He slid a plain white envelope across the table.

"And this is?"

"An unsecured loan granted by the Manhattan branch of International Equity to the Fragrance Club, the sum is being deposited into your Bahamas account as we speak. It is a reckless loan. The bank will write it off as bad debt later this year. It is as clean as money comes. We went to the trouble of washing it for you. It covers the loss of your commodity, the purchase price, not the potential profits.

The careful tactician opened the envelope and read every line with great of care.

"This is not necessary," he said pocketing the slip. Dr. Kennan smiled.

"That kind of hypocrisy is never lost on our schizophrenic patients."

"Thanks anyway, for leaving us alone."

"We try not to interfere in human affairs."

The words 'human affairs' gave Andrea Fassati an odd tingle. Was there any other kind?

"This is personal deal. Do not reveal it, even to the most trusted consigliere. Never mention our information or use it as a bargaining chip. This is not an easy story for the authorities to accept. You would be the only one telling it, and you would not get to tell it twice."

The doctor reached over and withdrew the printouts that Fassati had taken care to withhold.

"If ever one word comes to you with an urgent demand for support, no matter how reckless the request, even death of your people, stalling will be a worse option. It is not a common word, and you will never mention it to anyone.

"One word?"

"Heimdallr." Dr Kennan spelled it but didn't hand him the slip.

Fassati rose nervously from in his chair, as the doctor opened the door. The secretary had vanished from the anteroom. So had his bodyguards. That was a blow; after telling them to stay put.

"Where are my men?"

"Don't worry, Mr. Fassati, they were tended to."

They walked side by side to his car.

"I am sorry, Doctor. I had no idea."

"About what?"

"Everything!"

Dr Kennan smiled reflectively.

"That is a very good start, Mr. Fassati."

They had parked the car to the side, probably out of concern for the greater good of Asgard Park. Fassati appreciated their attention to its spot free image. A public scandal in a place like this, with dozens of eminent scientists, would be like firing a shotgun in a field. Everything with wings took off.

Dozing in the car were his four men, all dressed up in straitjackets. Fassati decided not to utter another word. He gave Kennan his hand, tried on a weak smile and made his grip firmer, intending to inspire trust in a deal he aimed to keep to the letter.

The information in the Asgard Park dossier had touched him like a live wire. There were liaisons to nurture and others to sever. It would be a fruitful episode.

The knowledge would ease his path to the inner circle, and he would never speak of it. The clandestine organization he had come across was powerful enough to operate by its own rules. That kind of clout probably meant it was government sponsored.

Back in his Manhattan office, he started to search for that strange word. Fassati was not a religious man but a text from Old Icelandic mythology told him all he needed to know.

'Heimdallr is the watchman who settles social order among mortals. He is alert enough to hear grass grow and a single leaf fall. He never sleeps.'

Chapter 1

BURTON CRANE STOOD AND stamped the early hour's mist on a gravel road to nowhere. It had stopped raining, but the wetness and the wind persisted. The clearing was in a river valley surrounded by woodland eight miles east of the old Ducal town of Landshut in Lower Bavaria. There were nine of them waiting for police backup to arrive from the Federal Criminal Police in Munich, eight officers of the German Verfassungsschutz and he as a lone liaison officer from NATO intelligence. Strictly speaking, NATO had no intelligence assets but got the professional staff it needed from various countries, in his case the American NSA. Salary-wise, Burton Crane was on loan from SIS, the United Kingdom's external security agency, more commonly known as MI6. They too were temporary masters as window-dressing for a different case. It was complicated.

The blankets of morning fog were thinning, suspended in slivers above the ground. A canopy of twisted virgin forest covered the slopes where the impregnable thicket converged on a dried-out riverbed.

Burton Crane from NATO was technically here as an observer. The inspectors of the German security police were in charge; but the action was his brainchild from the start, and he was angrily impatient. He had stepped on too many toes to get this search underway, and someone was making a deliberate muddle of it. They didn't like Yanks meddling in the backyard.

The spooks of the BND intelligence agency in Bonn had washed their hands of the affair, for leverage. If it was a dud, they'd file a complaint to undermine his standing; what was left of it. And since the Verfassungsschutz had for historical reasons been stripped of its authority to arrest the citizenry, they were compelled to wait for the regular police to arrive from Munich. Crane had hoped to return to London in the evening. Evelyn expected him back by then and given the account of broken promises, it was amazing that his chipper wife still missed him.

It was getting light. The BKA police backup from Munich was an hour late. Crane had chosen early morning to strike, the time of docility and disorientation, but his window of opportunity was closing fast.

Up ahead, under the veil of the black German forest was their objective. Buried under the black canopy, heavy in the mist, were the barracks of the biker gang involved in the Berlin incident. The information was reliable. It told him that this place was accessible by footpaths only. The land belonged to the powerful patron of this club: Baron Keltenbrunner von Geisenhausen. Until the police arrived with the search warrant, he, and the rest of them were trespassing on private property.

Crane broke off a twig to chew the sprout. The taste was bitter, and he spit it out. He had been compiling circumstantial data on these particular bikers for some time. Links connected them to the arms caches dug up near Zwiesel at the Czechoslovakian border several hundred kilometers to the north; on another of the baron's estates. A pattern was emerging. Unfortunately, sightings of bikers near the arms caches were circumstantial. The club carried no insignia.

This particular gang was a brawling army of drifters. They were partial to heavy drinking and a fatalistic contempt for danger. In this they differed little from other clubs. These unsavory louts ran constant feuds all over the place. Crane had seen enough in the line of fire and had no sympathy for brainless cravings.

They kept a curiously low profile, though. The absence of markings made them hard to trace. He found no evidence that the club ran chapters outside Germany. Were it not for the Keltenbrunner connection, they might have been what they claimed, motor enthusiasts!

For most clubs, franchising was the road to respect, the action was drugs, protection, and prostitution. Scratch the surface and these bikers were a different breed. Interpol inferred that the club stood aloof from illegal dealings. As the BKA would have it, this unruly bunch was picking flowers and watching birds. It seemed more like an undercover army, but for what purpose. These guys were never short of funds. He recalled the different and more distinguished guests in that cavernous room of the Geisenhausen estate. All of it seemed bigger than the parts.

Crane stomped the gravel with polished military boots that were a trifle heavy for civilian clothes. The leader of the Verfassungsschutz was on the phone to a colleague at Köln headquarters. They confirmed that their telex to police headquarters in Wiesbaden stated the correct time. This was an internal police foul-up. Someone at Merianstraße 100 had given the wrong rendezvous time to Kriminaloberkommissar Brechter in Munich. The police buses were half an hour away.

After a lifetime of law enforcement, starting out as a teenage MP on American bases in Germany, Burton Crane was used to people screwing up his schedule. He could do without the hassle. The shadows in his private life were growing darker as the demands of the job kept him away.

Pushing his fists deeper into the coat, he turned to face the road, fixing his stare at where the crooked road disappeared into the black forest, waiting for the bloody Volkswagen buses, looking back in time.

His posting to NATO signaled a changing emphasis from his purely military orientation. Engaged in the mundane world of infiltration, he came well equipped for the job. The intelligence communities knew one another intimately. The cloak-and-dagger stuff was long gone with the glory and the glamour. The secrets had lost their luster, and everything was boringly predictable.

Germany was officially reunified since last October when the six reestablished federal states of East Germany formally rejoined West Germany. Having accidentally met the Treuhand president at that Bavarian Mausoleum, he did not envy her the task of fusing the parts. His team had infiltrated one of the fastest growing crime syndicates within the former Eastern Bloc, peopled with old-timers from their former intelligence communities. These guys were into all that could be sold off, and potential progress into nuclear materials was a real concern. His NATO team had succeeded in attaching a mole: his friend Konrad, a German citizen with a valid passport and a fictive past. His second life as a German with a former East German party card was supported by carefully tailored, well-worn documents, smudged by more stamps than any person should be forced to suffer.

After months of menial jobs on the syndicate's fringes, Konrad was now a trusted driver. He worked for Helmut Mayer, one of their executives, a man of unknown origins. Three days ago, the crown jewels fell into Crane's lap, in the form of a Berlin dossier from a former STASI general. The dossier outlined the detailed network of STASI agents and their present positions in West Germany. The syndicate intended to use it to plant operators on various levels of business and government to ease their way to the money trough.

Konrad had tipped them off that Helmut Mayer would receive the dossier in a bar in Memhardstrasse. Konrad was to drive him to Dresden afterwards. Everything was under control. There would be a simple maneuver to detain Helmut Mayer; a case of mistaken identity, based on an all-points bulletin with a drawing that vaguely resembled him. This would force his driver, Konrad, to continue to Dresden with the STASI dossier. Mayer would follow after a speedy release. A laboratory van would escort Konrad at high-speed to Dresden, recording every piece of paper, with no lapse of time for Konrad to explain. He would hand over the dossier in Dresden.

As it turned out, a woman blew it all to pieces. She had intercepted the STASI dossier before Mayer got to it and made a perfect drop to a motorcycle courier. Their barracks were now within Crane's reach. The biker network, as he thought of it, baffled him. They had snatched the reward of his hard-earned labor from under his nose and made a fool of his team. Unwisely, this had caused him to throw his weight around. Faint motor vibrations irritated the morning air and snapped Crane out of it.

It was not the sound of buses and it came from the wrong direction. "Scheize!"

The sound of large bikes grew in consistency, but not in volume. The bikers were starting up but not yet on the move. They were out in force, judging by the sound that issued from under the sickly carpet damped by the soggy underbrush of the black deadwood forest. Crane checked his watch. The BKA troops were fifteen minutes away.

"Guys, we got to go in now. We cannot let them waltz out. The BKA will be here any minute."

The circumstances demanded this last rite, a gesture of protest. After decades of serving in Germany, he knew how hard it was for a German officer to bend the rules with other agencies looking over his shoulder. They would do this by the book.

"Impossible, Herr Crane, not without a search warrant. They will make trouble. We cannot arrest them without the police." As the tall officer from Verfassungsschutz shrugged in a helpless gesture, he did not seem a least bit sorry.

"Wir warten!"

The sound was on the move and coming closer. No doubt they had plenty of paths in the woods. They could easily scatter and evade the police. Crane knew he was beaten, an observer without influence. His father had once told him, that observers in the Second World War had a special badge that consisted of a central O with wings. The soldiers used to call these guys the feathered assholes. That was how he felt at this moment, like a feathered asshole.

Headlights flickered thought the foliage up the path to the right as the sun broke through the morning fog behind him. He tried to untangle the knot in his stomach. It was a long, rugged procession, at least forty bikes. The leader halted at an intersection about two hundred feet down the road, looking them over. Crane guessed it took more than a bunch of civilians on private land to impress him. Slowly the procession started towards them. The fingers of the Verfassungsschutz inched towards their 9mm Heckler and Kochs.

The moment grew tense, the morning silence filled with the powerful strokes rose to stir the air into a macho orgy of machines. The escapades of these guys were legend. They were crazy people on pointless suicidal excursions. They clashed with organized crime and came out on top. Not protecting their interests, if that was picking flowers. Just for the hell of it. By all accounts these guys were harbingers of bad news, and not only in Bavarian beer halls.

What should have happened and didn't happen puzzled Crane. The bikers made no attempt to drive them off. They did not question their presence. They didn't stop to chew out this bunch of trespassing civilians. They knew!

And not only did they know who they were, but they knew why they were waiting. It turned the mystery a darker shade. These guys were privy to information from high within the Intelligence Services. It was the first direct sign Crane had seen of ties to the establishment. This delay had been precisely planned.

The leader was a big gaunt guy with light brown hair combed back and tied in a bun. As he passed, his scarred face betrayed no expression but an intense stare. Crane felt his eyes search him out. For a moment he held his gaze.

This was no friendly tip from a police sympathizer. No BKA buddy in Munich could give this guy the goods on Crane. Why did that not surprise him? One of his minions had the gall to snap a picture where Crane found himself in the crosshairs. So, he grimaced as sweetly as he could under the circumstances. It was only appropriate for a snapshot of a feathered asshole.

Book 3, Burton Crane

Chapter 2

IT TOOK THE PROCESSION of bikers a couple of minutes to pass. The men from Verfassungsschutz watched them gun down the road. Some shook their heads in relief. A lost STASI dossier was nothing to them. As the last bikes rounded a curve in the road and disappeared from view, the sound died away. The murmur of the brook came back to hold sway over the empty domain. A few birds saw fit to serenade Burton Crane in his discomfiture. A few minutes later, four white buses appeared around the same curve.

Although nothing incriminating would be found in camp, the BKA went about securing the grounds with all the Sturm and Drang of the Teutonic tribes. They would be back in Munich for afternoon beer. Crane trailed up the front path behind a stout Kriminaloberkommissar Brechter and his megaphone.

There were three large barracks made of joined prefab units of good quality. The drab camouflage paintwork made the setup less impressive than it was. Long open sheds of corrugated iron over metal frames set on concrete floors confirmed its role as a bikers' club. The deserted compound was tidier than a Boy Scout camp with not so much as a mud puddle to soil your shoes, or an empty beer on the graveled grounds.

The greatest surprise came to Crane in the form of a gleaming BMW parked in the drive to the side of a square building with large windows and sturdy tables out front. Set apart from the barracks, the building served as a combination kitchen and dining area. The BKA had insisted that it was impossible to get a car up here; another bit of false information, expertly planted. In the back, an old geezer in a white spotted apron scraped food out of pots and pans.

At an outside table sat a middle-aged man drinking orange juice. The warmth of day had returned with the morning sun. As a metallic voice told of the impending search, the man rose to pick up his briefcase. Glimpsing armed police in full sprint between the trees, he waved a wasp from his juice and drained the glass in a long swig. Crane watched him pick a folded pinstriped jacket from the table and put it on as he stepped forward to greet his guests.

"I am Doctor Martin Langer, attorney from Landshut. I represent Baron Keltenbrunner von Geisenhausen, the owner of this land and buildings. You have a warrant to search the property leased to our motor enthusiasts?"

"Correct", barked Kriminaloberkommissar Erwin Brechter and presented his credentials.

"We have a warrant to search the premises. That includes all the buildings," interrupted Crane. He was out of line, but this farce had to stop.

"May I see the warrant?" The lawyer was in no hurry.

They were all swimming in his pool now. This was a man who relished the strict formality of a legal document. They must have pulled him out of bed at two o'clock at night to get here. Crane suspected that the lawyer found this meeting undignified. It was rude even for his eccentric employer who did not suffer any objections with good grace. The word was that Baron Keltenbrunner was one of the most influential men in Germany, a secretive autocrat, famed for his unbending ways. And like other forces of nature, he did not forgive refusals. The attorney from Landshut must have been escorted to this camping place in the middle of nowhere in the dead of night by motorcycle freaks.

Crane watched the lawyer read and reread the short document as the police relaxed or stole leaks after a long ride.

"This warrant allows you, Kriminaloberkommissar, to search the property rented by a motorcycle club on this land. There is no mention here of the private cottages or cabins rented to individuals. This large compound has hundreds of buildings on it, Herr Brechter!"

Skillfully, the lawyer was making Brechter personally responsible for any action outside his brief. He waved a hand at the square clubhouse behind him. "This is the building rented to 'Die Vogelscheuche', our biker club. I cannot allow any breach of the privacy of others who rent cabins here unless you have specific warrants that state their names and cabin numbers."

"Do you have these names and numbers?" asked Crane who had far too much prestige staked on this exercise to be careful.

"I am certain the baron's estate office in Landshut can help. It is incumbent on law enforcement to know what they want a search warrant for, is it not? You have me at a disadvantage, Herr . . . ?"

"Burton Crane."

"And what law enforcement agency do you represent, Herr Crane?" The lawyer was using a condescending tone.

Crane was wondering if he had to stand for this, and decided he probably did. "I am here as an observer for the North Atlantic Treaty Organization, as granted by German law."

"Oh, I admit I am unfamiliar with the terms of the NATO treaty, but this is irregular, Herr Oberkommissar, and perhaps unlawful. The Bundesgerichtshof will uphold my interpretation of your warrant," he put the emphasis neatly. "If there is a breach, the court will deal with any irregularities without delay."

"I am sure you are correct, Doctor Langer." Brechter was not about to cross swords with Baron Keltenbrunner. "Herr Crane's presence here is in holding with that outdated treaty. It has regrettably remained on the books. I assure you that we will search the clubhouse and nothing else."

Crane knew he was flatly beaten. The Germans were furious; bullied into this mess. At least he had a name for the bloody club. And what a fitting name I was, 'Die Vogelscheuche', the bunch had even looked like scarecrows.

The security police went through every inch of the clubhouse, a worn-down bar and dining room. They combed the kitchen cabinets. Apart from a stack of dirty magazines, this was a Boy Scout camp. The papers clipped to the large notice board were lists of summer festivals and restaurant menus. The big irregular empty areas on the board indicated that notices had been removed.

One small curiosity turned up, a snapshot of a young man in a white rock, a stethoscope protruding from the breast pocket. The white blackboard behind him indicated that he was holding a lecture. Crane found the photo slipped into a copy of Der Spiegel to mark an essay on STASI methods.

The lecturer was hardly gang material; he looked like a doctor who removed bullets without filing a report. The letters on the breast pocket were too small to make out. On the back someone had written 'Wallenberg'.

Wallenberg?

Raoul Wallenberg was the Swede who helped out Jews in occupied Eastern Europe during the war. Arrested by the Red Army, he disappeared. The Swedish government was still demanding an explanation. Rumors were circulating, and the thaw in the Russian deep-freeze was releasing dirt. Some said Wallenberg died under interrogation in the Treblinka, the Soviet state prison, others that he had lived until recently, an old broken habitant of the Gulag.

How did a Berlin dossier with the names of former STASI who had climbed to positions of influence in the West remotely connect to that? The

Scarecrows mastered the switch of the STASI dossier; a picture marked Wallenberg turns up in their clubhouse, as a marker for an article on STASI methods. The woman who engineered the snatch took the Sassnitz ferry across to Trelleborg in Sweden. There had to be a connection.

Crane knew that Dr Langer and the old geezer would fail to identify a face if he showed them a mirror. He slipped the snapshot into his pocket. It wasn't much, but it would fit somewhere. The technicians dusted the place for prints, carefully sifting the pornographic magazines. They would feed prints to their computers back at headquarters, making this pointless exercise seem professional.

The Oberkommissar offered insincere apologies over the flop and dropped Crane off in Landshut. Checking into a small hotel, he phoned the wife to tell her the story of his life; stuck for another day. Reluctantly he left a message on her machine as he studied the snapshot under a magnifying glass. He made out a name over the breast pocket: Lunds Lassarett. He'd have it enlarged in the morning.

The Swedish hospital would be a dead end. The Baron had a large stake in the Midgard Group, a mammoth international conglomeration that controlled a large number of eminent health institutions, but Lunds Lassarett was a State-owned hospital. The more he dwelled on it, Raoul Wallenberg made less sense.

Kriminaloberkommissar Brechter called from Munich to confirm that no further warrants would be forthcoming without clear evidence of wrongdoing. Baron Keltenbrunner had protested in person to his friend the minister of the interior. The baron was influential in Bavaria, and that included all the Security Services. No prosecutor would put his hand into that hornets' nest.

Three weeks earlier, with incidents concerning the baron dropping into his lap, Crane had foolishly decided to attend a banquet uninvited at the Geisenhausen estate to check out the host. A young captain in Wiesbaden had agreed to feel sick for the nigh and Crane had stepped in as a general's adjutant. The Bavarian family fortress was a block of prewar concrete, minimalist in all but size.

Inside the entrance, amid a darting shoal of male secretaries who hustled guests off for introductions, the baron had not afforded Crane a glance. In retrospect that was just as well. The hall was the size of an aircraft hangar and was roughly as inviting. The several hundred guests were top politicians,

Staatssekretar this, Innenminister that, mixed with business leaders and military brass. You could rule Europe from this room; the world if need be. That was not the surprise.

What startled Crane was to see Director General Zhou Shaozheng of the Chinese Central Investigation Department chatting with his Japanese PSIA counterpart. That was unheard of. The last thing he had expected to run into were dozens of senior figures at the helm of state intelligence and security agencies from a wide political world-wide spectrum. You got to be there to see the implications.

The talk had the flavor of an armament fair between deals. Was there some repeat of the Third Reich brewing, an embryo of re-armament behind the façade? If there was an underground movement on this planet better infiltrated than the Neo-Nazis, Crane had not heard of it.

And why was NATO in the dark about this top-level meeting that had been flagged as a routine low-level dinner? Crane had aborted his surveillance. He faded into the shadows and waited out his general.

Back at headquarters, his subsequent urgent report vanished without a trace into the classified labyrinths of the NSA, which of itself was not surprising with their own deputy Director at the banquet. What was it all about?

Had he gate crashed some secret cabal? Today, at the biker camp, he had been blindsided again. Intuition is a smell. Often you cannot tell where it belongs. Then, one day, you walk past the source, and suddenly you know.

That is the beauty of smells.

Chapter 3

IT WAS A PICTURESQUE building of medieval character with sagging red beams. The Baron's estate office in Landshut had a brass plaque beside the wide hardwood door with a cryptic inscription: "Urdr".

The middle-ages were a pretense.

As Burton Crane crossed the threshold, he entered the air-conditioned efficiency of a modern computerized office. On a stand near the front desk, a prospect on the Urdr investment fund gave a list of companies in which the fund held substantial interests. Partly owned by the Baron, the fund was controlled by him. Crane guessed that a lopsided part of the profits lined the Baron's pockets while the fund carried the costs. Smart and probably legal.

Crane presented himself to the lone secretary, prim, able and pretty, giving his name and position.

"I need an appointment with Baron Keltenbrunner on an urgent security matter. This is regarding arm caches dug up on his land near Zwiesel at the Czech border."

The young woman was well versed in dealing with the starchy upper crust. She was not enthusiastic.

"I am afraid the Baron is a busy man, Herr Crane. May I suggest that you discuss your questions with one of our lawyers? The Baron does not concern himself with unsolicited matters. This is not his office."

"If the lawyers include Dr Langer, we met in a bikers camp, would you believe, and he was no help at all."

"In that case I cannot possibly help."

"Does Doctor Langer work here?"

"Yes. He is not in at the moment."

"Alright, give me a piece of paper. I will leave a note for Dr Langer. Tell him the Baron will be cross if they keep him in the dark."

"I will make sure that Dr Langer gets your message."

"By the way, what does Urdr stand for? An acronym, is it?"

The secretary was flustered by his innocent question. "I don't think so, Herr Crane but I should know."

It made her a thoroughly modern secretary.

"I won't tell the Baron."

The heat of the medieval sun met him on the doorstep. He decided to walk back to the hotel and knock back a beer or two on the way. It would help him mull things over.

When he had left, the secretary cursed herself for not knowing what Urdr stood for. She made a note of it and was about to slip the folded message into the mail slot marked Dr Langer when curiosity got the better of her. What cheek to imply that the Baron would concern himself with a common message dropped in off the street!

The Baron was a breed apart. That kind of wealth and power gave her the creeps; the way these people used it, that most of all. The brutal will to use it. The Baron was the most powerful man in Germany. It would come as a surprise for many. People like that scared her. She smiled on recalling how uptight and nervous the lawyers became if summoned to the Baron's estate. The common help like she simply did not exist.

The Baron ran a tight ship, and he never mingled. He had visited this office once in her six years with the firm and had not exchanged a single word with the personnel. He was the rudest man she had ever witnessed. The lawyers had private lines to the Baron's staff that would tear into them for the smallest oversight. She didn't like the Baron's staff one bit. With them, courtesy came last. They did their work under heavy pressure. She respected that. An unsolicited inquiry to the Baron would be hard to explain to his private staff. She did not envy Doctor Langer the task to broach the subject.

She folded out the sheet and noted that the American had written his name and phone number at the top. There was no message. Only a single word in longhand slashed across the center page. She stared at it for a suspended moment. Just that one word.

'Wallenberg'.

Six years ago, when she started here, she was given a confidential briefing by the baron's private secretary, a rare honor. It was strange because it concerned one name. The name was 'Heimdallr'. She was never to mention it, even privately. She was told not to think it. If there ever came a request citing that name, or if she heard it used in any context, there were urgent instructions to follow.

She had never heard anyone use the word, but every year she got a visit to keep the urgency alive. To forget what Urdr stood for was easy, but to forget Heimdallr would never happen. Then out of the blue, last week, the baron's private secretary came by in person on an exceptional visit, to add another name to her memorized list, the name that now stared back at her.

Half in shock, the front desk secretary at the Urdr investment fund unlocked her top drawer and took out a small book of names and codes. Calling up a file on her computer, she punched in a code and was immediately asked to identify herself. It was then she knew there was no turning back. The phone number flashed on the screen.

With a heart ricocheting in her breast, with trembling fingers, she dialed, for the first time in her life, the unlisted number to the private den of the feared Baron Keltenbrunner von Geisenhausen.

Book 3, Burton Crane

Chapter 4

WITH HIS DAY IN Landshut all but over, most of it spent on the phone, Burton Crane stretched his legs and enjoyed the afternoon breeze outside Gasthof Trausnitz.

The word from headquarters suggested conflict on the home front about his investigation. He had to play this by ear, which was fine. The beer made him sluggishly comfortable. Clouds on the horizon suggested rain by nightfall. In the morning he would be winging his way back to London. A deep swig left a string of froth across his solid brick face. His wife had just told him that she missed him, in spite of another delay. That made him unreasonably happy, another whistler out of the blue. He was no good at patching up broken crockery. He had been expecting a painful reunion because Evelyn was taking flack as a producer at the BBC, being routinely passed over by a bunch of pedigreed highflyers. He was her shoulder to cry on. The woman was the one wonder of the world that Burton Crane cared about enough to let under his thick skin.

He consulted his notebook, the jotted records of a busy day. Some smaller pieces fell into place. The tracer he put out on the Vogelscheuche gang rocked his day. This was no chicken-shit outfit. The club's large stock portfolio was shrewdly managed by the Urdr investment fund. The annual earnings of the Scarecrows were enough to keep them out of crummy camp, and from drifting without pushing or pimping. Their recruitment methods were a mystery, which was an oddity for a biker gang, but it had the advantage of preventing infiltration by law enforcement. Why was that important?

He took another long swig and signaled the no-nonsense waitress for another jug. She was bigger than the Alps and he expected her to burst out in a Wagnerian onslaught at any time.

He had found there were other property leases by the Vogelscheuche from an array of German corporations. The Urdr investment fund had a stake in some but not all. Why would the giants of German industry put their property into the hands of vandals? Up to now, the enigma of gangs had occupied a handful of men in the services and rated low priority. Politicians wanted their conquests high tech and classy. Even now, Crane held out little hope that he might shift their position by ramming this whistler up their candy asses.

He had been astonished to find the Urdr Investment Fund to be one of the biggest sources of private capital on the Western Hemisphere. It controlled many interests in other less known funds and institutions. Its mesh of tentacles formed an opaque maze. Earlier in the day, he had called a history professor in Heidelberg to ask about the name. Turned out Urdr was one of three witches that weave human destiny. They accounted for the past, the present and the future and had the daily duty of watering the world-tree from a holy well.

"Thence come the maidens, mighty in wisdom. Urdr is one, Verdandi the next and Skuld the third. Laws they made and life they allotted to the sons of men and set their fates."

A name out of the Nordic past. No surprise there. Crane felt silly leaving his stupid note for Dr Langer. If he had emphasized the arms caches near Zwiesel, it could have gained him a low-level audience where he could have irritated his way upwards from there, which was not easy with powerful players. The Baron had the financial muscles to lead any conspiracy that appealed to him. The man followed a ruthless strategy. The Baron had tactical logic behind every move.

If the involvement of Germany's wealthiest baron of industry might call for a revaluation, it could not explain how a dead Swedish diplomat was connected to a biker gang storing arms all over Germany? It was certainly not a theory to loosen the strings to the committee purse.

Crane walked back to the hotel; Landshut was one of those Bavarian towns of gables on the Isar, going back centuries. It gave him a good walk. The sun was lost in the gathering clouds when he reached the hotel where he would order an early wakeup call. He was going home to make love to the wife. In the foyer a pleasant young man in expensive clothes, of the sort that cultivated the air of authority, stepped out to intercept him.

"Herr Crane." It did not sound like a question.

"Yes?"

He ruled out the hotel manager and decided police. The young man's authoritarian bearing and self-assurance changed his mind: it would be the BND, the intelligence agency. The spooks in Pullach were about to tramp on his toes.

"I am Gerhard Mühler. Baron Keltenbrunner von Geisenhausen has instructed me to inquire of you whether a two-thirty appointment tomorrow afternoon would be satisfactory."

Out of the corner of his eye Crane saw the reception clerk drop his pen on the desk and leave it. If he left that wakeup call, that clerk would be there in person. Keltenbrunner was a big name around here.

"I am booked out of Munich in the morning." No way was he going to lose this opportunity to meet the reclusive Baron. No reason to give the game away either.

"Shall I relay that to the baron?"

The fish were not biting. The interest was tepid.

"No, I asked for an appointment. I will postpone my return for a few hours; two thirty, where?"

Rumor had it that the old castle that housed the baron's private office was strictly off limits. It was unlikely to be the old concrete fortress he had visited as a general's adjutant.

"The Baron's private office, and on time. The Baron is a busy man."

"That goes for us all, young man; how do I get there?"

"By car or chopper; Geisenhausen is on the map, Herr Crane," the younger man smiled. "NATO will provide you with a map."

Snotty little devil. He probably wasn't kidding about the chopper. This was a perfect BND recruit.

"Tell the Baron I'll be there."

On his earlier visit to the concrete estate bunker, Crane had studied the baron from a safe distance. The man never conversed with his so-called friends. He asked questions and he issued orders. He seemed to believe they were all his employees.

Watching the young man walk away, Crane recalled the oath of allegiance sworn by the boys of the Hitler youth: To be tough as leather, quick as a greyhound, hard as Krupp steel.

Did all the intelligence ambassadors summoned to the baron's banquet swear allegiance to one leader? He hoped to God that was not true.

Book 3, Burton Crane

Chapter 5

THE DAMP HUNG IN patches over the lake as Burton Crane drove past the large gate down a mile-long gravel drive. The showers had dried up, but the wind was fresh. The ancient fortress by a small lake fitted the grounds, but the lawns needed tending. The whole place had the natural smell of decay. In Britain you'd expect a fashionable country restaurant on the ground floor with a liveried waiter to greet you at the door. The top floors would be open to the public; the best wing reserved for the old family, squeezed by inheritance taxis.

The thought made him smile. The only reason for untended grounds was that Baron Keltenbrunner liked it that way. This aristocrat was still collecting his feudal dues.

Crane had heard the stories and read the tidbits about the loveless breeding of the young baron, a brutal stem of old Geisenhausen stock. The boy had a barren life, a single child, watched and harassed every minute of the day, taught to waste not a word. Trendy psychoanalysts had dissected dinners in the family mausoleum, the lack of feelings and strict regime. Fearful servants and gloom in rituals of silence; two parents, each with an army of spies.

The son of the House was cast as a piece of steel. Started off on the floor with the machine division in Munich, the foremen were under orders to ride him hard. If reports to his father failed to show this, the old man would sack the foreman in question. The boy was good material for molding. Still, the Old Baron suspected that he kept a soft core hidden where he could not get at it; and God knows he tried! It was the stuff that sold glossy magazines.

Crane walked across the parking lot. The three-story fortress of stone was topped off by a later addition, medieval of light facades and dark beams, turrets, and all. He had spotted the chopper pad earlier, a large ugly asphalt circle set in a green field, large enough to handle an army; practical but unsightly. The man needed a woman's touch on the grounds.

There were swans on the water, nestling in the sedge. It was a fine touch, as were the small pier and a couple of dinghies. Hidden by foliage on the wall beside the large door, something piqued his interest. He could push leaves aside enough to read the green copper plaque with the castles name, SchloZ Heimdallr.

Having pestered his friends in the Services about the old fortress, Crane found it surprising that none had called the estate by its name.

In the large airy hall, a somberly attractive and effective woman sat behind an antique desk with a leather top. Both the desk and the young woman went well with the high rustic beams and the flagstone floor. The atmosphere was pleasant and strictly business. Baron Keltenbrunner was expecting Herr Crane.

Burton Crane was no dandy. As a cop he had met too many fancy dressers on the opposite side of the law to develop the taste, but he wore a conservative tie. Nothing gained by upsetting the aristocratic eccentric. Crane recalled his wife's disdain for the descendants of the high-and-mighty that spent time squandering the rewards of parental toil and resting on inherited laurels. Not that Keltenbrunner did any of that.

The secretary relieved him of his parka and ushered him through, closing the door behind him. The room felt small after the high-beamed hall, more of a library. It was the Baron's private den. Crane found himself looking at a naked man with a book on the top of his head. The thick leather-bound volume lay open and balanced. It was the sort of thing small boys might do with the family Bible while their parents were out of the house.

The man stood by a grand viewing window and stared absentmindedly out over the small lake. Stirred by occasional gusts of wind, its grayish surface almost reached floor level. The nature of his reverie was hard to fathom. He seemed lost, apparently unaware of Crane's presence. It occurred to Crane that this was willfully so. He studied the man and his den in silence, biding time. If this was a deliberate ploy to put him off balance, it was off the mark, but it allowed him time to glance about the half-domed unlit room. Bookshelves crammed with old volumes scattered the sparse light as spines glittered with gold.

Crane wondered about the string of eccentricities that flirted with madness. It had often affected the barons of German industry. This stone fortress could not compete with Alfred Krupp's monstrous concrete villa of a hundred and sixty candlelit rooms, some the size of railroad stations. Krupp kept no library, as books could burn, and so could paintings and carpets and tapestries. Alfred would have none of it, but then, he had his private den above the stables and open to them. It allowed the odor of manure to percolate and inspire his creative thinking. Baron Keltenbrunner had a long way to go.

The sight of naked skin did not disturb him either. Crane had cleared out too many drug-infested nests of naked bodies rolling in filth. As a former paramedic, he could take the emotional jolts with the best of them. Thankful for the melancholic stillness, he studied a room that proved surprisingly airy when his eyes penetrated the dusk. It was large with beams and vaults in the high ceiling, and a panorama window. The dark water in the moat lapped against the wall below a windowsill where a bearskin rug covered a large bed.

Into his field of vision, meters away, outside the grand window, a pair of swans swam out of the sedge, heads dipping in dark water. Crane inspected the Baron's desktop with interest. There was a large silver-framed photo: a man with harsh features and a manic stare that was almost unsettling. It would be the father.

The naked man did not move, nor stop his brooding study of the lake. Without greetings or gestures he addressed Crane in a voice without hesitation or rush.

"What is on your mind, Herr Crane?"

The directness and lack of presentation was not a baronial approach. Crane had to remind himself that he was dealing with a general of a secret army, and, according to all sources, a formidable piece of ruthless energy and intelligence. Plainly, this man did not respect rules.

"I wanted to ask you, Baron Keltenbrunner, if you are aware of the large cache of small arms and explosives found on your land near Zwiesel at the Czech border?"

"Yes." The answer came without any follow up. It gave nothing away.

"May I ask how you know?

"I cannot see that as your business, Herr Crane. Bundesnachrichtendienst saw fit to inform me, as is their duty by law."

"Do you know to whom these arms belong, Baron?"

"Herr Crane. Stop wasting my time. Your superiors will get a detailed report from the BND, the MI6, and your NSA. I hate overlapping reports. I take no part in waste. Was there anything else?"

And it suddenly dawned on Crane why he was here. The Baron had granted this meeting solely because of that name. He was not about to come clean about arms or biker clubs. It was the name that troubled him.

"Baron Keltenbrunner, do you know a young man named Wallenberg?" Crane was not sure how to handle it, only that it was crucial. The shaded silence in the room had been empty of feeling, a slack cord, neither hostile nor friendly, if anything bored. As he spoke the name, it changed. A tightly wound string waited to be struck. If only he could hit the right note, but the response was tentative.

"I know many by that name, some of a Swedish family of industrialists and bankers for generations. Why?"

Crane was acutely aware that he could not elaborate without giving himself away. He had not the faintest idea what this was about.

"I meant personally, baron Keltenbrunner."

"You remind me of a young bear, Herr Crane; a bear I came across in Canada. It had come to a river to fish like you. The water was not familiar. There were shadows moving beneath the surface. The beast did not know how deep it was or how strong the current. It did not feel secure enough to jump in. It stood and pawed the water, Herr Crane. Have you come here to fish?"

"Tell me baron; you would not know the whereabouts of the missing Raoul Wallenberg?"

The string went flat. It was plain. The charge fell away. He had blown his chance, hit the wrong note. He should have left it alone. Baron Keltenbrunner did not even try to mislead him. He didn't care that he was showing his adversary that he had struck the wrong note. They had warned him: you did not dislodge this unflinching character from his path.

"No more of this nonsense. Stop wasting my time, Herr Crane. You work for a bloated organization with a staff in the hundreds of thousands. You are a cipher to the men who run your National Security Agency. I know the men at the top personally. I am a valuable ally. Your administrative branch can be full of surprises. The next departmental reshuffle could wind up your career."

Baron Keltenbrunner turned to face Crane; pushed a button on his desk. He put the bible on the desk. He was a fine-looking bloke, a perfect recruit for master race, down to blue eyes and blonde hair. He was also a perfect candidate to drive a conspiracy, a man of immense wealth and influence. The German government would easily fold on his command.

Yet he had set all that aside because of one name; Wallenberg. Crane could not imagine any bigger forces at play than the Baron. How could this unknown doctor be central to a brewing conspiracy. Why did this brutal warrior stand here talking to him, a mere cipher? Crane had not dented the surface.

"Don't threaten me, Baron."

"Do not misunderstand me, Herr Crane. How you fuck up your life is your business. This is a free world. Stop meddling in my affairs."

The secretary was standing in the door. She took no offense at the Baron's balls. Crane noted that he was moderately well hung. The secretary handed him his parka by the door. He turned.

"Tell me, Baron, what happened to the bear; did it lose its nerve?"

"No, it did not, Herr Crane."

"Catch any shadows?"

"Herr Crane, I did not intend to take this fable any further. Your persistence has a knack of pushing matters too far. You might find a lesson in that."

"So, what happened to the bear?"

"I shot it, Herr Crane. I was hunting, a single shot. The bear never stood a chance," and Baron Keltenbrunner gave a loud bark of a laughter that had all the charm of an exploding grenade.

Chapter 6

BURTON CRANE CAUGHT THE afternoon flight from Munich to London, two hours after his snub-nosed meeting with Baron Keltenbrunner. With no time to spare for a report to Wiesbaden, he called in from Heathrow to tell the station chief he was going home to see the wife.

Angry disapproval found Crane long past caring.

The German minister of the interior had dispatched a protest against unauthorized meddling to NATO's Wiesbaden headquarters. The Innenminister was one of the baron's cronies, and he controlled the Cologne Verfassungsschutz, charged with the surveillance of anti-constitutional activities in Germany. but who was minding the minder?

There would be no wriggle-room from under a full report. This was no laughing matter, tramping on tender Teutonic toes in military boots. Crane was called to an early meeting the next morning at headquarters in Lambeth. The punctilious nature of the military mind made it ten o'clock sharp.

He had arrived home late to their nondescript bungalow in Schoolbell Mews. Loafing around the empty house in the dark, he fought the cold hand of jealousy. Why had not Evelyn returned from work?

Back in the old days, they had put off having kids to have fun and travel. Later, when the urge set in, nothing came of it. For years Evelyn kept a manual of periods and temperatures. It was a circus. They both checked out. Wasn't meant to happen. With their workload, adoption was a bad choice. She had settled into resigned acceptance, and the editing job at BBC became her escape.

In the light of the lamp on Evelyn's working desk, Crane studied the photo blow up. He hated desks; refused to get one of his own. His wife complained of him messing up hers. He liked these small conflicts of family life. Lunds Lassarett confirmed a Swedish connection, but it was too vague. His mind drifted to the baron and his secret army. How could a Swedish doctor impact on that beast? And what was with Baron Keltenbrunner, that familiar arrogance? Was it hurt national pride on confronting a NATO occupation officer? The Baron knew more than he was telling about this lowly doctor. The Baron was a soldier, pure of heart, no Machiavelli that hid his feelings. Crane had touched a nerve. That was why the German establishment was ordering him off the pot. It was a bad omen, going naked to a meeting in Lambeth.

He heard the car in the driveway, small steps and fumbling of keys, and his innards began to thaw. He had shaved and showered in case Evelyn would stand by her proclamation of need. Evelyn was off to the shower, shouting for him to prepare a bite. Her voice held promise. He picked a wine she'd like and put out some cheese and garlic bread. He was no wine buff, but the stuff agreed with his wife, and she needed pampering. He never could explain his delays. In his line of work, conjugal openness led to complications. You had to choose between half-lies with the right ring, and the perfect cover stories sounded flat. Silence was the gold standard. Crane was not an imaginative lover but tonight he aimed to please. This was the measure of his tenderness towards his wife.

It was the morning after, sunny but windy. Crane sat at a long, gleaming table in a leather chair swiveled to the side. He watched the snake of the Thames weave its glittering path far below. In spite of single glazing, the view was eerily silent on the 16th floor of Century House in Lambeth. You could tell the spooks from the buildings they hid in.

He had heard that the Secret Intelligence Service was talking about new headquarters. The chameleons would take their cue; it would have everything but character. Crane foresaw cubicles packed with blow-dried bureaucrats knee-deep in gadgetry. It was an Orwellian vision. He was no outsider. A head office without personality was a bad omen in an intensely personal business where you needed passion born of conflicting traits. Having drifted through many quarters in his day. He recalled their smells and flaws, the hot and airless summers, the cold and drafty winters. Grimy windows fogged over, the smells of pipes and stale cigars.

It was over a decade since Crane had been recruited into army intelligence, after serving with the military police in Wiesbaden, learning his less than perfect German while driving an ambulance.

"You have a nasty habit of flying solo, Crane?"

He ignored the question because it wasn't one. He felt like a worker brought up from the factory floor, treated with superficial respect by pinstripes out of academia. They felt a need to reiterate who was running the show.

"Wiesbaden is wondering if you are out of control. They reminded us that we are a team. Frankly, it is nobody's jolly idea to bother Baron Keltenbrunner like that. You are supposed to be the resident authority on our German friends, have you no idea who the man is? This is a private chap."

"With a big ballroom."

There were three of them present, Sidney presiding. He lowered his big black Parker.

"You met him in his ballroom?"

"In his study actually." There was no point in being facetious. They could trip him up badly. They excelled at that, taking your legs out from under you.

"The Baron met me in the buff, you know, with his Bavarian pointing at me. And while he showed off, he balanced an old Bible on his head. Not my definition of a private chap, Sidney, but if you say so."

The tidbit seemed to have softened Sidney's attitude. Unconfirmed rumors had him bent that way. There were always rumors. Crane's provisional boss was unhappy to have a German cockup dropped in his lap. He left it to his operative to elaborate. Crane changed the subject.

"What was it that bothered the Baron, exactly, did he say, Sidney?"

"The BND in Bonn informed us that you pressured the security police to get a search warrant under false pretenses. You then compounded this by asking the federal police to overstep its authority on that warrant. And when Baron Keltenbrunner agrees to see you in person to clear up the muddle, a rare courtesy, you feed him drivel about the long dead Raoul Wallenberg, the Swedish diplomat who died in the Second World War."

Sydney looked fatherly at Crane and made a small wave of a dainty hand to silence any objections, signaling the handsome Eaton boy to read out the version since Berlin, the version according to Wiesbaden.

Crane settled back to listen to his own plan to detain Helmut Mayer long enough to allow his team to film the file on the Dresden run. His undercover man, Konrad, present whereabouts unknown, had recently become Helmut's driver; a fine plan until the mystery woman ruined it.

The young man underlined that this foul-up could not have been predicted and that nobody could be held responsible, meaning nobody but Crane.

The mystery woman had approached the former STASI general at his table, a middle-aged barrel of a man who handed her the dossier with obvious reluctance. The woman slid it into a leather portfolio and left the bar, passing

Konrad, parked at the curb. Helmut Mayer had just stepped out of the car. He was their key to a syndicate that sold Ukrainian armament to any willing buyer. Their progress to nuclear materials was a matter of time. Mayer recognized the woman and stopped to stare after her. After a heated exchange with the former general, Mayer ran out of the bar, but she was gone.

The unknown woman had walked away in the shadow of Crane's eight men standby team while his other team continued the surveillance of Mayer. The young Etonian was modest about the finer points of tradecraft.

"Not easy to with dozens of observers in a desolate East Berlin Street." Crane smiled encouragingly.

"The woman had engineered a flawless switch of folders with a passer-by who minutes later passed it to a motorcycle courier. It was moving fast, and our choices were limited when the bikers started to harass the team members. In the commotion, nobody could vouch for the lost dossier. The woman unlocked a Sweden registered Mercedes in a side street and drove out of Berlin heading north. Soon afterwards, Helmut Mayer took the same E6 route to Sassnitz with our man Konrad at the wheel. Mayer could not know where she was going without some prior information. Mayer boarded the same ferry as she to Sweden and he told Konrad to meet him the next morning in Swinoujscie, Poland."

The Eton boy glanced at Crane, who smiled proudly back.

"Konrad called in from Sassnitz after the ferry left. Mayer knew the woman, something about an East German visa. Helmut Mayer was see searching the ferry, as did our people, but the woman vanished into thin air."

Crane looked over Docklands far below. A week had gone by. Helmut Mayer had arrived in Swinoujscie the following morning on the Ystad ferry as planned. The bikers took two days to journey to their barracks outside Landshut, their progress charted by a full team and a chopper. The Scarecrows had drifted aimlessly, probably to throw them off the scent. According to Wiesbaden, aside from getting up everybody's nose, the biker gang could have nothing to do with the woman or the dossier. Wiesbaden did not know, so why tender an opinion?

In Trelleborg, a man approached Mayer in his car and got in. The observers were on unfamiliar ground. It was essential not to compromise Konrad. When Mayer took the motorway north, Crane had ordered them to drop the tail on the outskirts of Trelleborg.

The young Etonian, needed to make an important point

"After losing the woman, Burton Crane, after locating the biker base outside Landshut, decided to go solo. His unorthodox methods caused an upheaval in the German intelligence community. Baron Keltenbrunner, a major source of goodwill towards NATO is raising the roof. And, this morning, Central Command Stateside has proposed a full inquiry."

The young Etonian, deferred to his master.

"Care to fill in the colors, Crane?" Sidney did not expect an answer.

"Wiesbaden thinks the woman is SÄPO, which explains why NATO is not in the loop. The Swedish security police deny any involvement of their agents, but they would. In addition, Wiesbaden has presented a list of respected and wealthy citizens who are members of this particular club of motor enthusiasts, which rather explains their financial assets."

Sidney picked up a large photo with a yellow fact sheet clipped to it.

"We traced the young man in your photo. His name is Wallenberg, as it indeed says on the back of your pilfered snap. I trust this puts your mystery to rest. Dr Birger Wallenberg practiced at the Lund University Hospital until recently. He is a respected scholar, now director of The Asgard Park Institute in New York, and beyond any reasonable suspicion. Wiesbaden suggests that you contact this man only in his professional capacity. He is an accredited psychiatrist."

"Who owns this Asgard Park Institute?"

"Who owns it?" Sidney shook his head wearily and nodded vaguely at the Eton boy who left the room.

Chapter 7

"THE SHORT OF IT, Crane, is that Wiesbaden has formally requested of your masters across the pond that you make no further inquiries without a nod from the NSA. That is where we stand; any thoughts?"

"I have a gut feeling about this, Sidney."

"That is not the way we work." The voice was softer than the summer wind. "Wiesbaden put a painstaking year into planting Konrad with Helmut Mayer. They are not about to blow their chance on your wild goose chase. There is too much at stake in Germany. They actually want your head. All we want over here, is that you take a few weeks off on paid leave."

Crane threw back his chair and barely avoided kicking the transparent burn basket as he rose. Sidney waited for an outburst. Best not give it to him.

"There is a secret empire out there, probably run by a barking madman. For all I know, the world's greatest conspiracy to defraud humankind. These guys own half the world!"

"Which is not altogether criminal," said Sidney, "the world is full of crackpots, Crane. Frankly you are beginning to sound like one."

The Eton boy was back with a slip for Sidney who glanced at it angrily.

"The Asgard Park Institute for the Criminally Insane is owned by the well renowned Midgard Group. They are legendary in the international health sector. I hope that puts the matter to rest. Either you are part of the team or you're not. Frankly we are waiting for the answer to that, from Stateside."

Crane took in the view towards Westminster and the Houses of Parliament. An institute for the criminally insane? If the Baron controlled Asgard Park. Had he just recognized the name of its director? Was he checking if something was wrong?

A secretary interrupted with a telex. The message did not improve Sidney's humor. His face turned disappointed, as he put it down reluctantly.

"There has been a development," he conceded.

"Let's hear it." Crane's mind was on Konrad.

"Interpol got an open request from Stockholm on a fingerprint trace, from Kriminalpolisen. We had a flyer out on any requests. The thumbprint matches that of Helmut Mayer. That is quite a breakthrough for us. It ties him to murder. One would assume of that he murdered the Berlin woman in," he studiously raised the telex, "Falsterbo."

Sidney turned to Crane, "look it up will you, Andrew. How do we play this, do we confirm to Interpol?"

Crane relaxed.

"Sure, but don't give them Mayer; all in good time. Give them a match, a suspected terrorist, classified but working on it."

It was another whistler out of the blue. Crane resumed his study of the Thames. "So now we know! Mayer caught up with the woman, but the dossier was not there. The Scarecrows got it. Mayer fails to cover his tracks. I can see this coming in handy. We got him on murder one."

Crane knew there was more to it. Sidney was having too hard a time living this down.

"The woman wasn't SÄPO, was she? Their security police would never trace that as murder; not in the open like this. Who was she?"

"A business magnate of sorts, run a large corporation with worldwide connections."

"Have a name, does she, Sidney, old top?"

Sidney couldn't have produced a sourer tone with the help of all the queens' bugles, nor a melody sweeter.

"Catarine Wallenberg, it seems."

Crane sat down heavily. He had no malice in his heart. Long faces were in order. The ground had shifted under all of them.

"Don't channel this through Wiesbaden, Sidney. Get MI5 to put the lid on this end. Confirm to Stockholm that we are working on the print. Ask SÄPO to comb her house and keep it under wraps. They owe us. You can bank on the Swedes, but for God's sake leave Wiesbaden out of it."

"Eventually they must know."

It was odd. Why did a billionaire tycoon, Catarine Wallenberg step into the danger zone to snatch a STASI dossier in Berlin? It made no sense. Like the Baron, such people delegated sensitive or dangerous errands to professionals. She used the baron's private army of scarecrows. Was it the use of her name that upset the baron, or the name of her now absurdly wealthy son? With all the choices open to him, why would a young scholar bury himself in an unknown asylum in upstate New York? The smell was there, stronger than ever, but he should not be looking for a German conspiracy. The tentacles were spreading. Who was controlling who? What was the role of Asgard Park, or Baron Keltenbrunner? There was something else. In all the objections flying around over his handling of the case, they did not want his head for a lost STASI file, the only thing he screwed up.

This was pure diversion. Asgard Park settled on his mind like dye. The more he rubbed, the deeper the stain.

Burton Crane knew it was only a matter of days before Sidney would revert to the fold, given the pressure from Wiesbaden. As the man in the middle, he had no reason to hold his hand over a runaway Yankee, operating on borrowed time.

Chapter 8

HITCHING A RIDE ON one of America's biggest military transport planes, Burton Crane touched down more heavily than usually on a C5 Galaxy at the eastern Long Island air base of the New York Air National Guard.

New York was pleasant, hot, and humid. With Wiesbaden calling for his head, the smells of youth felt safe. He attended a long lecture given by Dr Margaret Kirkpatrick, an iconoclastic physicist speaking to a small gathering of interstellar physicists on the uneven texture of mass in space, and variations in spatial heat. It was all well above his head.

With the woman's facial recovery in the third week, the lecture took will to deliver. Crane had come across this young woman in his study of Birger Wallenberg. If experience was anything to go by, she and the doctor were straight shooters. Her fling with Jack Gradidge, who fronted a few downtown clubs, had ended when she found out about his affiliations. Her toilet had cost the Mob ten million, and Jack Gradidge his life. Crane could not figure it.

He called to tell her that somebody at Asgard Park might be privy to a cache of missing secret documents; guessing that a Kansas farm girl who cleared Yale on a scholarship, had a dose of natural curiosity. She agreed to see him right away.

Her Park Avenue apartment was one of those places Evelyn admired in refined magazines; an apricot-sponged wall with a small glassed-in Nolde in a gold leaf frame. Not bothering to change from a gray training overall with dark patches of sweat after a workout, she offered coffee with a view of Central Park. It was hard to imagine how disfigured these strong features had been weeks ago. She had caked over the stitches on both sides of the nose with cosmetics.

"So, who are you, Burton Crane?" The well-modulated professor's voice was superior, "and what does NATO want with me?"

"I do my bit in the intelligence services. I'm what they call a floater. The down-to-earth variety. I am looking into a Berlin disappearance of a confidential dossier some days ago. Nothing earth-shattering. We believe in keeping things tidy. I would prefer that you did not mention this to anyone."

"A floater?"

"A roving troubleshooter."

"I cannot see how I can help you."

He showed her four photographs one after the other. Helmut Mayer, the former STASI colonel, a blowup of the Berlin woman, and a photo of Baron Keltenbrunner, the only photo available in the NATO file, and didn't even look like him. They drew a blank. There was, however, no mistaking her smile when he handed her the enlarged snap of the doctor.

"Birger Wallenberg!" She said it in a way he would like to say Evelyn but seldom did. He had just left his wife after one of their little spats. She had this tendency to become excited and angry. It was a deep character trait. His reserve would feed the fire while he passively withstood the onslaught. She had this wildness in her. This time she chose not to nurture it into row. His life was worth shit without his wife and his work. He was doing his darned best to lose both.

"That's right; I am planning to meet the doctor."

"Where did you get this photo?"

"That is an interesting question. There are almost no photos of him to be had. This one we found in the barracks of a biker gang in lower Bavaria, in Germany."

"Bikers? That does not sound like him." She drew her legs into the sofa. "What is this about?"

"Puzzling isn't it, unsavory guys running feuds across Europe; fatalistic contempt for danger, brainless cravings for the joy of battle, fencing government documents. It does that sound like your friend?"

"I think you've been spying on me," she handed back the photo without a trace of anger. "I never told you he was a friend. Birger is a hard-working scientist, and he is not into gangs."

"What exactly does the doctor do?"

As he had feared, she spoke at length about coupling neurological advances to the revolution in information processing. Settling back to enjoy the sun as it lit up the treetops of Central Park, he noticed an old bronze Buddha by the window; the green speckled face pondered him back with wry humor, so he barged in on her elucidation.

"I understand that you turned down police protection, Margaret. The Mob has a long memory. I noticed you did not check my credentials."

Margaret made a face.

"I suppose! My heart is a careless trustee. I better stick to the exact sciences. The security officer at Asgard Park told me that the threat had blown over."

"How would he know?"

"Even gangsters read the papers, Burton. Two minutes as a punching bag gave me more fame than several years of hard work. Everybody knows I flushed their drugs down the toilet. The Mob has nothing to gain by coming after me."

"Your daughter is doing well?"

"Yeah, thanks. She is on the farm with my parents for the summer. You cannot believe how I miss her. There is never enough time."

"When admitted to the hospital, you told a nurse that you had phoned Asgard Park, and that they sent men to save your daughter. Questioning by the police later one, does not bear out your first version. Why is that?"

"It is what I thought. I had drinks in me. I came close to losing my child and my life. The last thing I remember was the beating. Somebody intervened. Guess I felt saved. Later I made a more levelheaded assessment after therapy. The mind can play tricks on you."

"Why on earth did you make that call?"

"Well, years ago, before he died, Bill Rayman, Amelia's father, gave me a number to call if I got into trouble. I used it once when Bill himself vanished. He died in an accident abroad, you know. The man who took my call to Asgard Park back then was of no help. Weeks ago, the same man took my call, and told me to take it easy."

Crane sighed and consulted the black scribbles in his notebook. To anyone else these spidery jottings looked like a cracked riverbed.

"Bill Rayman died seven years ago. This is an unlisted number to Asgard Park that you used only once before. Are you telling me you recalled an unlisted phone number after seven years?"

"Not really, but back then when I dialed the number, the letters struck me."

"What letters?"

"The letters matching the numbers; it's an old habit. I have a way with combinations. They are a great help when the letters spin out."

Margaret grimaced at the lukewarm coffee and gave Crane a fine smile, parting with a private confidence.

"The Asgard number was easy. The letters form a word."

"They form a word?"

"Well, sort of!"

"What word would that be?"

"Heimdallur."

Without interest, Crane made a great show of writing this odd word down in his leather notebook. This time the letters really looked like bird droppings and the message was even less comprehensible.

"How do you spell that?"

Heimdallur or Heimdallr, whoever or whatever; a new bolt out of the blue had laid bare a secret hub that tied Baron Keltenbrunner to Birger Wallenberg.

Jumping to criminal conclusions on the bases of this information was not a theory likely to loosen the strings of the committee's purse, much less getting his head off the block.

Chapter 9

HIS FBI LIAISON WAS an old acquaintance from back in the seventies. Special agent Hugh Miller had given a lecture at the National Police Academy when Burton Crane was a greenhorn. Only rarely did the public halo of the FBI reflect its real work behind the scenes. Miller had allowed him close enough to see the halo slip.

Ages ago, Miller, lured by the image of the FBI's clean ideals, took the lifetime plunge, a survivor determined to stay the course. He bent in the storms that raged through the Bureau. Cleared the hurdles of autocratic dictates and did the dirty legwork. Worked his plodding way upwards or downwards as some would have it, to clandestine wiretapping and illegal surveillance. Graduating to political intimidation and arm-twisting, he did his unselfish best to serve Hoover's personal brand of patriotism.

Now himself a grain in the great lore that his vast organization held up for public scrutiny, he had become part of the new untouchables: the exclusive little club who knew where the bodies were buried. Hugh was a perfect liaison for an old apprentice.

The head of the New York field division greeted Crane handsomely in a bright office in lower Manhattan. Better a king in New York, than glorified errand boy in Washington. He was of medium height, solid, aging body, close-cropped bristling white hair with a balding spot.

"How's the wife, young fella?"

"Great, thanks." Hugh had a soft spot for the family. "I hear you're interested in the Asgard Park case?"

"Is that what you call it?"

"Gut feeling, Crane, gut feeling!"

"I'm building a case profile on Dr Birger Wallenberg, their director; a matter of national security." Crane evoked the scepter of communism on purpose, a great spur for the old guard. "Someone snatched a dossier of sensitive East German documents from under my nose in Berlin a few days ago. Our search turned up a photo of this young doctor. They tell me he's as clean as they come. I'm fishing for connections."

"I'm your man."

"So, what have you got on this guy?"

"Nothing. Clean as a whistle. But you have to wonder. After he took up residence, the coincidences crop up faster than illegal donations in a primary."

"What have you got?"

"Well, young fella, it began with a missing cache of freebased Mob cocaine worth millions. A woman, a physicist no less, flushes all that crack down her toilet. I can tell you this is out of character for anyone graduating from Yale; a friend had stashed it in her apartment. The word on the street is that the Council pulls in the friend. They waste him, that is after he puts a finger on the woman. They find her in a downtown hotel. Come at her with a four-member team."

"Sure, but how does this tie in with Asgard Park?"

"I'm getting to that, son. You see, before these guys arrive, the woman puts in a call to Asgard Park to tell somebody of her troubles. The Sicilians were already working her over when they run into unexpected resistance."

"Any idea who?"

"We don't know. They winged an escaped schizo from Asgard Park, but was he involved? His doctors are not forthcoming. The guy's a certified fruitcake."

"This was all in the police report, Hugh."

"Young fella, this was a team of Mafia heavies sent in by the Council. You don't trifle with them guys. One got hit by two heavy subs No random fire, targeted, and controlled. Get my drift? Whoever sent in the cavalry; picked his pros. They let one man walk with a message."

"The child is protected."

"You heard that one. That was before the Yale woman lost her memory. We can't make head or tail of it, but we are very interested in Asgard Park."

"I can't see how an escaped psychopath could be part of the mystery team, Hugh."

"It gets better."

"Go on."

"The morning after, Dr Birger Wallenberg visits his fruitcake. He feeds the press a phony story about his guy being the hero. The press gobbles it up. Then he confers privately with the woman and declares that she has come down with post-traumatic stress. This is before anyone gets to question her. And the Yale woman promptly loses her memory."

"I hadn't heard, but the man is a psychiatrist!"

"Let me finish, fella. How's this? A few days later, a limo arrives at Asgard Park. Our spotters confirm five occupants connected to the Gambino family. The Bureau is working under the assumption that the guy in the front is the alias we've been hunting for years, Eric Schaeffer Spears. It was an important break for us."

"I've heard nothing about this visit."

"Why should you, son, nothing came down."

"That's a bit thick."

Hugh Miller laughed softly and stroked his sunburned bald spot. His close-cropped hair bristled in the cool office air. He was the picture of comfort.

"Wonders never cease at Asgard Park. Our road detail sees the limo leave, an hour later, the bigwig himself behind the wheel; four of his men propped up in straitjackets. The Institute security detail wrapped them up. I say that sacred cows make the best burgers. It is without precedent. We had agents on the inside. They were given a lecture on how to handle psychopaths while this went down."

"You are kidding."

"No kidding in that park. We are doubling our surveillance. Now, you'd expect reprisals. These guys don't swallow. I've kept a team on Spears ever since; nothing, zilch, and I should know!"

"There couldn't be a political angle to this, Hugh?"

"You've been away too long, young fella. These guys are for real. And there's more. It was open season on that Kirkpatrick woman; suddenly it's hands off. Like a bolt out of the blue, this woman is the holy virgin. We picked it up from multiple informers. Not your everyday local stuff either. It's an across-the-board tribunal directive. The whole apparatus below the belt of this nation was suddenly going bonkers over this woman. There isn't a punk from here to Vegas, who will piss on her sidewalk. It is something awesome, and that's the gospel truth."

"You don't walk away from shaking down these guys, Hugh. It's a matter of honor. Nobody gets struck from the list. The Council is biding its time."

"We can't figure it either, son."

"What do you know about the father of her child?"

"Bill Rayman, a straight arrow out of South Africa, killed in a hunting accident seven years back. There is no connection. I checked the coroner's report. They weren't even married."

"Still firm on the morals, eh, Hugh?"

"Family values are important, Crane. Any kids yet?"

"Not yet, but we keep trying."

"That's good. Keep it up. The family is important."

"You wouldn't have a photo of Karl Leamas, the former Director who founded the Asgard Park Institute?"

"Sure!"

Hugh Miller barked over the intercom at his secretary. A printout photo of Dr Leamas arrived with his file. The recognition was instant. It was the picture on the Baron's desk. The man Crane thought was the father, the same arrogant gaze.

"I know this face."

"Of course, you do. This psychopath is involved in a dozen murders. Mad as a hatter."

Crane leafed through the thick file. "These cases, he never dirtied his hands himself?"

"Way too clever for that. We suspect he used patients or paid mercenaries. His victims weren't exactly model citizens, and somebody was always being saved. Maybe the guy's a rich vigilante, high on Batman. We were never able to build a case.

"Tell me about this guy."

"The kind of millionaire we call billionaires today; a Harvard man; never a good start in life."

"Any German connections?"

"You sure on your toes, young fella."

"Tell that to my superiors."

"This is unofficial. Our friends in Europe picked up several connections that may interest you. Birger Wallenberg was a newborn, when a large German insurance company made good on a claim by his mother, Catarine. That was the seed money that started her off during the Cold War. She became a billionaire, as did her son. Ever ask why a wealthy doctor is running a two-bit funny farm, out in the boondocks? And guess what; a major stockholder on the board of the German insurance company that coughed up the money was Dr Karl Leamas in vigorous mental health."

"A public insurance company?"

"German owners mostly, the old aristocracy."

"Baron Keltenbrunner von Geisenhausen?"

"I'll be damned! Sure, that's the one; Geisenhausen, not Keltenbrunner. Fill me in will you; let's keep this a two-way street."

"That would be the Old Baron. I visited young Baron Keltenbrunner in his medieval Bavarian castle and made a mess of it."

Crane flashed the Leamas photo at Hugh.

"This character was in place of honor on his desk. Why would a baron keep a photo of a common shareholder on his private desk?"

Hugh Miller sighed deeply and contentedly. "Don't fit the social pattern. Think of it, Crane, the times before the hordes of Harvard and Yale descended on us, with all their pseudo intellectual crap. Before communism even. The days of the old aristocracy! They ruled the world for a long time. Where is this Bavarian castle? Have a name, does it?"

"That is the beauty of it. The castle bears the same name that helped Kirkpatrick to remember an unlisted number to Asgard Park seven years after using it once."

"The name!"

"Heimdallr."

On this note, the leisurely atmosphere swept from a sunny office space in lower Manhattan. Burton Crane looked up from his notebook and saw Hugh Miller slam shut. He could not have seen it clearer if a steel door to a nuclear bunker had slammed in his face. Crane had accidentally kicked the panic button.

"Should have told me that name up front, young fella."

"Heimdallr?"

"I have a bad feeling about this, Crane."

"It's a common enough name in Nordic lore, Hugh."

"I've a bad feeling about this, young fella."

"What is it, what does it stand for?"

"Can't tell. Bound by a blood oath. Goes back a long way. Hoover tried but he never got close. They burned him bad. In the end, he wouldn't touch it with a pole. Gave him the shakes. Look, Crane; I have a bad feeling about this. This is my advice. This is dead serious." He paused to stroke his bald spot with a dark worried expression. As if to make sure his head was still there.

"Drop it."

"Whoa, man, what's this about, Hugh?" Crane found this turnaround almost funny, but that reaction wore off quickly.

"Take advice from an old warhorse. Back off."

"At least give me a hint?"

"You've done me a favor, son. I owe you one. My division just dropped this case. The Bureau dropped this case, effective immediately. I'm calling off all my agents. The Asgard Park file is closed for all purposes. It is closed for reference. In fact, I'll go one further; I have never heard of this matter, nobody in the Bureau has, and I just told you that for a fact. We have no record of a Birger Wallenberg or Asgard Park on our files."

"Because of one word?"

"Look at it this way, son. If the Mob backs off after being humiliated and the Bureau runs for cover; is that a sensible question?"

The head of the New York field division stood up. His ramrod back straightened to a stern regiment. Once again, this incorruptible law enforcement officer with exacting standards had a job to do.

"Got a file to bury, son. No hard feelings, but there it is."

They shook hands. The older man wouldn't let go. It became a very personal handshake. Somehow his protégé must be warned not to be reckless. He was once almost part of his beloved Bureau. Hugh Miller cleared his throat. The watery blue eyes looked straight into Crane's. They held him.

"Don't dance with the devil, young fella. He knows all your steps before you think of them."

Chapter 10

THE VICTORIAN BUILDINGS OF Asgard Park lay basking in the sun, suitably framed in pastoral beauty, and cooled by the brisk summer breeze. The grassland and meadows had a fresh luster after yesterday's rain.

Walking from the parking lot, Burton Crane found this an idyllic setting for the world's best brains to study their alter egos. The Institute had no profitable defense contracts to offset its prohibitive costs; the work here was all pleasantly academic. It was hard to imagine, that a lurking colossus from the prehistoric days of Hoover, hid behind this cultured varnish. Still shaken after his meeting with Hugh, the implications were enormous. Old hands like Hugh did not use Hoover's name lightly. His warning was serious. If Hoover shrank from these guys, they were able to hurt him more than he could hurt them. It was the only equation that counted. A vast ancient conspiracy, alive and kicking in the heart of his nation, was the last thing Crane had expected to stumble over.

It had surprised him how easily he got an interview with Birger Wallenberg. All it took was a mention that he had met his mother in Berlin, while shadowing her suspected murderer. The man at the center of this deepening mystery immediately set aside half an hour between meetings.

Cooling his heels in an antechamber, Crane watched the doctor's flack catcher, an older lady, field anything incoming with calm competence. On the dot, the secretary ushered him into a scholarly office, with a small library. He noted none of the trappings of power; the windows were thrown open to the sounds of nature; foliage rustling in the breeze. Showers of seeds floating on the air.

"You met my mother in Berlin, Mr. Crane. That makes you somebody's official."

After meeting the Baron, meeting the man who could yank his Doberman's chain, Crane had expected a more ruthless character. Not a guy in his shirtsleeves.

"I'm affiliated with NATO."

"I thought you were an employee of the National Security Agency?"

"May I ask how you came to hear that?"

"Mr. Crane. My security staff runs a check on people who come here. They are thorough, and it costs money. I plan to look into their budget later this year."

"What else do you know about me, Dr Wallenberg?"

"Nothing; I read the first page of their printout, and saw you were NSA. If it tickles your fancy, you can take it with you when you go. I am pressed for time." The Director had a disarming smile. "What can I do for you, apart from stroking your ego?"

Crane shifted his legs uncomfortably. Better not butter this toast on the wrong side. "In Berlin your mother, Catarine, met a former general of the East German Staatspolizei and received a dossier with an extensive list of names. Have you any idea what her interest were? Why she took part in such dangerous covert games?"

"Mother went her own way. Her funeral was two days ago. I have my hands full. After her death, I have come across puzzling inconsistencies that she omitted to tell me. I am now a major shareholder in the Midgard Group that controls this Institute. I was under the illusion that I was chosen for my job on merits. Contrary to what you may think, my owning the place was a bit of a let-down."

"Any idea what she wanted with STASI documents?"

"She could want the names for legitimate reasons. She owned shares in several German companies. I don't suppose STASI agents are no worse for wear, as people go, but one can see that they can be vulnerable to threats of exposure."

"You are jumping me one here, doctor. How do you know that this was a list of former STASI informers, presently employed in West German companies?"

Crane expected a stumble, but the open smile did not falter. Clear as an arctic summer.

"I suppose one of your superiors told me. Your NSA and the Armed Forces handle billions of secret documents. He grinned disarmingly.

The information was a matter of national security, and this guy waved it off. There was every reason to haul him in for questioning. The young man clearly did not grasp what he had just said. It was the Baron all over again. Crane decided he did not want a repeat performance.

"Your mother outsmarted us by excellent tradecraft. We watched her pass the STASI file to a biker gang, or so she wanted us to think. Picking up the pieces after our debacle, I visited a German industrialist, Baron Keltenbrunner von Geisenhausen. Ever heard of the man?"

"Sure, I may have met him as a child. I think he knew my mother."

Crane half rose and handed him a photograph of the Baron; the only one available.

"Ever seen him?"

There was no mistaking the troubled recognition in the young man's face.

"I saw this man in Mother's album. She never mentioned him by name or his title."

He was telling the truth. Crane was sure of it. Why was this young man being so open and up front?

"On the desk in the Baron's private study, I came across a framed photo of Dr Karl Leamas, your predecessor. Can you explain that?"

"Sure, before his illness Dr Leamas was a respected scientist and a wealthy entrepreneur. Most likely they had many investments in common."

"They have you in common, Dr Wallenberg; you and your mother. What got me into his Bavarian castle was your name."

"As I said, Mother knew the Baron."

"We searched the barracks of an unsavory biker gang on the baron's estate. It gave us nothing but one hidden photo."

"Yes?"

"A snapshot of you, Dr Wallenberg, between the pages of a magazine, marking a STASI article; you in a doctor's robe from Lunds Lassaret. The snap had your name penciled on the back."

"A photo of me?"

"I'm curious about that."

"Mother's murder defies explanation. I can tell you that when one of our patients got involved in a downtown shooting, I wanted no suspicion to fall on Asgard Park. I invited the FBI to take active interest in the case, and they provided several undercover agents. They found nothing wrong at the Institute."

"The FBI told you this?"

"And then you show up."

"When was this?"

"Yesterday afternoon. A Hugh Miller, the FBI officer I invited to stake us out, called me to give Asgard Park a clean bill of health. He assured me that they had found nothing wrong with the Institute's handling of the matter, or any other matter. He commended our respect for the Bureau. His judgement did not exactly fit my impression."

"I happen to know Hugh Miller. I have great respect for his judgment. Why would he lie?"

"And why would your friend assure me that any private inquiries made by an NSA employee named Burton Crane, had nothing whatsoever to do with the Bureau?"

"Which answers my question earlier about the NSA. Thanks for clearing that up."

"Your thanks may be premature."

Dr Karl Leamas, your schizophrenic patient, can he be behind this?"

"A schizophrenic split does not hamper intellectual capacity. It often gives a rational sense of superiority, but it tends to prevent complicated planning."

"The man may have multiple murders on his conscience."

"I am reasonably sure that his secret is not sanity."

As the young man rose to cut off the interview, he turned to Crane with a question. "The terrorist Helmut Mayer, the man they are hunting, do you know if he has a burn mark on his right hand?"

"Yes, he did, and that is another fact you should absolutely not know."

"Ask my secretary to fit you into my schedule, Crane. We must talk."

They shook, and the young doctor handed him the background file, with a rushed smile.

"Since I don't have the time, you better read what my security people have to say about you."

There was a knot of doctors arguing heatedly in the anteroom, waiting to be let in. Burton Crane walked back to a car, cooking in sunshine. If this young man headed a powerful secret organization, he was the world's greatest angler, friendlier than a wet dog. Crane was ready to throw in the towel. He opened the windows to air the car, and flipped open the file, reading the staccato pages of bank accounts, house mortgages and dates due; his private medicals; the names of his superiors, outlines of his most important cases; all top-secret material.

These career details did not come from the NSA data bank. They had no proof that his British liaison, Sidney, kept a Kensington flat with a Henry Gaudier installed in it. Where was this stuff coming from?

Worst of all were the matter-of-fact lines on his bank accounts in Gibraltar and Guernsey in the forged names of identities used over the years for backup; the first line of defense for a field man that needed to protect his back from friend or foe alike. All out in the open.

To see this information about his secret funds on print was nothing short of devastating. And his wife's gynecologist's journals outlined failed efforts to bring a child to the world. Who would break into a doctor's office for background checks on a wife, twice removed? This was no casual handover of a routine background check. This was a humiliating threat, handed over with a charming smile.

Helplessly, Crane stared back at a Victorian idyll basking in the sun. The tipoff about his NSA ties had not come from Hugh Miller. In this, his gratitude had indeed been premature, as the young man pointed out.

Heimdallr had just shown its teeth.

Dr Wallenberg had revealed his position at the center of a deep conspiracy. His security was thorough, the young man said. This was way beyond what was even possible. Crane gunned the car down the drive, eyes fixed on the rearview mirror, and still his heart was singing. One sentence in that file made his life complete.

'Heimdallr confirms that Evelyn Crane has remained a faithful wife.'

Based on their uncanny insights, he had every reason to believe that this bit was true along with the rest. If this clandestine operation was out of government control, it was truly the mother of conspiracies.

The guard at the far gatepost saluted army-style as he went by.

Chapter 11

WAITING FOR FLIGHT SR 458 to Tirana, Burton Crane left the transit bar at Zurich Airport. He was going back to the Middle Ages. Swissair was the airline allowed into Albania. The party bigwigs needed the Swiss connection.

He missed this morning. Having rustled Evelyn up an English breakfast, he had taken his wife on a walk up Okeford Hill.

From that point, the day got worse with urgent summons to Lambeth. Konrad had reported in from the British Embassy in Tirana. Evelyn had dropped him off at Century House, his "concrete penis", she called it.

In Albania, it had blown wide open. Helmut Mayer was dead. He was the German tourist who ran amok and battered a dozen men to death at a country inn. The item had made a splash in the news a few days back. Konrad had been on the run from the Camorra through the Albanian countryside for two weeks. He had reached Tirana in the early hours and was holed up in the British Embassy.

Crane had asked the Embassy to arrange a visa for Reginald Murray. He was using pristine papers from his safe. He did not trust the Foreign Office to hold a hand over him in Tirana. Konrad would meet him with the visa at Shqiperi airport. Sidney voiced his doubts, finding him overly reckless, as always. They had argued. Crane asked him to stop treating Albania as the crown jewels. At the bottom of the barrel, they were a third-rate target, plain as Monday, no pedigree, no style, no class, of interest to nobody.

"How very singular," was all that Sidney offered.

The flight took less than two hours but peeled away two hundred years of civilization. Out of the Fokker 100 window on its descent towards Shqiperi airport, he saw fields and hills peppered with gray concrete mushrooms, like a rash on the landscape. These domed defense bunkers numbered over 700,000 in the poorest country in Europe.

Getting off at Shqiperi Airport took longer than the flight. The airport had no local equipment, so Crane stood patiently on top of the Fokker's build in ladder, watching them check papers on the concrete apron below. Wild discussions in broken English. He scoured the area, but Konrad was nowhere in sight with his visa. With Sidney as his sole protector, this could become tricky.

When it came to his turn, he tried to explain that his visa waited in the arrival hall, but they did not speak the lingo. Shunted aside, they kept him under guard in the shadow of the aircraft wing. He made an ugly scene to test their stamina, but these guys had stoic patience. The rough hands fingered well-worn machine guns with casual familiarity. Their youthful brazenness allowed no sympathy. This foreigner was clearly a danger to their country.

Wearing a two-piece suit, Crane pocketed his tie. Even in the shade, the heat was oppressive.

Two hours later, when all passengers had left the plane, they took him into the steaming arrival hall. Here the smugglers and officials were in full commerce, bribes flying thick amid handshakes and backslaps. Wisely, the Swiss flight crew remained on board. Later, when the last baggage was manhandled into the hall, Crane rescued his valise. Nobody stopped him. He waited, resigned to the medieval pace, sweating by the pint. They processed the passengers again, this time having them file by a wooden cage with a round hole in the glass.

Biding his time, he studied the sullen routines of the three men inside the cubicle. It was all window dressing. They had trouble reading the passports and hardly looked at the visas. A sight of one off-white, badly typed and illegibly stamped paper was all they needed. After that, a feigned routine of checks, and a grudging stamp.

Konrad did not show up with his visa.

Early on he had noticed a man of classic Balkan features giving him the eye from the door to the outer hall where the custom women searched more unseemly baggage that no official was willing to vouch for, things unworthy of a small bribe. The man was waiting for something.

With the arrival hall almost empty, Crane made another row and demanded a call to the British Embassy. Witnessing the shouting match, the man by the door came over to explain in broken English that the British Embassy had sent him to fetch Mr. Reginald Murray. Crane quelled his fury and stomped up to the glass window, pushing across a stamped badly printed slip of paper, his visa, and the Albanian text worked its magic. The stamps came down after pointless scrutiny.

"Five dollars."

"How much is that in sterling, sir?"

"Sterling?"

"English pounds."

"Five English pounds."

This place was truly the backwater of Europe. The women in customs made eyes at his suitcase, but his new companion returned an angry glare.

"Businessman!"

This explanation worked well enough. They were outside the shabby steam cooker with commendable haste, only to enter another. It was a prewar Mercedes so antiquated that, if renovated, it might be worth more than a new one. It had none of the modern comforts.

"Why isn't Konrad here to meet me?"

They were rolling on uneven asphalt along an empty country road from the tiny airport. It had taken him that long to simmer down. In the merciless sun, the breeze through the open windows was roasting.

"Mr. Konradi dead."

For a moment Crane was too stunned to ask. Accepting the hazards of his profession, the anger rose against this godforsaken land. The road of mirages to Tirana took half an hour, the only traffic an occasional peasant on foot. It took Crane all that time to make some sense of it.

The story was that Konrad had left the Embassy for the new Swissair office, set up recently in two rooms at the nearby Hotel Dajti. On his way back, less than two hundred meters from the fenced-off street of foreign embassies, he was mugged. The police suggested he resisted. There were no witnesses. A common criminal had shot him dead and got away.

His body was in the city morgue.

It was not a credible lie. If Konrad had resisted a mugging, the body in the morgue would not be German.

"Mr. Murray go to Hotel Dajti for beer, yes?" Embassy drivers also wanted the good life.

"Take me to the city morgue. I want to see his body. Now!"

If the embassy errand boy had learned anything in life, it was taking orders from assertive men. He consented; unable to fathom how anyone would rather pay a visit to a city morgue than to the oasis of the Hotel Dajti.

As protection against the heat, the morgue was a few steps down in a cellar in a low, nondescript backstreet building. The entrance from the small, pebbled backyard was covered with fine dust. Outside, in the shadow of a wall, an older supervisor and two young men in dirty tarpaulin aprons, passed the time-of-day smoking cigarettes in the brutal heat.

Burton Crane suffered the sun while the driver introduced him to the supervisor, a big comrade in a sleeveless shirt, fronted by a gleaming apron. His deeply weathered arms were covered with an awkward jumble of ugly, amateurish blue tattoos.

The supervisor complained about the lack of papers but the driver, who moved in more exalted circles, smoothed it over with a ten-pound bribe from the well-dressed foreigner. When the Embassy driver wanted to stay behind in the yard, Crane insisted that he tag along. None of the others understood a word of English.

The stench in the cellar was unbearable. The cooling system was out of order. Nothing serious, they assured him. The electricity would come back in a few hours. The light from the small windows barely moved the dark to half dusk. In the front room, a couple of half-carved-up bodies lay on wooden tables in a heat that was slightly less palpable and twice as stifling.

The supervisor lit two oil lamps and held them up. The third body was Konrad's. There was no doubt about his identity; killed cleanly by a bullet to the side of his head at close range. It was not the wound to expect on a well-trained agent fully able to take down a mugger with his eyes closed.

The staff was using the cellar as cool storage on the side. This was not a place people were keen to burgle at night. They had placed a crate of vegetables on Konrad's naked stomach. Crane closed his friend's eyes and accepted that the old supervisor was an official first and a human-being second. These guys left their humanity at home. They knew no respect for the dead. He had found this attitude prevalent in the state organs of Eastern Europe, especially in those set to the odious task of processing the dead. A corpse does not protest. A corpse cannot pull strings, and it was treated accordingly.

There was little Crane could do. They had never heard of lead coffins. If they were dealing out vegetables off the corpses, they hardly grasped the need. His attempt to use Konrad's to infiltrate a syndicate within the former Eastern bloc had been effectively terminated. There was no way to win dignity for his agent other than get his body out of the country. He offered the supervisor another ten-pound note for having his friend taken out of service as a vegetable rack and have him covered with an empty sack of coarse jute.

He asked if they still had the crazy German who had massacred all those people. They did, and another fiver got him into the inner sanctum. The supervisor pulled open a rickety door to a side-room. His blue tattooed arm hung an oil lamp on a hook and waved him into a grisly scene. In this small cellar chamber, the air was still cool, but the thaw caused everything to glisten with condensation. Now and again drops fell on them from the low roof. On a long table of rough-hewn timber, twenty or so naked bodies lay stacked three or four deep, feet forwards and bellies up. The nameless bloated corpses carried genitals of both sexes, but all looked the same. The faces towards the wall were out of his field of vision.

On a separate table, on a buckled metal sheet covered with droplets of water that sparkled in the light from the gently rocking oil lamp, seven other bodies lay in a single row. Their badly maimed heads hung throat up over the front edge of the table, dull eyes staring at the visitor. These were the remaining victims of the hammer massacre, the ones that nobody wanted.

The only head with an intact skull was Helmut Mayer; body and face covered in cuts and holes. They had washed away the caked blood. In this crappy light it was not easy to spot the half-healed scratches on his face, the scratches made by Catarine Wallenberg before he gagged and tortured her. Distractedly, Crane pondered the skin scrapings from under the nails of the woman, the semen, the DNA; things for others to pursue. He took the oil lamp and studied him closely; somebody had used the German for target practice, long after he was dead.

As they stepped up into the solar furnace, the two underlings were still hanging about smoking, waiting for more bodies to stack in their thawing cellar. Pale from the ghoulish undertaking, the driver made no comment when ordered to the British Embassy, but Crane recalled a rule of thumb; never make bad blood with the locals. The man had earned his beer at the Dajti.

He was cornered. You got away with insubordination if you brought home the bacon. He would not be doing that. And nothing in this bloody mess could by any stretch of imagination be connected with Asgard Park.

Book 3, Burton Crane

Chapter 12

MANY AMBASSADORS HAD FLED Albania for consultations in better-stocked capitals; so too the British. The chargé d'affaires was a young lion from a line of blue bloods; a man Crane tipped for an easy rise within the ranks, if he could crawl back out of this hellhole with spotless marks of distinction.

The British Counselor did not want the case channeled through the Embassy, as they were already handling the exhumed body of Charles Grenville, a Canadian mining magnate who was at least Commonwealth. Both Konrad and Mayer were German citizens. Unimpressed by American meddling on his turf, NATO or not, the young lion resisted.

He was put straight by urgent instructions from the Foreign Office in London.

"The bloody country is going to the dogs, Mr. Murray," he said resignedly to keep the peace.

"It's the Balkans, son. The only way to get civilization into their heads is to ram it in with a rifle butt. I sure as hell don't want my agent rotting in a morgue with no electricity. There's a wife waiting at home to bury him in decent soil. You get me a lead coffin on the first available flight out of here.

"I'll do what I can."

And do me another favor. Set up a meeting with the Tirana Chief of Police, and please, son, on the double. These people have no sense of time."

The Chief of Police was a handsome man with a broad strong face, and bushy graying eyebrows. His impressive cap could not tame his head of hair. He had the languid movements that come to a man charged with the destiny of proud and explosive people. A simple man who carried weight, he was openly despised by his ragtag force who hated him for his paltry privileges.

They met at the Dajti, where Crane had checked in and paid off the Embassy driver with a cold beer. The Chief of Police spoke halting English. As other high officials, he was a frequent visitor on the embassy circle, and eager to ingratiate himself. It was one of the most coveted privileges. The young lion had been kind enough to change Crane's pounds into dollars, the only respected currency. Crane befriended the Chief with a bottle of White Horse whiskey.

The Chief looked around the Dajti dining room and studied every person with a long lazy stare, then made a broad slow gesture. "My men question all people around Konrad murder place. There are no witnesses, my friend." After a while he made another broad, well-trained gesture. "What to do? Everyone steals and robs in Tirana. Chief of Police is not safe on the street."

"What about the hammer killings, any witnesses there?"

"Yes, spy go crazy."

"I heard that two witnesses survived the massacre inside the birrari."

"Yes, two witnesses inside; two German spies." Another broad gesture and a slow look for reaction. Satisfied there was none, he continued.

"A whore who slept with crazy German, the widow of Emir Avxhiu; good family. We question her many days. She knows nothing. I released her before I come here to meet you. She will not live. Families of murdered people will kill her."

The Chief of Police gave a slow wave of his hand to underline how unreasonable it would be for the families not to pursue this goal.

"I heard the victims were criminals."

"No, no, innocent people, my friend."

"And the other witness?"

"Brother of whore, Spiro Shituni; he is very criminal. No worry, we find Spiro Shituni."

"I'd like to talk to the widow; what was her name?"

"Shequere Avxhiu. This is no good idea. Dangerous idea. Many want to talk to widow."

"Which is why I need to see her now."

"She is free. How do I know where she hides? This is not your good idea, my friend."

"It is a formality." Crane mirrored the man's slow throwaway gesture with his hand.

"The British Embassy and the German Foreign Office demand that I see this witness. NATO wants to ask her a few questions. If I cannot, the embassies will assume that you refused to cooperate. There will be retributions. You know how it is. If I can see her for a few minutes, everybody will be happy. Give me her address, so I can get it over with."

"I take you there. One never knows, my friend."

The Chief knew all right. Somebody was about to take up the questioning where the Chief had left off, with less refined methods. It was not his business of course; the girl was unlikely to know anything about Helmut Mayer, and much less of Konrad or his death. He was clawing at straws.

"NATO recognizes your help, sir."

On the steps under the hotel portico, the Chief called out to a driver, loitering among the men under the palms. Before leading them to an old Mercedes, the driver took his sweet time about the handshakes. Insubordination like that got you sacked in the real world. Among proud people it was the norm, if you could afford it, a man marking his independence. A man of a good family.

It was a short drive across town to a crumbling two-story house where the witness lived in a defunct photo studio on the ground floor. What looked to Crane to be an old Zil limousine in the street with open windows outside the small house. Couple of men in the front seat smoking. Crane didn't like the look of them.

"Are these your men, Chief?"

"No," the Chief had a worried look, "Sigurimi."

"They disbanded the Sigurimi."

The Chief of Police answered with a gesture that suggested that words and deeds are not always the same. He was sitting this one out on the fence.

"Now no good time, my friend, we come back tomorrow and talk to whore." He muttered angrily to the driver and the car was moving again.

"I have urgent meeting," he added for good measure.

After a short ride, Crane feigned illness, and waved them to a stop. The Chief of Police acted with admirable resolution. He was not about to have his official car soiled by foreign puke.

"Sorry, chief; must be the heat. I get easily carsick. I shall walk back. It will do me good. What time tomorrow can we talk to this Avxhiu woman?"

"Tomorrow afternoon."

"Alright, thanks."

Book 3, Burton Crane

Chapter 13

CRANE TRAILED BACK TO the place, crossing from the street into the communal backyards, a few houses down from the run-down store. The backyards were a scrubby waste of dust and refuse. The afternoon was cooling but the sun was still up. The well-trodden paths through the backyards lay empty and deserted.

There was no time to case the building; only one door in the back led to the ground-floor studio. There was no option but to give a determined knock and barge in. A split second brought him through the doorway; enough to survey the scene and sum up his odds. This was, after all, as Evelyn would say, his natural habitat: bursting in on people.

The girl was battling to raise her shoulders from the floor as she gathered the torn shoulder of her dress, an act of importance. Her hair was wet. A low wooden barrel of dirty water where she had recently bathed stood in the corner. Crane could imagine that her days in jail had not been her cleanest. The girl had suffered some slapping around but did not appear hurt. Her jaw was set in a stubborn frown of anger and panic. She used the disturbance to pull herself together. The young soldier hovering over her let go of her ankles in confusion.

"What the hell is going on here?"

His American accent commanded the authority of a quarter century in the field, but here it stood for nothing.

The Commandant came up with a start from the single rickety chair. Draped in a long blue felt coat, his corpulent body defied the heat. His squashed cap sported the red star. Enraged, he moved to confront the intruder. He had the typical broad features of the Balkans, large wide mouth, and strong teeth. Built like a bull; a choleric man who had spent his life sending people off for twenty years for disturbing his afternoon nap. Now the lowest of them all, a foreigner, challenged his authority on his territory, in front of an underling.

"You have no business here. Get out!"

He came straight at Crane. His assault pounded the American backward, towards the door as he pummeled his chest and shoulders with heavy palms, expecting a quick and humiliating retreat.

"You have no right! You have passport? Your visa is no good! You go to prison! Get out!"

But the American was no stranger to body contact. He used his bulk to slow and break stride. Gradually it brought the advance to a stop, as he backed off just enough to give him space. The angry breath in his face reeked of garlic.

He had often come across these senseless instruments of tyranny. They were in demand with despots around the world. Men who never listened, not even to confessions. The point of the game was not information but control. Their masters would look the other way if they covered their tracks; often when they did not.

He watched the broken veins on the Commandant's nose redden with rage. Losing face in the presence of lower ranks was a serious matter. The man grappled after the handgun in the worn leather holster at his side. That move cut out the time for protocol.

Crane knew by experience that problems of this nature are best worked out later by level-headed bureaucrats.

He moved with an agility belying his size. His left hand took hold of the Commandant's left arm and twisted it sharply; then he struck the back of the straight elbow with a powerful punch with the flat of his right fist. It laid no claim to great skill, but it was effective. Something gave way.

The surprise of being on the receiving end elicited the start of a whimper that was terminated at source a heavy blow to the side of his head. Gratefully, and without grace, the Commandant collapsed. Within the space of two seconds his dumfounded soldier came down to join his general. The girl scrambled to her feet. The noise would not have reached the men in the car. Crane knew he had to move fast. These guys were out of government control. The disbanded Sigurimi was like a Camorra in its nascent state, a free operator with a promising future.

"You come with me!"

"Sigurimi take money, yes please, sir!"

"Forget the money. There is no time. Come!"

Angry over the lost money, she sprang in his wake into the yard and down the dusty paths behind the houses, over footpaths strewn with ruined bricks. Hailed by scruffy chickens in wire coops; the only eyes watching from the shadows were those of despondent underfed children.

"We must talk. Where can we go?" Crane slowed; a brisk gait would draw attention.

"Tirana stadium, yes please."

Her English came as a relief, and she seemed to trust him, grateful for his timely arrival.

"You Helmut Mayer man, please sir?"

There was hope in her voice, and that was helpful. The question had more significance than he could account for.

"Yes, Burton Crane is the name!" He used his own because it would mean nothing to authorities around here.

She smiled at him; trust confirmed.

"You are in a fine pickle, young lady!"

"Pickle, please?"

He ignored her. They were in the side streets now, with a few people around, passing over a narrow canal by a pedestrian bridge. The canal was dry. They walked under a sinking sun across a rubble-strewn square in front of a locked soccer stadium. The thin wooden partitions that blocked the main gate were more symbolic than real. Until recently they were enough in a country where nobody dared cross authority. He pulled the flimsy partitions aside and edged through into a silent circular stadium, home of the Tirana soccer team. The shadows were longer now. Crane looked around. It was abandoned and quiet.

Her beauty surprised him. The Chief of Police had said she was a widow, and he called her a whore. The girl had raven hair against a complexion of milky white. It gave a startling contrast, and she blushed easily. She stood five foot four, tall for her race. He tipped her age around seventeen, noticing she was barefoot. She had run through the rubble without complaint, a sturdy, proud sort with a fine figure.

Crane didn't like to conduct a debriefing without refreshments but bringing her in was not a solution. The girl had just had a brush with officialdom. She would clam up.

"Why did you ask if I was one of Mayer's men?"

She gave a shy smile, and a passing blush.

"Mayer say his men take care of Avxhiu. You take me to Paris, yes please?"

There was his inducement; a strong hand to play.

"If Mayer made you a promise, I only have your word for it. And, if I am to honor his wishes, you must tell me what Mayer said from the moment you met him, till he died?"

As they sauntered in the shadows, she began in broken English to tell him the tale of the day she met the German as his translator. How she found, after what was likely a mild heart attack, that he spoke fluent Albanian.

Crane assumed his brush with death affected his mind, it would explain a lot, but speaking Albanian didn't fit his profile.

"Did you ask him about the scratch on his chin?"

"Yes. Woman put mark into Mayer."

"Did he tell you why she scratched him?"

"He said this woman has more courage than Avxhiu."

"Helmut Mayer did not tell you he raped that Swedish woman, on burning stove after tying her hands and feet down with wire. Can you imagine a death like that?"

The girl went numb, immersed in disbelief; then shook her head violently, stuttering alive.

"New Mayer not do this," again the deep unruly blush, "he love Avxhiu."

"New Mayer? You were lovers, were you?"

"Yes, new Mayer say his men take care of Avxhiu, yes please."

Her proud white face was scarlet now. True, she had bedded the bastard without knowing; but she defended him too readily. This was not the first time a woman tested his faculty of understanding. Perhaps she sensed his disgust. She looked at him with new doubt.

She told him the story that she had told the police. It was the truth. Finally, she came to the gathering at the birrari, and spoke of the hammer singing, the sparing of her brother.

A childhood memory came to Avxhiu, the slaughter of an ox out in the open. From a distance, the immense animal tugged at the ropes, tossing around the men that steadied it for the kill. The sound of the muffled shot arrived long after she saw the bulk of an invincible beast turn into falling mass that obeyed only the call of the earth. She had seen that again in the roadside birrari. The torn mass of her lover, held up by limitless will, oozing blood, hoarsely croaking a strange word, and in one instant he became falling mass that answered only the call of the earth.

"Mayer say name of man who take care of Avxhiu," she stumbled as it had no meaning to her. Maybe Valennbi," she offered with downcast head.

"Wallenberg?"

In his surprise, Crane pronounced it sharply.

It was a revelation. Avxhiu had heard the word croaked at her once and thought she misheard. She had not. So much elation swept through her that she jumped in joy and struck his chest in joy

"Yes, Wallenbergi, yes, yes, yes. Wallenbergi!" She danced around him.

"Did Mayer ever mention that name before?"

"No, is Wallenbergi Mayer's man?

"In a way, but tell me about Konrad, his driver. Why did he leave before you went into the birrari?"

She realized that all Burton Crane wanted to know seemed to concern Mayer's driver. He was moreover oddly relaxed. To assault a Sigurimi general carried the death penalty. She knew nothing about this man. Was this a show, to gain her trust? Was it a trap? She had already told him too much; told him about Rakipe, the Kid who worked at the Dajti for the Sigurimi. How careless she had been. She smelled liquor on his breath.

The man had inside knowledge. Who had told him about her in the Birrari and about the driver? His information must have come from the Sigurimi. The police had told her that the Sigurimi had killed the driver who was a NATO spy. Avxhiu had to make sure.

"Have you met my brother Spiro?"

"No, I understand your brother is on the run. If you can arrange it, I would like to meet your brother. I can help."

No, Spiro had told this man nothing. This was not one of Mayer's men. This man was police, a NATO spy like the driver, a devil with a silver tongue. She did not reply, angry to be so easily duped.

"Tell me Shequere, did Mayer say something to Konrad, the driver, before he left?"

It was all about the driver. She hated her eagerness to trust in people she had never met. Her desperate lack of options was no excuse for naivety. In the car, in the heat of passion, her lover had told her that the driver was a NATO spy. She would test this foreigner.

"You good friend to Konrad."

"Yes, he was a good friend for many years." Mayer had told her one month.

"The driver was NATO spy. Are you NATO spy?"

A ragged man had entered the stadium through the flimsy barricades at the main entrance, to eye them with watchful hostility. The girl grew fidgety by his side. Crane walked across the hard trodden soccer field to challenge the stranger. Halfway over, the stranger decided they were harmless. He signaled to a woman with two children, who stepped out of the shadows to follow him inside. Like the thousands adrift, they traveled light, seeking a spot to rest for the night.

Crane turned. The girl was gone.

Having sensed her mistrust, he should have known better. Raised around here, she would know other ways out of the arena. The girl was a fool not to trust him. They'd find her, and her story would be of no interest.

And having disposed of Catarine Wallenberg, why would Helmut Mayer make her name his last word? Or was it about her son?

Outside the stadium, having lost his orientation, Crane got a boy to show him the way back to the British Embassy. The young ones are always the first to pick up phrases. He gave him a dollar for his trouble and found that happiness could still flower on this barren soil.

Chapter 14

"WAS OUR CHIEF ANY help, Mr. Murray?"

Crane was back in the British Embassy, taking tea with the young chargé d'affaires.

"No, I'm afraid our friend chickened out; left me holding the bag, as it were. I needed a word with a witness from the birrari massacre. The Sigurimi got there before me. I intervened just in time."

"Mr. Murray, you have no jurisdiction here. These are volatile people."

"They disbanded the Sigurimi, son. The government of Ramiz Alia confirms it. They have no jurisdiction. Let's just say that I tried to stop a domestic brawl. It is a field in which I have some experience."

"You mean to tell me there was trouble?"

"My wife told me once to live each day as if it was my last. It's called failure of communication. I haven't helped with the housework since; see what I mean? You British have always been better at buttering up the natives than we Americans. So, I ask a favor. Talk to your friends in their Foreign Office. Pat the right people on the back. Talk to Sali Berisha, their reformist; tell him a funny story about a stupid NATO officer who came across some guys crowding an important witness. Tell them how the NATO spy boasted of saving the girl; that he broke a few bones. Let it slip that this fool insisted that the criminals were Sigurimi."

Crane helped himself to some more bread with English jam and grinned at the young man.

"Then you can all laugh together about Americans, seeing as the Sigurimi has been disbanded. And when your sides stop aching, ask them to confirm, I mean officially, that the NATO spy was imagining things. For Christ's sake, these guys want to join NATO. They want to rent us an air base. Nip it in the bud, will you son, before they get the wrong idea."

"You broke a few bones?"

"Nothing serious."

"Where is the girl?"

"Gave me the slip; story of my life."

"Go home, Mr. Murray. I have booked you on the next flight to Zürich, the day after tomorrow."

"I'm not leaving without my agent, son. Get me that lead coffin and book us out of here."

"Mr. Murray. The British Empire was always efficiently run. You may recall that it was built by educated bureaucrats."

"True, the educated backbone of all Empires is built by bureaucracy and nepotism, hand in hand."

"The lead coffins for the two dead German's and the exhumed body of my Canadian friend, Charles Grenville will arrive from Zürich on Thursday at 15:10. I have arranged with the Italian aid workers to put up a military tent by the runway at Shqiperi. The coffins will be taken off the plane and to the tent where the bodies will be placed in them. While the coffins are disinfected and put back on board, I want you to wait in that tent under military guard, for your own protection.

As far as Her Majesty's Government has any say in the matter, you will be on that flight."

"This is why we love the British."

"Stay in the Embassy till then, Mr. Murray. Disbanded or not, the Sigurimi is a force to contend with."

"You got that right, most of their officers transferred to the SHIK, but why they now call it the National Informative Service is beyond me."

"The thing is, Mr. Murray, the Fokker 100 cannot cope with a fourth coffin. If the Sigurimi for some reason decide to kill you before that, I will be forced to charter a special transport plane for the bodies; think of the paperwork."

With his support crumbing back home, this investigation was coming apart anyway. Even here, there would be military music to face for American meddling. Crane assumed that with Asgard Park setting the tune, the young official's complaints were sure to find a sympathetic ear back in London.

"You are most kind, old son."

Book 4, Heimdallr

Chapter 1

BIRGER WALLENBERG WALKED DOWN the marble steps from the glass and brass offices of Verdandi, his mother's Italian investment company. It was another in a long row of companies that were his to deal with under the watchful eyes of the Midgard Group.

He appreciated the snappy style of their staff but suspected that Italian emphases on flair in secretaries did not bed for efficiency in a less literary meaning. Maybe his weeks of celibacy were weighing in. These educated girls outperformed their testosterone brethren in going after what they desired. Being fabulously rich made him no drawback; unvoiced invitations veiled with flushed smiles. They all but whispered of love to him; te Amos in the sustained looks and assertive moves. Te Amo in the fall of staccato vowels. Invite me to dinner. Have my well-oiled fanny for dessert. Make me a child. Buy me a palazzo in Tuscany, and invite my parents to live, the herds of my garrulous family to visit, roughly in that order. How could one help not to love them?

Walking down Via Mario Pagano in the center of Milan, he tried to enjoy the first week of a month-long vacation from Asgard Park. Officially he was in Italy to attend the 5th World Congress of Biological Psychiatry in Florence. It was a flimsy cover for a less flattering mission.

Karl Leamas had made him an offer he could not refuse, promising him full disclosure in lieu of a single errand to Albania. There was a girl, to be brought out of that country. Why she found importance in the eyes of Karl Leamas was the same old; a hint from Heimdallr.

His predecessor had the excuse of being verifiably insane. With no excuse, Wallenberg accepted to go to Trieste personally, to check if there was an envelope waiting for him in the shipping offices of the Adriatica Line. No need to implicate others in this folly.

Whatever else he might be, Leamas was a man of his word. Winning his trust might reveal the nuts and bolts of his secret sway over Asgard Park and the Midgard Group. To walk away, leaving the questions of his mother's association unexplained was not an option. Wallenberg flagged a cab to Stazione Centrale. They would have a train to Trieste. With any luck, he could make it back for the planned dinner with the CEO of Verdandi.

With lines snaking in front of the ticket counters, and clerks minding their own business; spur of the moment communications in Milan, in the summer of 1991, should be left to the hired help. On his own, he wanted to go via Venice, but the train was about to leave. He decided to pay the fare on board. The platform was crowded and the train already moving. Its first-class compartments were up front and out of reach. Running along the carriages, Birger Wallenberg tried two doors, before he found an opening in the human wall, sufficient to squeeze in. Pulling the door shut behind him, he was grateful for the audible click.

The first train ride in his youth had been with mother, a luxurious recreation of the Oriental Express. Descent into cramped third class, on a local Italian train in midsummer, was a rude awakening. He took in the impressions and found himself studying a Brueghel masterpiece.

Pushed up against him in the crammed coupling corridor, was a middle-aged pair with cardboard boxes bound up with strings and a scuffed suitcase from the fifties. The man was a graying, stocky farmer. The short brown fingers of his plump dark wife carried a heavy ring of gold with an ornate crown. It went superbly with her dark-rimmed nails. The pair was eating bread, with a lethal-looking kitchen knife, passing hunks, and throwing unwanted pieces on the floor.

Wallenberg drew back to avoid the knife, as the train shook itself free from the labyrinth of Stazione Centrale. The old couple eyed him, not unkindly. He saw that they understood perfectly that he was an imbecile, and that his rich parents had dressed him up, and set him on a train where he had been unable to find his first-class seat.

For no reason, Birger Wallenberg laughed. His mind was overloading him with impression. His outburst did not seem in the least surprising to his fellow travelers.

Pressed up against the exit door with one foot on a fold-up footstep, he peered out at plain villages and sunburned fields that passed in monotone review. His body started to protest the heat. The rattling train shook the sweat off him. Was his deal with Leamas worth it? Why had his mother never mentioned Baron Keltenbrunner as a friend of the family? The photos told him differently. They had an extensive business relationship. Knowing his mother, probably more personal than he liked to dwell on. Sooner or later, he would have to pay the man a visit.

As a learned man of sound mind, why was he accepting this bitter bait laid down by a mad Machiavelli? Why this odd happiness in acting outside the cloak of responsibility? His senses seemed sharper, drunk on the details of a pungent new world; kept from him by the comforts of wealth. No conductor checked for tickets. There was no way to move through the carriages.

This was the first free ride in his life.

He changed trains, and to first class in Venice, his clothes drenched in sweat. The air-conditioning didn't work. Nobody seemed to expect it to. In a window seat opposite him, sat an emissary of the Pope, a gray eminence in gray clothes, gray shirt, gray stockings, and dark blue woven shoes, his demeanor set to the studied air of the cloth, reading the history of the Medici's'. His gold rimmed spectacles were not really gold, and his mousy face, and inward pointing teeth not really human. Wallenberg found himself in a very peculiar frame of mind.

In Trieste, he had no difficulty in finding the office of the Adriatica Car Ferry Network, where a clerk handed him a small envelope, and made him sign for it. A white slip of stamped paper with his name on it was presumably his visa to Albania. He had no way of telling if it was for real, or if he was the target of a practical joke. Albania was off the grid. It took more than money to arrange their unobtainable visas, and forge passports. How did Leamas get away with it?

The black and white photo in the Albanian passport disturbed him. The face was that of a young woman, Shequere Avxhiu, with a visa to Switzerland. He stood a while and brooded. Nobody could know that he had talked to this girl in an empty soccer stadium in one of his spooky visions. A letter confirmed that the girl was due for urgent cancer treatment at a Midgard hospital in Geneva.

"How do I get to Albania from here?"

"You need a visa."

Wallenberg had considered flying in on a company plane, or an ambulance plane, but Albanians were touchy about foreigners. There would be red tape, and if the was one thing he wanted for this errand was keeping it low-key.

"I have a visa. How do I get there?"

"The ferry that leaves tomorrow, docks at the port city of Durres, one hour's drive from Tirana. We are arming the crews, you know. The thousands of refugees fleeing the country are hijacking any boat they can get their hands on."

"In Durres, do they have trains to Tirana, or taxis?"

"You can take your car, but I wouldn't."

"This is a car ferry?"

"The best there is!"

"Where can I rent a car around here?"

"To take to Albania?" The clerk shook his head smiling.

"What money do they use?"

"Anything but their own."

"Credit cards?"

"Forget it!"

"Book me on the next boat with a private car. I'll have it before departure."

Wallenberg had never sailed the Adriatic. The cruise liner would dock in Durres on its way to Greece. The trip would calm his nerves. Checking into one of Trieste's best hotels, he phoned his CEO in Milan to cancel dinner, and to arrange a car, then rested on his laurels. The good thing about having powerful friends in Italy, especially on your staff, was that things got done. The car was brought before nightfall by the Director in person. Instead of dinner they had long drinks at the bar and discussed longer term investment strategy. Wallenberg was pleasantly surprised, how highly this investment guru valued his layman's opinion.

Getting aboard the ferry was more trouble than he had expected, with endless delays, and checking of passports and registrations. He felt conspicuous driving a gleaming new Jaguar through a sea of broken-down Fiats the Italians had given up on. They were being exported as luxury items to Albania.

The boat trip took two days, with nothing on his hands but self-analyses. As far as he could ascertain, using the tools of his trade, he had no major behavioral problems. His inner angst was a natural reaction to his visions. They differed from dreams by being driven by repressed emotion and could cause neurotic symptoms. Dream analysis was never context predictive. So how did you approach visions that proved to be records of incidents as they happened?

With the coastline of Croatia hidden out of sight, Wallenberg sat alone in the shaded bar, for hours. The alcohol infused him with hilarity. On the deck outside, against the shimmering Adriatic, passengers shuffled by on a never-ending treadmill; a procession of cut-board cartoons against the blazing backdrop of the reflecting sea. What ghastly profiles passed in this parade, the double chins, the triple chins, the no chins, imbeciles and upturned noses. Only rarely the flickering traces of beauty, the one thing worth a young man's time. Barrel-chested women of forbidden shapes, and foreboding sizes, potbellied men with misshapen heads and stumbling gates; they all shuffled across his altar of beauty.

The jocular grew as his mind careened out of control. God, what have you passed upon your chosen creature? The ice cubes in his glass shook in spasms of merriment. Of all the nasty minds I have met, and in my profession, you sooner or later meet them all, you take the prize.

In your image, was it? Lord.

There was that other thing that troubled him. No matter how wretched the exteriors of people in this parade, the thoughts he encountered in every individual surprised him no end. They all had zones of thoughts that were infinitely pure and chiseled like Shakespearian sonnets. These thoughts never reached the surface and were hidden to the person who thought them.

They were virtuosos, like people who eke out time in an autocracy that gives no access to any expressions that are not uttered by the imbecilic tyrant. In human terms, that would be the brain.

Birger, the expert on the human brain, had started to realize that he had seriously underestimated the human mind. It had little to do with the simple executive system of the brain. It was the domain of huge numbers of individual cells, throughout the body. The logic was clear as day.

Book 4, Heimdallr

Chapter 2

WALLENBERG WAS DOWN ON car-deck in time for docking. The fleet of aging cars started to disembark, in a black outpouring of toxic fumes. They immediately hit a snag, as officials checked papers and cars shipside. The air in the cargo hold turned into a disgusting black smog. This prompted the drivers in newly bought old cars to keep their motors running with the headlights on. His fellow travelers seemed curiously partial to the smell of exhaust.

Wallenberg opened the window and choked. He was glad for the sealed interior of the Jaguar. After an hour, a handful of cars had rolled out. The rest kept spewing. Unable to run the air-conditioning, he abandoned the Jaguar, and made a run for the exit where he could breathe clean air. Now and then he braved the fog to move the car a space or two. After an endless wait of hours, many still had their motors running. These were proud people.

Passport control and customs showed his gleaming car great respect. The search was superficial, and his papers rapidly processed. A man with such a car had connections.

He could have spared himself the bother of a car. A couple of taxis waited outside the enclosure of Durres harbor, a few old and battered Mercedes Benzes in the pride of place. There were no service stations or maps to be had, so he hired a taxi to drive ahead of him to Tirana. The trip offered good clean air and several near misses. The pedestrians milling along the asphalt road with animals, refused to take slightest note of motorized traffic.

Within an hour, he had checked into the Hotel Dajti, the best in town, the taxi driver claimed. Grateful for his foresight in Trieste to fill his suitcase, he washed off the exhaust soot in the shower and changed. Refreshed, down in the lackluster lobby, he decided to get the task over with, and turned to the desk clerk.

"I am trying to locate a young woman. I have her address." He wrote the address from a memory he did not know he had and handed the slip to the clerk.

"I need a guide who knows the city. Can you arrange that for me?"

Another factotum joined them to take charge of a situation that commanded a tip. Speaking English with a high-toned pleasant voice, he wrote off the address in his notebook. This surprised Wallenberg who had never in his life paid much attention to hotel porters.

"We can provide an English-speaking guide who knows this part of town, in half an hour. Will that be all right Mr. Wallenberg?"

"Sure, you'll find me in the bar."

Two hours went by before a guide who spoke passable English turned up. The desk factotum received his tip without interest, but with an observation. "It would help if you gave us a name," he said. "We here at the Dajti have access to the city register. It would save you time. These are difficult times. Many families have moved."

"Her name is Shequere Avxhiu," he didn't offer up her passport, as he had no business holding it. "She is due for a cancer operation in Switzerland."

Wallenberg was a good judge of body language. Both men knew the name, jolted by instant recognition with aborted exchange of glances.

"Let me check the register Mr. Wallenberg," said the master of ceremonies. He was gone for a short moment but returned nonetheless with new information.

"The woman is no longer registered at this address."

"Do you have her new address?"

"We think she may have left the country."

"Right," Wallenberg turned to the interpreter. "Take me there; the neighbors must know." He was not about to argue the case, halfway out of the hotel entrance.

They drove along roads packed with pedestrians. His guide, trying hard to mask his awe of the royal blue Jaguar and creaking amber leather, kept staring at the telephone in its moorings between them. It occurred to Wallenberg that running this errand for Karl Leamas to gain information about Asgard Park, put him and that telephone on equal footing. He was out of his depth, out of contact, without a network. It was a disturbing thought.

The land was agricultural. He had expected bustling small-town markets and merchants touting farm produce, envisioning thickset, white-frocked women, courted by ruddy-faced men. Here he found the depressing sight of cartloads of onions being handed out in a corner of an empty lot; people appearing in droves, out of nowhere.

Nobody paid attention to traffic signs. When he stupidly stopped at a red light, a truck rumbled past him, and blasted its horn.

They had traveled a small distance when the guide gave a sign to pull over. They stepped into the sun outside a dilapidated two-story house with a boarded up downstairs shop. Like the rest of the city, it was a sullen place. On the other side of the Adriatic, there would be flower baskets on the houses to refresh the arid heat. The guide led him to the door of what seemed to be a closed photo studio. The young woman who came to the door was no match for either his vision or the passport in his pocket. The alarmed girl disappeared.

"What did you say to her?"

"I tell her get husband!"

"She's sure to know more about the girl."

"Better ask man in the house."

"Bloody hell, I will do the talking. You are my interpreter, nothing more." He felt better having alienated the guide, the sly bastard wriggled like a cut snake.

The husband, a young swarthy man with a shifty eye, knew nothing about the girl. Wallenberg had them check with the family upstairs. It turned out to be the same family. The grumpy white-haired gentleman from upstairs was less alarmed than his stepson downstairs. After taking the guide aside to sound him out, the older man told Wallenberg in broken English that he knew nothing of the young woman who had squatted there. She was a tramp and a whore. He was the Tirana soccer coach. His family had received the apartment downstairs legally.

"She must have told somebody where she was going."

In Albania there was no such thing as asking a simple question, certainly not for a foreigner in a suit with a beautiful car in the street. There were invitations into a run-down apartment, setting him down in a seat of honor, waiting for thick black coffee and mismatched glasses filled with suspect spirits that did not agree with his stomach. When they finally accepted questions, nobody knew what became of the Avxhiu girl, much like his mind had claimed from the start.

Wallenberg was a methodical stubborn sort, working the surrounding houses systematically, growing sluggish in the slow-moving time. Knocking at doors with a sly shadow at his side, accepting coffee and more drinks, trying to take a few sips and leave as much as was polite. Flutters of nausea came and went, his stomach acting up. Asking for a toilet caused commotion. He got the feeling that it was not a proper request to spring on people. There was a scramble to prepare the toilet. Once there, he got wretchedly sick with the awful smell. When he was done, there was no water and no way to clean a mess.

The people were curious about him, warm and friendly but a deeply rooted suspicion turned their performance into unintentional rudeness. They regaled him with their stories of hardships and dreams. He sifted through it for scraps about the girl he sought. Putting his back into it, he was obliged to look at family treasures; a simple outdated color calendar from west, a priceless icon where olive oil patina blackened with age hid gold leaf inlays. There were ancient coins, crosses of silver; exquisite workmanship; dear enough to hide at the risk of state reprisals. While their acumen for peddling was impressive, and their need for currency dire, they had no sense of value. In his alternating fog of nausea and loose stomach, he got no closer to his quarry.

His cup runneth over. A thickset middle-aged man who claimed to know the Avxhiu girl, put him through a charade with his dying mother in the room. The man had covered the old woman's body and head with a blanket and rolled her barely breathing smelling body off her resting place to pull from under it a few small woodcarvings of no talent. He offered these works of his youth at a fair price, a thousand dollars, testing the waters, a few hundred dollars?

The Avxhiu woman? No, he had no idea where she had disappeared to, but could he possibly put him in contact with an American art gallery? The airless smell in all those apartments, the evil coffee and homebrewed liquor, proved too much. His palm came to his mouth to prevent him from dispensing vomit over the woodcarvings. His mouth filled up. He rushed to the door, leaving a dumbfounded artist and his dying mother.

After a while out in the rubble, supported by a crumbling wall, Wallenberg gained a degree of balance. Washing his hands with sand, he told his infinitely patient guide to take him to the car. They would be returning to the hotel.

The fresh air did him good, but the new Jaguar was a sight to see; its side mirrors pried off, electric wires hanging out, wipers and antennas snapped, the royal blue paintwork scratched with a nail. The car had not been entered. Nothing was taken but the mirrors. This piece of luxury had just proved too great a thorn in somebody's eye. The guide made a nonchalant gesture; it was to be expected.

Half-drunk on bad liquor, Wallenberg drove back to the Dajti, less careful of the strollers on the streets. They sensed his aggression.

He killed nobody on the way back.

Book 4, Heimdallr

Chapter 3

AVXHIU HAD LOST COUNT of the days. Keeping track of time was never easy with the irregular movements of her watch, another wedding gift. Spiro's bringing guts, the State-run distribution of bread, rumors of vegetables in the square. These were measures of time. The anarchic moments of hit-and-run electricity, and water, made any other use of time meaningless. She longed for the happy hours of morning breadlines.

After a few days out in the hills, having run from the NATO spy in the soccer stadium, she hid in the Kid's room. The Kid had a special standing with the Sigurimi. She was one of theirs; everybody knew. She had renounced Avxhiu to the Sigurimi. It had not prevented them from searching her room earlier. This was not a safe solution. They could come back anytime.

The Quarter Council's committee secretary, who had arranged the airless laundry room in exchange for an open account of the Kid's naughty favors, had found a new fancy; for now. The Kid was her umbilical cord. The days passed with insurmountable slowness. Avxhiu hung on every word Rakipe brought home. It was mostly bad news. The family above her studio had taken possession, claiming that it was abandoned. Losing her home was the drop.

The soccer coach on the second floor had a dirty mind and fast fingers. He had connections to bribe his way. He brought foreign goods to the right people when the soccer team was sent abroad. The Quarter Council had confirmed his rightful occupation of her studio for his stepson, and his stupid daughter.

She was grateful to Rakipe for her foresight in picking up Avxhiu's motorcycle from her cousin Fatos, while she was questioned in jail. With help from the guards, who thought it was hers, the Kid parked it inside the gates of the Embassy Street compound. Avxhiu dared not ask how Rakipe repaid the favor. The Kid passed the compound on her way home from the Dajti, every night.

The heat was suffocating in close confinement; they were all looking for her: the police, the Sigurimi and the Camorra. She could not trust anyone but the Kid, and Avxhiu had begun to wonder, how long that could last. She hated the thought, but nobody had heard from Spiro. What hurt the most was that the promise that Helmut Mayer made to his wife had come to nothing.

The tiled laundry room allowed little movement. She kept quiet, so as not to alarm others in the house. They assumed the room to be empty when the Kid was out, so it was impossible to step across the cramped gangway to the joint toilet. Avxhiu kept a covered pot in the room, for her needs, and the Kid emptied it. She could not wash properly or clean herself from the bucket of water the Kid brought in every day, except oftentimes there was no water. Then the bucket water got filthy, and it stank, and she could not wash away the sweat.

One day the Kid came with news that had an ominous twist.

"They found his body, the foreigner you killed, you know, the old guy, Charles Grenville, where Spiro buried him."

"Don't say killed. It was an accident."

"They sent the body away on an airplane. If you ask me, this is so stupid." The Kid shook her head. "Why buy a seat on an airplane for a dead man? Who wants a seat next to a body that has been dug out of the ground? I mean, in an airplane to the West?"

"Did they say how he died?"

"No, they are blaming the murder on Spiro, and you. Spiro's contact in the Sigurimi ratted, the one who got the computer. Do you know what this means?"

"They already want me for the birrari murders."

"Oh, this is worse, Shequere. He was a foreigner. They ask the police in other countries to look for you, the Interpoli! You can never get visa or a passport because the Interpoli is looking for you in every country in the world, and they must send you back if they find you."

After this speech they were both quiet, until the Kid broke the silence.

"I had to renounce Spiro as a friend. Some people say he escaped to Greece. They have asked the Interpoli to find him too."

Avxhiu despaired. These people had long memories. They did not want her tongue-worn testimony. She heaved a listless sigh. It was another turn of the screw.

A few days later, the Kid brought her a book in English, from the Dajti Hotel. A foreigner who had come to Albania to teach people about God had given it to her after a deeply depraved act. Rakipe had accepted the book in lieu of extra payment. She knew that Avxhiu was stuck with nothing to do. The man had told her that it was the most famous book in the world.

Avxhiu found the Bible remarkable, so unlike the other novels she had read from the west. She had heard of it from her mother but reading it made her doubt tall tales from the West. All the scenes reminded her of Albania.

Often, she would find herself minutely exploring the seams of her short fling with Helmut Mayer. She would close her eyes, and recall his words, and his body, the emotions he evoked, his indulgent generosity. Feeding her obsession with this man and reading the Bible, kept her from falling apart. Mayer could not have told anyone about his promise to her, except his driver. And now the driver was dead.

She worried mostly for the Kid, having told the NATO spy about Rakipe. They said he was a NATO spy. The careless words in the soccer stadium hunted her. The Kid was her ears at the Sigurimi. How could he be one of them. The spy broke the arm of the Sigurimi Commandant. Had she made a mistake? Avxhiu suffered another bout of confusion. Why did he say that Mayer murdered the woman who scratched him? Mayer would not do that.

Early she had learned to accept first impressions, to trust her instincts. First impressions told you who was an informer and who was not. Strangely enough, although the foreigner was no friend of Mayer's, her impression had been to trust him. Now there was nothing to be done but wait for the Sigurimi to find her.

Book 4, Heimdallr

Chapter 4

TWICE IN ONE AFTERNOON, there had been heavy footsteps out on the landing, followed by an official-sounding knock on the door. Avxhiu took refuge in her shelter, with a pounding heart. Her hiding place did not stand up to a search. Twice the visitor went away. When the Kid finally returned in the afternoon, Avxhiu was beside herself.

"They've been looking for you, knocking on the door."

"Who?"

"How should I know?"

At that moment they both heard steps on the stairs. Someone had been watching the house and seen Rakipe enter. They both knew what to do. Silently and quickly, Avxhiu crept into the old wooden cabinet for laundry that came with the room. They had prepared a space for her by removing the lowest shelve. The hideout was curtained off with a thin piece of gauze. It took her seconds to get in, and she was already in place when the determined knock sounded again. The smell in there was not fresh. This was where they kept her covered pot.

Avxhiu recognized the deep official voice. For days, it had harassed her with questions about her German lover. It was the Chief of Police in Tirana, a frequent guest at the Dajti, and well aware of the Kid's profession, she brooded feverishly. Had someone reported the hotel food the Kid stole to sneak to her. They all did that, but the Kid had no family. It could arouse suspicion.

The man stood squarely in the small doorway, his bulk filling the frame. He greeted the Kid as a friend and came to the point.

"I have come about the motorcycle you parked, within the diplomatic compound. This is illegal, Rakipe. There is no registration plate. Is it yours, or is it stolen from the State?"

Avxhiu heard the Kid laugh, and could see her grab him by the arm, and give him an inviting tug. Of course, she thought, if he had law enforcement on his mind, the Chief would have sent his minions. Then he could give an underling the blame if a culprit had official backing.

"Chief, we both have friends. The Sigurimi is aware. Why rock the boat?"

Avxhiu saw him sit down heavily on the bed that creaked under his weight.

"Nonetheless it is illegal. I'm not taking steps. This is a friendly warning, and there are better ways of looking after your motorcycle. I might be able to help."

Something made the Chief chuckle in a guttural whisper.

"There is always a way, kid."

"Tell me, handsome, how you can help."

There was the sound of a belt buckle, and the chief of the Tirana police started to speak in a voice that was not his firm Chief of Police voice.

"Put it in the police garage. My men can keep eyeeee, and watch ooovrr..."

It dawned on Avxhiu what was going on, and she couldn't believe it. How could the Kid do this to her?

"The compound guards won't be happy," said the Kid.

"Fuck the guards."

"I do. There are six of them, and only one of you."

"That's right, come here, kid."

In fear mingled with disgust, Avxhiu listened to him satisfy his lusts, and her pretending to. The whole house was privy to the debauchery. The sounds were so close; it felt that she was in the bed with them.

The Chief was a married man. Avxhiu felt vain anger over his misuse of office. There was nothing she could do to stop it. The Kid had told her that all the officials wanted girls who fucked foreigners. It was a status thing.

The Chief was roaring like an angry bull. The creaky bed screamed its objections. The Kid talked him through the onslaught, and when the ruckus died down, Avxhiu heard a small voice escape.

"This is like having Skanderbeg himself in bed."

The deep rumble from the Chief of Police seconded her opinion. It nearly caused Avxhiu to burst out laughing in her shelter. They all learned of Skanderbeg in school, the Dragon of Albania, the hero who defeated the armies of the Ottoman Empire.

"All right, we do this my way, kid."

The Chief was on his feet now, putting his clothes back in order. He bent to pick up his big solemn cap. It had rolled to the floor outside the thin gauze that had separated Avxhiu from his immoral act. She could see him clear as day, but he was not in an attentive mood.

"Bring the motorcycle to the main station. Keep it there, as long as you like. I'll throw in some petrol for you, now and then."

He did not mention that further favors were due. They both knew that. On a gruffer note, the Chief of Police left with a few official words out in the passage, as if the whole house did not already know the nature of his visit.

After a while Avxhiu climbed out of her hiding place to stretch her aching joints. She watched in silence as the Kid nonchalantly washed her private parts, with a towel and water from her bucket; it took a while for Avxhiu to get her voice back.

"How could you let him?"

"Let him? Oh, Zote, you are so stupid. I used him, Shequere, not the other way around."

"You believe that?"

"You think I like this shit. You think it is easier to service six young guards, on rotating shifts, than an old sock like him, and you never know who is on duty. This was a godsend, Avxhiu. It is your motorcycle; would you rather do this yourself?" Her voice grew bitter. "I didn't hear you protest, while he was at it. You were mute as a mouse's ass in a storm."

"I couldn't get a word in edgewise."

They both laughed, and Avxhiu found it best to draw back. It was a difficult lesson to stomach.

The days passed, and Avxhiu turned to the Bible for solace, the novel the Kid brought her. It eased the hunger that gnawed at her every day.

'I am Alpha and Omega, the beginning and the end, the first and the last.'

Food lost its luster with the solitary contemplation of life. She felt an odd upheaval of emotions, reading about this man Jesus Christ. The NATO spy had said his name when she told him about Mayer. Vaguely she recalled her mother talking about this man. When the government screwed up his life, he had not flinched. Constant hunger in combination with the tension, made her miss her period, and caused her to nag at the Kid, but she just cut her short.

"Where would you be if I did not help you? You are such a hypocrite. If I could take customers home, I could keep more of the money. At the Dajti, the Sigurimi keeps almost all of it."

They knew that this was impossible. The truth frightened her. Every night when the Kid left for the Hotel Dajti, they embraced long and sincerely.

Then, one evening the Kid came home in the early evening. She had been crying. Avxhiu hadn't seen her cry since she was a child, and it broke her heart.

"What is it?" she whispered and put her arms around the narrow shoulders.

The girl was trembling. Avxhiu brushed her loving palms over her streaky child's face. Had a man mistreated her? One look into her eyes, and it was infinitely worse. In panic she hesitated to speak the name, out of fear it might come true.

"Spiro?"

And up came the answer through the racking shoulders. Avxhiu fought to be the strong one, but this was too big. She could not fathom it; no lodestone cast into her well of sorrow would find a bottom. It was like dying. Her own fear lost all meaning. It took a while to summon up the will to ask.

"What happened?"

"The Sigurimi shot him two days ago. He was living in the Gradishka prison camp for political prisoners. Many of the prisoners still live there after the amnesty, and they never cooperate with the police. Spiro was hiding with friends. There was an informer."

"Spiro is dead?"

Grief doesn't allow rational thought. Her protecting sky was a flaking laundry roof. Silently they embraced in a spiritual union, reaffirming commitment. It brought Avxhiu the sense how one-sided this had become. After a while she rose, and pushed the Kid away, to look at her.

"You must not show your tears to them, Rakipe, you must be strong."

"I laughed when they told me!" The Kid had amazement in her voice. "I laughed when they came and told me, that the traitor Spiro Shituni was dead, shot like a dog. I never thought I could be so hard."

"It is good to be resilient, Rakipe. There's no shame in that."

That night Avxhiu stole out of the house into the cool darkness of a summer night. She walked for hours without aim or purpose through dangerous quarters of a silent city. The veil covered her face, and nobody approached. It was as if people knew that this flighty creature moved under a phantom spell of bad luck. When she returned, the Kid had gone to the Dajti to reaffirm her commitment to the table of plenty.

The next morning Avxhiu woke to merciless light that held no promise. There was no escaping the death of her brother. Any morning could be her last. She would flee, she decided, but in the end, she stayed put. The hunger made her submissive. She didn't have the drive. She waited for news of Spiro's funeral, twice bereaved, unable to attend.

Later, the Kid told her that nobody came except diggers and the Sigurimi. The State would demand the cost of his casket, no matter if they buried him without one, naked in the ground, and urinated into the grave. A member of Spiro's clan took over his room and stole his stuff. Spiro Shituni left his family nothing.

Endlessly, she and Rakipe planned their escape to Macedonia, or Greece. The motorcycle's tank was full. The Kid got police mechanics to check the tires, bringing home extra petrol to prepare for the long trip, a little at a time in a milk bottle. Avxhiu recalled the face of the Sigurimi Commandant when the NATO spy broke his arm. It infused her with a transitory flash of pride.

There was no escaping the long arm of the Sigurimi.

Book 4, Heimdallr

Chapter 5

IT WAS EVENING WHEN Wallenberg woke, smelling of puke, having collapsed onto a bed in his clothes. After a shower and a shave, he went downstairs to eat. Dinner lacked appeal but eating calmed the queasy sensation.

He made a call to New York on an antiquated phone in the lobby, and got through to Dr George Kennan, his Chief of Psychiatry at Asgard Park. The line was so bad he had to shout into the black Bakelite handle.

"George, you won't believe it but I'm in Albania."

His Chief of Psychiatry expressed no surprise. You could tell that the man had practice in dealing with the insane.

"I'm running an errand for Dr Karl Leamas, in exchange for information, George. I cannot begin to explain this, but I need to talk to Dr Leamas. Can you arrange that for me while I wait on the phone, however long it takes?"

It took exactly eight seconds on his Rolex for Leamas to come on. Wallenberg noted this because he was timing the call; the hotel had no other way of keeping track of the charges.

"How are you, Birger? I cannot tell you how pleased I am. Glad to have you aboard. I'm thrilled you accepted my offer! Have you found our young ward?"

"Leamas, you have landed me in a lot of bother. The girl is nowhere to be found, and I have a feeling that nobody wants me to find her. Is there something you are not telling me? Because if there is anything illegal you are asking me to do, or remotely dangerous, I'm taking the next flight out of here."

"I think you better find the girl. As the new vessel of Heimdallr, you must stay the course or perish in the attempt. The god has left me. I seem to be cured, as you would say. My visions are gone."

"Bully for you," Wallenberg mumbled inaudibly. "I am not letting anybody take over my mind."

"Look, Birger, my promise to you stands, total access to our organization. The god chose you for a reason. Stop resisting him. Do you feel any change?"

"What do you mean?"

"Have your perceptions changed in any way, are you better at reading people? This is a building process in your brain. They are setting up a system to serve the god. Heimdallr will enter your mind first when that time comes, not before. Please understand that the god will not enter you uninvited. You must invite him. You will…"

In mid-sentence, Wallenberg hung up the old Bakelite phone in fit of desperation. It had taken his Chief of Psychiatry eight seconds to get his most isolated patient on the phone. He needed no further proof that his right-hand man was also deeply involved in Karl's schemes. Dejectedly he told the phone operator the elapsed time and waited for a slip to take to the front desk, where the factotum took him aside to ask about his fruitless search.

"May I say, Dr. Wallenberg that I think it was a bad idea to go looking for this woman?"

"Why is that?"

"I don't want my guests to get hurt. This girl is bad news, and please don't say I told you so."

The situation was preposterous. Was his predecessor stringing him along? If he was a true believer, why do that? He needed a cold beer to marshal his defenses. In the bar, he struck up a conversation with an Australian cameraman whose TV team had run into bureaucratic difficulties.

"This is one crappy place, Birger. I've been doing the Aztec two-step for days. My shots are all jumpy."

As he talked, Wallenberg noticed a kid watching him from across the room. Few foreign women stayed at the hotel, but there were others, younger and prettier, who kept a low accessible profile. He had frequently met prostitutes and felt them up, but always in an emergency ward, practicing his profession.

"What is the Aztec two-step?"

"Diarrhea, mate, the food here doesn't agree with capitalistic intestines." The Aussie eyed the kid, who sidled up on Wallenberg's far side, then muttered under his breath. "I had that one, mate. She's good, but if you are interested, you better wear a diving suit. This is public property."

"Hi, hansom!"

"Hi there, I'd buy you a drink if you were old enough to be served."

They did not seem that particular because, without prompting, the waiter brought her a welcome drink. They both waited for him to draw back. He took his time.

"You want meet Shequere Avxhiu?"

"I'm looking for a young woman by that name, why? Do you know her? Does she work here?"

"No, and you are rich, I see your car, Avxhiu has no cancer."

Wallenberg somehow understood that the desk pimp had gathered the girls in the Sigurimi room and told them about a hospital in Switzerland. Although it did not show, he could feel that the child was on edge. Steps had been taken. They had told her not to crowd him; to tell him nothing, to get him talking, preferably in his room so that the Sigurimi could listen in.

"Do you know Avxhiu?"

"Avxhiu traitor, come walk," the Kid proclaimed without hiding her voice. She beckoned him to a lover's stroll through the uninspiring lobby. In the corner, she spoke quickly, her words barely audible.

"Avxhiu friend but no tell."

"Sure," he lowered his voice, "I want to meet her."

"Why meet her?"

"Can you keep a secret?"

"Yes."

She was sweet. Without her makeup put on with a bricklayer's trowel, this kid could drive a young man crazy. He looked around as he whispered in her ear, trying to take a lover's suggestion.

"I want to take Avxhiu out of here. Her cancer treatment is a cover."

He saw that the word caused her trouble, "a lie!" he added. And she burst out laughing, as if he had made an outrageous if not wholly unwanted proposal. He was unsure how much she understood.

"Where take Avxhiu?"

"Swissair has an office in a hotel room here, the first of its kind. "I will buy her a Swissair ticket to wherever she wants." As the Kid led him into a dark corner, pretending intimacy, he knew it was out of range from the hidden microphones.

"Avxhiu no passport, no visa."

He showed her the passport, briefly, and put it away. She looked at the picture and up at him, and he felt a truly massive shock of revelation flow through her mind.

"You know German?" she whispered.

"Yes, do you?" He knew it was unusual for people here to speak German here. Mostly it was Italian or French.

"No!"

The answer puzzled him, but she seemed pleased, and he dropped it.

"Can you take me to Avxhiu?"

"Maybe!"

"What will it take to make up your mind?" He expected it to be money and he was prepared to pay a lot. Wouldn't that be something; beating Leamas at his game.

"I go now," said the kid, "maybe later, yes?"

"Thank you. What is your name?"

"Rakipe Hallidri!"

"See you later then, Rakipe."

After the kid slipped away, he went back to the bar and ordered another beer. His stomach was not up to hard liquor. He needed to calm his nerves. The idea proffered by Dr Leamas of the ongoing cancerous restructuring within his brain, was too unpleasant to dwell on.

Chapter 6

"HALLO, HANDSOME." A DIFFERENT young woman; the same mating call.

Birger Wallenberg found the phrase amusing; the animal warmth of delivery was not. Had it been culled from a Sigurimi handbook under the section on how to woo foreign spies, picked up by their chief while visiting the Reeperbahn red light district in Hamburg?

The girl was small and a few years older than the kid, dark and winsome. He had a feeling she had been selected for this approach. The question was by whom. She spoke almost without an accent.

"You bored, big fella?"

"Never, too many interesting people about."

"Want some company?"

"No, thank you, miss, but allow me to buy you a drink."

"I hear you are looking for my friend Avxhiu."

"Your friend, is she? I heard she was bad news. And what is your name?"

"Vera Capani. Yes, we are good girlfriends." This dark vixen was not hiding her voice. She had a scar down the side of her left chin that went white when she smiled.

"You wouldn't know where your friend is hiding?"

"Avxhiu's not hiding. She is staying with her mother in Tirana."

"Great news, if you give me the address, I'll make it worth your while."

"Why do you want to meet Avxhiu? Are you friends?" She smiled impishly, "lovers maybe?"

"I never met the young woman. She is scheduled for a cancer operation in Geneva. Can we call her from here?"

The girl laughed loud and naturally. He was unaware he had told a joke.

"Don't be silly. Her mother has no telephone."

"I see."

"But I can take you to her. I know the way. We can drive there in your new Jaguar."

"You mean like now?"

"If you like, or we can go up to your room first, I'll be very good for you."

"Let's go find her right now."

Outside, under the lights of the hotel entrance, Vera Capani studied her reflection off the Jaguars glistening patina. It had a chic look. She did not comment on the deep cuts in the paintwork. Wallenberg had noticed a similar mark across her chin. She sank into the soft leather, in clumsy elation. Easing the car onto the empty boulevard, he slid in a disc, and she smiled as the music vibrated through the car.

"Do you want to make love in the car, sir?" It was asked easily, an off the cuff remark; might have been about the weather.

"No thanks, I've outgrown cars."

The young woman was a stunner, the most attractive he had seen at the Dajti.

"It will cost nothing. I give great pleasure."

And while she was at it, he assumed, she would dispense the litany of infections that plagued her profession. He caught a sudden whiff of her mind. It was strange. In the luxury of this splendid car, she was part of a charming world, not her sordid one. She wanted a secret memory of making love on this luxurious leather among hardwood panels. He would not be part of that memory, and his precarious psyche was causing him to imagine other people's minds.

"Later perhaps," he said to tidy her over. The girl reacted like a soldier, too disciplined on rejection, with no show of a sullen side.

"Okay, later!" A silence fell between them. They both knew there would be no later.

"Where to, sweetheart?"

The roads went from potholed to worse. He was getting goosed by a pro. It was the rush hour back at the Dajti. The Sigurimi run a tight ship. The pimp at the front desk had given her the go-ahead. They had been crawling along in the treacherous maze of the city outskirts when Vera Capani signaled him to stop in front of a small run-down stone house.

"Avxhiu lives here with her mother and her brothers. I go in and tell them about your visit. This is the custom. They want to prepare the room for a guest, a foreigner."

"Believe me, I know!"

He sat in the car and listened to opera. He turned it off and listened to silence. The darkness did wonders for the neighborhood. What was he doing here, running a dangerous errand for a psychopath? The warnings from his mind fell around him, like snowflakes in hell, and vanished unheeded. Was this a sane way for one of the world's wealthiest men to conduct his life? He pushed a button, and the window came down, then up again. The air reeked of piss. For some reason, Wallenberg was seized by a fit of hilarity. Fighting his own mind, was too absurd.

Vera Capani was back, knocking on his window.

"You can come in now!"

He got out of the car and locked it, dismissing the acrid stench.

"Is Avxhiu at home?"

"No, they are sending for her."

"Will that take long? I am out of time."

"Not long."

There was an ugly character standing in the doorway. He was friendly enough, offering a hand in greeting, presenting himself as the brother. Wallenberg entered a small room to shake hands with another man, also claiming brotherhood. That there was no mother was a minor snag. They served him compulsory black Turkish coffee that no Turk would admit to. It had a bitter taste he could not place. Due to the absence of electricity, an oil lamp had been put into service. Vera Capani sat demurely in the corner, used to the squalor. She had done her part.

His mind had told him that the Kid who approached him at the Dajti was for real. He had ignored that. How could he trust a mind that offered sensations and insights beyond the realm of reason?

The raki tasted bitter too. The two men insisted on the traditional welcome. He knew better than to toss it down and wet his lips instead. They didn't speak English. The pretty one translated when she cared to.

"What do you want with our sister?"

"Avxhiu has cancer. A friend asked me assist her to Switzerland."

"What friend?"

"A doctor in New York."

"But you are Swedish."

Wallenberg shook his head. They were not playing this well. They had no way of knowing that. They had spiked the coffee and the raki. They were waiting for him to pass out. If he had his senses intact, he should be savoring his scholarly life at Asgard Park, with the world of science at his fingertips.

"Our sister has friends in Germany."

"Sure, I have friends in Germany. It does not preclude me from having American friends."

The two men exchanged knowing nods.

"Avxhiu had German criminal friends."

The Kid had asked if he knew German. She was talking about a German man. He took comfort that his reading of minds was awfully lacking, but it was a chilling delusion.

There was movement by the bedroom door. A young woman entered on a secret cue, a scowl on her dark face, shy of the foreigner. As he stood to greet her; the men didn't bother. He felt wretched, grateful he had drunk little of that ghastly stuff. His stomach was aching up after the bad spell this morning.

"This is our sister, Avxhiu."

Wallenberg extended a shaky hand and drew her into the bad light from the oil lamp. It was not the same girl, no likeness. This was a primitive creature, full of fear. He was probably having a nervous breakdown. All his thoughts centered on bitter drinks and cups of bituminous coffee. The girl withdrew, having played her part unsuccessfully without conviction.

"Don't you know that Avxhiu is a wanted person?" The ugly character asked in a friendly tone.

"Dead or alive," his companion added.

"No, I didn't. What crime is she wanted for?"

"She murdered a Canadian businessman and stole his money," said Vera Capani without prompting. "The police are looking for her all over Albania. The Sigurimi in combing every town and village. Avxhiu works for the German Mafia. Her German friend killed twelve Camorra bosses with a hammer in a birrari. Her brother Spiro Shituni planned it. We in the Camorra are also looking. Why are you looking?

"Are you sure we are talking about the same girl?"

"Same girl!"

In one of his visions, he had interviewed the girl in a soccer stadium. He got her story firsthand, but he knew that the Avxhiu girl was an innocent bystander. This was no longer a practical joke. Why would Leamas want him involved with this treacherous lot? This girl was the stalking horse of three armies of half-wits. He raised his glass and lost his wind as the pain shot through his midsection.

He tried to stand, but he was going nowhere. There was no strength left to draw on. He grabbed his abdomen. The room was swimming. They were looking at him, curiously detached, waiting.

"Get me to a hospital. I am sick."

Nobody moved. His mind had been right about that too. They were waiting for him to pass out. He had flunked the test. He was dying in a filthy robber's lair. They relieved him of his Rolex, and he felt hands go through his pockets: wallet, keys, passports. The pain throbbed in his veins. Hanging on, he refused to pass out. A case of defensive living ensued, worse than any. He closed his eyes to swim in his private pool of pain.

There came to him the sense of being bundled into the trunk of a car.

He lost track of time as the car careened through the night on crooked roads; coming to briefly when the potholes rocked him. Once he came to because the car had stopped. He heard Vera Capani being humped on the leather luxury of the back seat. They were in his Jaguar. The young woman was having a memory implant a few inches beyond the event horizon of the black hole that engulfed him.

Wallenberg slipped into oblivion.

Book 4, Heimdallr

Chapter 7

FROM THE SLANT OF the sun, it was midday when Wallenberg woke. It was not pleasant, but he had gone through too many visions to care. The pain ate at his gut and parched his mouth. For a while he lay grasping after a hold. His bed was a mound of straws thrown on a floor of earth or manure or both. His clothes were gone. So too were his shoes, his watch, papers, and money; all that went with his stratum of society.

When his feet carried him, the curvature of the roof allowed him to stand straight in the center of the round floor. He had seen these bunkers in the hills, upturned concrete caldrons dotting the landscape, the fossilized swamps of a dictatorial hallucination. Every patch of communal earth would be defended; every beach and field watched from a bunker, which, as it turned out were perfect targets from the air.

Streams of sun came from the long narrow firing-slit in the concrete wall. It cut the semi-darkness on the earthen floor and danced with dust and the gnats that had fed off him during the night. The itch had set in. He could not localize his aches as he stumbled towards the slit. The opening was blocked by an iron screen that did not budge when he reached out to shake it. The corroded threads flaked against his palm.

In the darkness he tripped over a pair of old boots thrown on the floor: army issue, hard and unyielding, with worn down heels. The shoestrings had been removed, ostensibly to prevent suicides. Wallenberg suspected that desperate needs brought even bartering for shoelaces. The oversize boots chafed intolerably. He was torn between torture and the disgusting surprises the soiled floor held for bare feet.

He had a room with a view. His eyes adjusted to the glare of the vista spread across the ridge before him. Below lay a sprawling valley of black abandoned buildings and gutted factories. Acres and acres of calm thrust their abandoned smokestacks to the sky; silent reminders of a country that had forgot how to breathe.

He had almost forgotten to breathe last night. If it was last night. What poison had they fed him? They were no pharmacists. If not for his abstinence and paranoia, he would be dead. Were they holding him for ransom? He was unknown in this part of the world.

Judging from the perspective, the bunker that held him was halfway up the mountain. The hills below were scruffy and barren and gnawed by the wind. There was no hurry in these hills. A woman was picking stones out of a field far below. The distances were great, empty, and cheerless as the people who lived here; without imagination, much like the mountains.

His jailer had been in the shadows but walked into view at the ridge to look at women scouring the hills for brushwood. They hobbled far below, beetle-like, with bundles on their backs, chatting as they threaded their way down the slopes, back to the misery of daily life.

"You! What the hell is the meaning of this?"

Wallenberg shouted angrily at his keeper, a man in a black jacket with an oily shine around fraying cuffs. The man stepped from the ridge up to the firing slot with a half-smile that reveal that all his teeth were to the right. Unwonted longevity had kneaded his flesh none too nimbly. Without a language, the prisoner was of no interest to his keeper, except as a paying job. Responding to body language, the man pushed a rusty bowl of water through the hole in the sturdy wire mesh that blocked the firing slit. A loaf of bread and a piece of sausage followed onto a broad windowsill.

The water tasted brackish but worked wonders. The chunk of sausage had been literally sawn off like a limb and air-dried beyond rigor mortis, tough as wood. As he gnawed on it doggedly, it surrendered but microns of its girth. The taste echoed white truffle salami from across the Adriatic. Or maybe it was the hunger.

Would anyone miss a bachelor roaming the world on his vacation? The odds were not favorable. He had no family. His companies were independent. The Jaguar would be on its way to Greece with a steep price on its head, and his Italian CEO would have replaced it with a snappier company car.

That night he rested on straws, plagued by bugs, his mind in turmoil. He had had started to waver on Heimdallr, and he resented the weakness. His mind told him that embracing the god would allow him to control his jailers. If insanity was his only option for survival, it was a steep a price.

His life would most likely end in these mountains, without anybody being the wiser.

Book 4, Heimdallr

Chapter 8

AVXHIU WAS IN UPROAR. There was no way she could sit still and wait for Rakipe to return. Anything was better than this suspense. She moved along the tiled walls. Her palm traced their coolness and familiar cracks.

Wallenbergi was in Tirana. He had come to get her. He had shown Rakipe her passport. She had no passport. But this one had her name and picture in it. She sprawled on the floor, swung her legs in the air. Solitary confinement made her behave in funny ways.

"Wallenbergi," that was what Mayer had told her as he died. Could he get her abroad with the foreign police looking for her? Could he bribe them? A new idea hit and curdled her thoughts. She made a bundle of herself on the disheveled bed. Could he be a conman like the NATO spy? She was out of bed, tracing her fingers on the ceiling, making transcendent patterns, feeling fragile. Would they go to that length to get her?

She was crawling on all fours when she heard the Kid on the stairs. Repeated stomps on the first rung spared her the purgatory of her hiding place. She could not wait for her to open the door. Desperately impatient, she pulled Rakipe into the room. "What did he say?" The harsh whisper came out too high, and she toned it down, "where will we meet?"

The Kid gave a dejected shrug and threw the white shawl on the bed. The headscarf was a clever ruse they had devised. Rakipe wore it when she left the house. It was a common sight. Many women in the neighborhood wore them. Rakipe hated it, but people had stopped noticing. This had allowed Avxhiu to slip out of the house at night wearing the Kid's clothes with a headscarf to hide her face. These rare trips kept her sane.

"Forget the foreigner, Shequere. He is no German. This man is Swedish. I thought he was smart."

"God, what do you mean?"

"They picked him up. The Sigurimi ordered it. They are keeping him for questioning. They used Vera Capani to trap him. She is their favorite. He was so stupid. Vera said you were her friend and he fell for it, just like that. He walked right into their trap. Vera was bragging about it. She said she made love to him in the car, but she lied about that. Lek Mandrea told me, it was he who fucked her in the car. They found dollars on him, thousands."

Avxhiu sat down hard on the bed. "Why does this always happen to me?"

"Keep your voice down, will you. Tell you something else: they found the passport I told you about in his pocket. They don't think it is forged. It is so good they cannot tell. You believe that? Vera said it was a real passport."

"What will they do with him?"

"Shoot him like Spiro. They cannot let him go. He told them he has German friends."

"He told them that?"

"As I said, stupid. They were not torturing him, just talking. They cannot let him go."

"Where are they keeping him?"

"Oh, come on, don't you be stupid."

"Rakipe, he is my only chance. Maybe he can get me out if I can help him. You cannot keep me forever. Maybe he can even get you a visa."

"Vera said they took him to Elbasan, to one of the bunkers across the river. She climbed all the way up and ruined her nylons on the bracken. Bitch should've known better. The Sigurimi would not pay her for the nylons because she had no business being up there."

"Please, Rakipe, please bring the motorcycle with the tank full. Tell the Chief you are taking a trip, to Korca or something."

"What can you do? They have guns. They are killers."

But the Kid was not unreasonable, Avxhiu knew. They both knew this could not last. If she pulled it off, she might escape. Rich men had connections. Rakipe would not rat on her friend or let her down. It would solve the matter, one way or the other.

They agreed that it was best to report the motorcycle stolen, after she left. If they caught Avxhiu, Rakipe was off the hook. The police never looked for stolen goods.

"If he is in a bunker, I can whisper to him, when the guards are asleep. Wallenbergi will tell me what to do."

While the Kid went to get the motorcycle at the police station, Avxhiu rolled a loaf of bread and the kitchen knife into a piece of cloth. It was no protection against guns, but it might scare off people who tried to accost her on the road.

That night she again felt the wind in her face, flying across the mountain roads to Elbasan, hours away. Except for her German, it was a long time since she had felt so alive. The road was empty this late. She met a couple of trucks, coming down from the north. After winding mountain roads uphill, came the steep slopes down towards the deserted steel town. Exhaustion from battling the heavy bike was creeping into her muscles. She geared down the motor, hoping the worn-out brakes would hold against the acceleration downhill. She was unable to see anything in the dark pot beneath.

Then suddenly the whole valley lit up. The electricity had come back on. Even abandoned factories came to life. They never turned the power off. It was nobodies' responsibility. It was a stunning sight.

After a scary ride down, she passed a small township where the road to Korca forked out of the valley. She pulled off the road. The night was dark, and she hoped to be off to Tirana before light. Leading the heavy bike over the tracks, she found a desolate spot among the sheds of an iron mine where she hid the machine with half a mind. Abroad, she could sell it for money. The fatigue made her hands numb and sweat caked her face. She walked across the pebbled banks and crossed the river on foot. The rushing water came to her knees. It was icy cold and felt good. In the shallows on the far side, she took off her dress, and washed away the layers of captivity, chilly and clean in the humid night. Slipping back into her dress and shoes, she took to the hills.

It turned out to be the third bunker she approached. The first two further down the mountain had cardboard covering the windows. They were being used for homes. The third bunker, high up the mountain, had an iron grating. Avxhiu studied it closely, squatting in the dark, her mind in flux. She held the sturdy kitchen knife in a tight grip close to her thigh, staring at the bunker's firing-slit.

She detected no movement. No matter how many guards there were, they'd be asleep. She knew her people. Slowly she made her way in the dark, until she could see the entrance. There was one man outside, sleeping. If there were more, they had gone down to the village. Men liked company. They liked beds better than rocks to sleep on.

There were no keys; the bunker door was secured from outside with two iron crossbars. Working them loose would wake the guard. She was no murderer, no matter what they said about Charles Grenville. Being young and strong was one thing, and the guard seemed old, but she could not stab a man in his sleep. She made her way back and moved in closer. The guard would be alone. The young ones had women and drinking buddies down in the valley.

Avxhiu rose to a crouching position. For a terrible moment she stopped breathing. She held the knife so hard that her knuckles lit up the dark. Eyes glittered in the dark. The foreigner was watching her from inside. It was a terrible shock.

As she allowed the tension to drain off, the foreigner gave her another start. This man was full of surprises. He started to bang his metal bowl, on the rusty grating. It shattered the silence and echoed around the ridge. He was waking the guard. They could have planned something. The man was mad.

Avxhiu threw herself to the ground and hugged the sticking underbrush; no longer sure she could cope with the old guard, armed, and awake.

Book 4, Heimdallr

Chapter 9

"WATER, I MUST HAVE WATER!" The foreigner kept banging on the grating. Avxhiu raised her head, and saw the moving silhouette of the guard, dark against the gray concrete, hobbling closer. A lackey she thought, used to orders, used to doing as he was told. Tending to the criminal would be his way to get back to sleep.

The prisoner kept banging the bowl. The cursing guard thrust his hand through the grating, to snatch the bowl. His impatience became his undoing. The foreigner grabbed hold of his arm and pulled. Avxhiu saw it plunge into the darkness, as his shoulder slammed into the grating. The man screamed in surprise and pain, thrashing about, going nowhere.

And for the first time, the foreigner spoke; not to the guard, but to her, and he didn't ask her to open the door. He simply gave a calm order, and she moved to it without thinking.

"Kill him."

In five or six steps she was behind the guard who was unaware of her presence. His scruffy frame fought for his jarred arm. He was a living, breathing man in ragged clothes, smelling of days in the mountains. His back was against her open hand. She instinctively probed the ribs on his back, her fingers measuring him for the knife.

Then she took the plunge and drove the kitchen knife into his frame. It pointed slightly upwards because she was smaller. Without a thought in her head, she felt the resistance of clothes, and tissue, as the dull knife came to a stop.

Fiercely she put her body against the wooden handle, weighing upon it, till it had sunk slowly through his chest, and stopped against the stone wall. The guard made a desperate halfhearted twitch and tried to turn but he had nowhere to go and went limp instead.

Avxhiu stood holding the wooden handle for a lifetime, and could not bring herself to pull it out, or move. Her hand was drenched in warm, sticky liquid. There was no need for another stab. She let go and stepped away. The poor man hung by his broken arm while the foreigner calmly checked his wrist for a pulse. When the foreigner let go of his arm, the guard became one with the dark ground.

Avxhiu scrambled to the bunker entrance to remove the crossbars, backing away as the metal door opened. She wanted out of there fast. Her thoughts veered wildly between pride and shame. She had killed a man. His blood was drying on her hands. Dry straws and mud clung to her cheek, after the dive to the ground. She brushed them off, an impatient gesture. She had bet her life on this man. It was a comic and embarrassing moment. Except for the boots, he was naked. They had taken his clothes. It was funny. The silliness broke the ice.

"Look at it as the emperor's new clothes," he said, and left it to the darkness, to hide his privacy. Avxhiu had no idea what he was talking about. On the mountain ridge, high above the glittering pearly band of Elbasan, they faced each other for a fleeting moment.

"So, you came to me instead, Avxhiu Shequere," said Birger Wallenberg. This beautiful man didn't ask anything; he knew her name.

"I come to you instead, yes please." The words came to her naturally. She wanted to tell him why he hadn't been able to find her.

"Avxhiu hide because Mayer, your boss, kill many Sigurimi, please."

"You are in quite a fix."

"Pretty pickle, yes," she ventured boldly. The NATO spy had said that.

"You can say that again."

"Pretty pickle, yes." She said it again, not so boldly this time.

"My feeling exactly," he said, and she beamed back at him, her proud face flaming.

"No boss no more. Mayer die in birrari. He killed many Camorra men with Avxhiu hammer." Could it be that he didn't know that his boss had been dead for weeks? "Mayer say Wallenbergi name, before he died."

The foreigner stared at her. "Yes, I know about that." he said. He shook his head slightly and walked to the dead man. Rolling him over, he took hold of the plain wooden handle, and withdrew the knife. It was as if she was not there. He had no shame of a naked body. As he began to undress the man, trying to put on his old grimy clothes. They no way of fitting. The transformation was scary. This new man seemed unable to help anybody.

The foreigner came and put both hands on her shoulders to look into her eyes. She was grateful for the dark, and that he could not see the crimson blush.

"Shequere, I thank you for saving my life." He spoke straight from the shoulder, and she liked him immensely at that moment. She was turning into a real tramp.

"Yes, please, how get out of Albania?"

"I understand everybody is looking for us, the police, the Sigurimi, even the Italian Camorra?"

Avxhiu nodded, and they started making their way down the ridge, through a ravine. It was risky in the dark.

"We better go to some embassy in Tirana. I heard the British one is open. They must have someone in charge."

"Sigurimi outside embassy, inside embassy. No go embassy, please."

"Alright but I need to get money. We can take a ferry or a flight, or a car to Greece. There is a bank in Tirana, right? I can have some money wired over."

Avxhiu was aghast. How could this man help anyone?

"Banka e Shtetit Shqiptar no good. Communist party bank. Sigurimi bank."

"Is there no other bank?"

"No other bank, please."

"We won't get far without money."

Her face flamed out of control. She was grateful for the dark.

"Rakipe help, Avxhiu friend in Tirana, yes please."

"Rakipe, yes."

They had come to the river. Wallenbergi offered to carry her over. There was no need for him to do that. It was silly, but before she knew, she had accepted. Jumping up on his back, she embraced strong shoulders. Holding her chin to the light skin of his neck, she liked the way he stumbled across the stony bottom, careful not to hurt her, putting her down on the other side.

"I will bathe if you don't mind."

He took off the peasant clothes, to plunge into the water. She sat with a hot face in the dark, to study a white shape move against the black water. She washed blood off her hands and did not take her eyes of him. What a stupid, weak woman she was. For a moment, he had become part of something stronger again. He washed blood from his clothes and boots but had trouble putting the wet clothes back on.

"Rakipe best friend, we hide her house. She maybe loan money, yes." The hushed confidential whisper reaffirmed their bond. Crossing the asphalt road, against a sinister backdrop of large hills of slag ore, she led him to a bike behind a rundown shed of corrugated iron.

"This is Avxhiu motorcycle."

"You drove this thing here? You are quite a girl."

She waltzed around him proudly as he led the machine across the railroad tracks onto the road.

"This is a British Gold Star," he said. The worn letters B.S.A. were visible on the tank, aided by the light from an electric bulb above a door of an old railroad shed.

"This is truly antique," he added.

She knew it was a prewar machine, its headlight out of function, which was fine. Emir had said it packed a wallop in its prime. The pistons had lost some of their potency, but they still had plenty to give.

He straddled and kick-started the bike and she mounted behind him on a wooden brick that replaced the original, pleased at his laconic way around her machine. Her aching hands would not have mastered the bike back to Tirana. Her arms held on to his waist. As he gunned the motor, and let go the choke, she felt well-trained muscles move against her open hand. The wind in her face brought old memories. He must know she had to hold on to him. The motor turned over easily now. She closed her eyes and buried her chin in the dirty coat between his shoulders; to shield her face from the wind.

The old Gold Star climbed the steep winding hills, and the man gave it full throttle. The sound worried her. The worn cylinders had plenty of spirit, but the pistons were slopping around with too much spillage.

When they got to the top above the valley, they stopped to pour the rest of the reserve petrol into the tank. She laughed when he complained about the road. It did not trail the mountain slopes but rather the top ridges. A few feet to the left the mountain plunged into vertical hills that rolled on down forever to disappear into morning fog below. To the right, the same view.

The sky was getting lighter. There were already people on the roads. They passed a straggle of refugees, stumps of families filtering back after forty years of internment and labor camps. Their dirty kids in tatters jumped in the way of the motorcycle, pointing to their mouths. Wallenbergi swerved expertly but kept going.

Avxhiu knew that there would be no more hiding.

Like the view from a mountain crest road, it was terrifying and exhilarating at the same time.

Book 4, Heimdallr

Chapter 10

IT WAS EARLY MORNING when they entered Tirana. Avxhiu told Wallenbergi to lead the bike the last bit, so as not to wake the house. The neighbors were city folks, and few were about this early.

She had put on the white headscarf. There was no need to hide the foreigner, he looked like one of thousands in ill-fitting clothes, unshaven cheeks with days of stubble. Come to think of it, very little beard for his days in jail. The body hair of foreigners was different.

The two of them made their way swiftly up the stairs. Their footsteps would tell the house that the Kid was bringing home a customer. Rakipe had not returned from the Dajti. The foreigner insisted on going to the toilet where he made sounds as if he owned the house. Avxhiu covered up the small window with cardboard, plunging the laundry room into darkness. They better get some sleep before the Kid returned. The darkness appealed to her modesty.

"The water disappeared on me!"

"Wallenbergi let water run?"

"I was trying to clean my teeth."

Avxhiu thought of her molar. There would be hell to pay. Now she really hoped the Kid would come home. If the tank that collected rainwater had been emptied, the family upstairs would be enraged and demand that she open the door. It would be a disaster.

"Where is the light switch?"

"No light and no make noise. People hear. We wait till Rakipe come."

The only big thing in the room was the bed. The committee secretary of the Quarter Council had seen to that. Avxhiu considered the concrete floor. The nearness of the man was unsettling. It might as well be. Gingerly she crept under the thin covers, in a nightgown Rakipe brought from the Dajti. On the other side, her foreigner climbed into bed, unashamedly naked.

The springs moaned, and she held perfectly still. He kept his distance. Surely, he must know that this was an open invitation, by the drum of her heart.

"God, I'm tired. A bed," he exclaimed, but made no move towards her. He was immediately asleep.

She judged this from his even breathing, and the relaxed way he moved at times. Avxhiu could not sleep. Once she put out her arm, and brushed against his shoulder, with the back of her hand.

A couple of hours later, she was still awake when the Kid returned. She heard the signal and slipped out of bed to unlock the door. His breathing didn't change tone. The time in the bunker had tired him. There was much to tell. They sat excitedly on her side of the bed and talked in low whispers. She could sense Wallenbergi taking up the whole center of the bed as she told the Kid how she had freed him, and how she had killed the armed guard. The Kid was enormously impressed and promised to lend them money to escape. After a long discussion, they settled down to get some sleep.

But Avxhiu couldn't. Her mind was in too great a flux. Time and again it returned to the foreign body she had held during the trip. Silly woman, she thought and turned away from him. She knew he was close in his nakedness. The Kid had edged in on the other side.

A little later Wallenbergi was moving in his sleep, muttering in his dreams, turning in the dark. He would wake Rakipe, and she was impossible when roused without a reason. The bedsprings sighed heavily.

But the bed didn't settle.

Slowly the truth reached her in a state of disbelief, like witnessing the moon fall from the sky. These were customer sounds. The rhythmic swaying of the bed was growing louder. So were the sounds of heavy breathing, and pleasurable complaints. She heard the tiny voice of the Kid escape from under his body, saying the stupid words she learned at the Dajti. The moon fell from a great height.

Wallenbergi was fucking the Kid.

Avxhiu almost screamed out loud. This was not fair. This was too much. This was her foreigner. She cursed herself for her stupidity, being so used to the Kid in bed. Rakipe always slept naked.

Unable to fight the impulse to raise herself in disbelief to look at them, she saw nothing. She felt his animal breath play across her face, strafing her like bullets. In its warmth, her nostrils sensed the angry groaning pleasure that should have been hers.

In a blend of shattering hurt and silent rage, she slipped out of bed, and sat bundled up on the cool floor by the wall. The shame of it was that the whole house knew. They went at it like two half-crazed cats. He had told her that he was exhausted, the liar. She smudged the angry tears from her cheeks, glad of the dark. How could the foreigner do this to her! She had saved him. How could Rakipe? Why should she care? She did this with everyone.

Wallenberg had been deep asleep when he found the first electric inklings of her body against him. He became aware of her narrow naked bottom touching him, burrowing towards him ever so softly. She had undressed, he found, half asleep, numbed with fatigue. The young widow was no tramp, a safe bet without protection. He owed the girl his life. It felt right to accept a refreshing fling after his month of celibacy.

His sleepy sluggishness was too uncaring, her willing greed too direct. The coarseness of her appetite amazed him, but there was no turning back from the blindness of passion. It proved supremely relaxing. He went straight back to sleep. His visions had evaporated. He was at peace. Asgard Park and Karl Leamas were a world away. His consciousness drifted away, but his senses were protesting.

This was not right. Was he being tricked by his own mind?

Chapter 11

AVXHIU SAT ON THE floor in silent misery, long after the bed grew quiet. She heard his breathing turn to normal, adulterated by an occasional drowsy lament of well-being. Hating him for it, she refused to creep back into bed with these two immoral creatures. Pulling the cushion from under his head, she threw it on the floor for comfort, and waited for the fury settle.

It was midday when she removed the cardboard from the small window and let in the light. It flooded the room. Then she stood by the wall, her mind calmer. The Kid had stolen the bedcovers and lost herself in them. It was a relief. It would take time till she could stand the sight of Rakipe again. She'd never forgive her.

Wallenbergi was so innocent in his nakedness that she stared at him. Why should he care for the feelings of a widow? Why should he not take pleasure where he found it? He was waking up, his eyes flickering open. He caught her looking. Quickly she averted her eyes, too late, blushing as anger flashed through her. He made no move to cover his body. Instead, he smiled at her, and held out his hand. The man had no shame. Was he expecting her to come to him too? She ignored his hand.

"Thank you for tonight, Avxhiu." The mellifluous voice was balanced, the voice of a satisfied man.

"Thank Rakipe, not Avxhiu," she retorted, and turned to look him hard in the eye. But her heart was not in it. Why should he care?

"I do thank Rakipe, he said cheerfully, and had the temerity to smile. She found the curl of his lip inflaming. "I thank Rakipe for allowing us the use of her bed. But I thank you, Avxhiu, for putting me so sweetly to sleep."

His words took the wind out of her: stupid! stupid! She realized the truth. He didn't know, ha! How could he honestly . . . !

Wallenbergi was thanking her for those sounds of lust that had plagued her. In a blend of anger and pleasure, she blushed wildly. He had wanted her;

thought he was making love to her. How could he be so stupid? She balanced between hilarious relief and rage. Now he'd only want Rakipe.

"You fuck Rakipe, you thank Rakipe, yes please!"

She couldn't help the quiver in her voice, pointing angrily at the bundle in the bed. Wallenbergi followed her hand and reached to rumple the small mound of covers. She saw him jump on finding a body underneath.

"Jesus!" He looked bewildered at Avxhiu fighting her emotions. He threw the covers off the Kid, who lay naked on her back. Gone were the stylish clothes and grown-up moves. In sleep, she was a defenseless child.

"Christ!" With some astonishment, Avxhiu recognized both names from the book in the laundry cabinet.

Wallenbergi was left with such a long face of disgust that Avxhiu clapped her hands in a spontaneous gesture of joy. Then, aghast at having revealed her feelings, she bit her lip in his astonished gaze.

"I thought it was you, Shequere. I could kill myself."

Avxhiu was immediately alarmed. The foreigner didn't have to take it that hard. It was a mistake. Her husband had hung himself. Mayer had killed himself, and now Wallenbergi was suggesting that he do the same.

"Please no kill! Avxhiu make mistake to let Rakipe is in bed." Why was she taking responsibility for his debauchery? Why was she excusing his mistake?

"She is a child." His shame showed as he moved to cover the Kid.

With all this talk, Rakipe was coming to life. She sat up and smiled impishly at them, her face creased from the crumpled covers. Then she stretched her bare-boned body in every which way, with a child's violent nature, making contented sounds. She rolled onto her knees in childlike nakedness and slapped Wallenberg's stomach. She had a faded green tattoo on the back of her right hand.

"Got a cigarette, handsome?"

Avxhiu knew the Kid was oblivious to the shadow that her escapade cast on this claustrophobic setting. There was no point in telling her or point to the futility of bumming cigarettes off a naked man.

"Buy me a drink, handsome?" And Avxhiu realized that she was showing off her lousy English.

"You pay me now, handsome?"

As a doctor, Wallenberg was familiar with the fallout from irresponsible sex. Apart from having knocked off a half-grown child, he had not used no protection, and the Kid was in the market for all comers at the Dajti. The girl threw herself naked backwards on the bed, oblivious to her friend's angry glare. Wallenberg had a terrible urge to go and wash, except there was no water.

He tried to cover himself. His intentions toward Avxhiu had been railroaded by his own mind. Why was that? Why was his mind set against sexual intercourse with this innocent widow? His limbs and muscles ached. He was aware of a dull ache in his stomach, a sharp unfamiliar sensation.

The Kid lit a cigarette from her own package.

"Smoking is bad for your lungs," he said, and the Kid could not stop laughing.

"I think I am hungry," he said. Now they both could not stop laughing.

The Kid liked to talk, and Wallenberg became an involuntary lightning rod as Avxhiu translated.

He was informed that all Americans had big houses with swimming pools. They had large families and small dogs and phones with wires that reached out into the garden. The kid's brashness masked her lack of security. As she dressed, she moved her skinny bottom suggestively at him, but when Avxhiu snapped at her angrily, she stumbled out of a well-trained repertoire, her boldness broken. With a petulant shrug of bony shoulders, she threw up her arms to become an awkward child again. Dressed in blue jeans and a black coat, she sat watching them in brooding silence.

On his haunches across the hall, Wallenberg delivered something nasty out of his bowels into a foul-smelling squat-toilet without water. It was a great improvement on the bunker. A bathroom mirror was an old rearview mirror from a car. He resisted the idea of trimming his stubble with a kitchen knife. A stubble would be a great disguise. The Kid had squirreled away several mismatched garments of varied sizes and bland tastes, filched one at a time from well-stocked clients, with her eye on the black market. They were an upgrade from the rags.

They talked. The older girl seemed more intelligent. He had been hoping to work out a plan but found it hard to rely on their judgment. With bands of robbers on the roads, Greece was too far without armed escort, they claimed.

"If I ask my friends to pick us up by boat from the beach south of Durres, do we have petrol for the bike to get there?"

"Sigurimi have boats."

"We can outrun anything they have."

Avxhiu welcomed his taking charge, and they agreed to borrow fifty dollars from the Kid who demanded a visa for the favor if he got out of Albania.

"Rakipe want receipt," Avxhiu translated hesitantly. "Businessmen need receipt so not forget to pay."

"Of course," he said and wrote out the receipt in longhand with a broken ballpoint on a page ripped out of a Fortune diary, filched from a trick. Underlining the $50, he signed the jagged paper. The Kid read it twice, carefully, and handed it back with the fifty dollars in small bills. He tried to return the slip.

"You must keep your receipt, Rakipe!"

"No, you keep," she insisted.

"You want me to keep your receipt?"

"With receipt, you will not forget!" He acceded because it was not the time for a lecture on economics.

The only place with a public telephone in the city was the Hotel Dajti where nothing escaped scrutiny by the Sigurimi. Having spent only one day at the hotel, he was not well known by the staff. The mismatched clothes and untended beard made him every bit a different man. It could take them days to discover his escape from the bunker above Elbasan, and if he spoke Swedish on the phone, they would need time to pick up the scent.

Chapter 12

The Kid had recommended the lazy hour of midday to slip in through the main hotel entrance. With a shawl to cover her face, Avxhiu sailed humbly in his wake to the corner room in the Dajti lobby. A female official behind a high counter supervised the use of the single wooden compartment that housed the telephone. Wallenberg let Avxhiu explain his needs to the official. That way he did not have to speak. The woman explained the procedure and handed over a piece of paper with a blue stamp on it:

"DEGA ALBTURIZMI HOTEL DAJTI TIRANA".

"You must dial direct," the woman said, looking at Avxhiu, "does he know how?" Avxhiu nodded and turned from the desk to explain to her man in Albanian, for the sake of appearance.

Wallenberg had a powerful feeling that he only needed to ask what was in that official's mind to be allowed to access it. He resisted the invitation, and they walked over to the single booth.

"You must get connection to other phone and look at watch. When you stop talk, you put time on paper."

"I know the procedure."

He could feel her surge of pride in a man who could apparently master anything. A man who was curiously on top of things.

"It is absurd, isn't it, leaving it to the customer to chalk up the time," he told her. Again, he sensed her reaction, fright over having made a mistake. It had been an insensitive remark. She had just realized they stole his gold Rolex. Was he reading her mind, or was he imagining things?

"Wallenbergi take Avxhiu clock, yes please." She handed him her scratched and cracked plastic watch.

He wondered if the thing told time, but it was a wedding gift, and it was her pride. She knew it was cheap and she felt ashamed. How could he sense all this? It was not a good time to be imagining things.

"I'm sorry they stole your fine watch," she told him.

"Don't be. When we get out of this bloody country, I will give you the best gold watch in the world!"

They both went into the booth, huddling inside the small cubicle, her back to the glass. It made them less vulnerable. He put his finger into holes of a numbered disc and turned. As the disc returned by itself with a clicking sound, the girl watched so intently that he had to laugh. In this closed confinement, he was at one with her mind. When he spoke in Swedish into the handle, nothing he said made sense to her. He was in her thoughts, with the awareness of his visions. She was thinking that this was a brilliant stroke. The Sigurimi would not understand a word. She also hoped that the man listening on the line was asleep. She knew the message because he had told her. Wallenbergi was telling his team to send a boat to the Adriatic beach a couple of kilometers south of Durres.

The official took her time to fill out the slip of paper with Wallenberg showing his back. He sensed deep suspicion. The $35 charge was to be paid at the desk in the front hall. The clerk at the front desk ignored the slip and continued with paperwork. Wallenberg sensed that Avxhiu who was shocked by the price, found this normal. Even she knew that something was wrong when the man at the front desk had to leave the desk before accepting the money that she held out for him. That was not normal.

Wallenberg accepted an invitation to access his mind, just this once. It was so sudden that it was startling. From a moment to the next, he was looking out through that man's eyes, entering the door to the Sigurimi headquarters. They were all reeling from the report that the rich foreigner had escaped from Elbasan. The man asked the agent in charge to check a suspicious visitor at the desk who left a woman in charge of his money; an Albanian woman at that. That was not normal.

Wallenbergi spun on Avxhiu and pulled her away. In panic, she threw the money on the desk, angry over his loss of nerve. He walked her calmly out by the currency store down the side steps. He had parked the bike some way off. Anyone who parked outside the Dajti was soon surrounded by men who wanted to do you favors. Over his shoulder, he saw men run out of the Dajti. Light blue parkas, caps with red stars, black visors, and white braids. Police uniforms.

The two of them raced to the bike.

One of the guards was holding a walkie-talkie. This modern communication came as a surprise for Wallenberg. The well-worn automatics were no longer slung over their shoulders. As the bike came to live in a mushroom cloud of smoke, as Avxhiu jumped on back. He gunned the old motor to the sound of automatic fire, as they sped up the empty avenue.

"Where is the embassy compound?" Wallenberg shouted.

They were weaving between pedestrians in the street, rounding a big square to pass between the old lion-colored buildings in the official city center.

"No embassy! Tirana no good!"

As she shook him by the shirt, he narrowly avoided collision with another motorcycle. Just their luck that the cop in a blue parka with a walkie-talkie strapped to his shoulder had woefully inadequate control of a heavy bike.

The Italian authorities had begun to shower the police here with equipment in the hope of keeping Albanian immigrants out of Italy. The girl screamed as the big bike slid past them, her arms hugging the wind out of him.

Their old bike was in miserable shape, and Wallenberg thought wistfully about his Harley Heritage, with its dependable brakes.

As the novice motorcycle cop tried to keep his bike under control, he had opted for a long turning circle. Wallenberg's mind settled. On the open road they were easy prey for the Italian power-packet, but he knew how to handle a bike. Without reflection, he took a sharp turn to the right into a narrow side street.

Avxhiu screamed out as they sped headlong into the rubble-strewn maze of the city.

Book 4, Heimdallr

Chapter 13

THE MIDDAY SUN CONJURED up mirages that rippled over a long gray strip of asphalt as Wallenberg raced the old bike down a sleepy road out of Tirana. It gave some relief from the jolts that issued from below. The springs mounted under his saddle were useless. Every time the bike hit a rough spot, the seat connected to the mainframe and kicked his butt. The girl was even worse off. She straddled the improvised brick mounted onto the frame itself.

The motorcycle cop was so inept that he had immediately lost them in the maze of potholed city streets.

"Where does this road lead, Avxhiu?"

"The road to Elbasan." She sounded dazed.

"Away from Durres?"

"Yes, Elbasan. Durres other way."

He wished he had a map. The government treated maps as national secrets, unaware that the capitalists had much better map, that international corporations that hired satellites to chart every inch of Earth for timber and mineral. They were unlikely to have skipped Albania.

"Where can we get gas?"

"Gas?"

"Gasoline, petrol for the bike!"

"No petrol! State petrol, Sigurimi petrol."

The bike had little juice left in it. They would have to ditch it to make it on foot or hitch a ride to the coast. They rumbled past endless rows of greenhouses in various states of dilapidation. The tattered plastic coating fluttered in the wind, broken panes of glass and withered plants. Acres of unattended sprouts were an astounding sight in a land where people starved.

This was State property, and the cost of democracy was showing. The reporters in the Dajti bar had been joking about it. The State had recently started the vote-buying tactics that went with democracy and offered its employees eighty percent of their salaries if they were too sick to work.

Why would they show up for work?

He spotted the police van as they bore on top of it, parked by a cluster of trees by a brook; three cops stretched out on the grass to enjoy the afternoon shade. Hearing the bike, one rose and run onto the road to flag them down. The policeman pushed back his cap and glared after them. Wallenberg sensed disgust over civil disobedience, but not enough to break up an afternoon snooze. The cop sauntered back to the others, knowing that their car could never catch that motor bike anyway.

Minutes later, climbing the winding slopes, the bike sputtered and rolled to a halt. Avxhiu stumbled off with uncertain steps. Wallenberg led the old machine out of sight, down a shallow riverbed, his stride barely firmer. They hid the bike in a small gorge, overgrown with reeds and shrubbery. He sensed her reluctance.

"We have to leave it behind. There is no point in dying for this thing."

Avxhiu's mind also told him that is someone found a ditched motorcycle, it would never find its way to the police. That made him smile.

"Can we cross on foot to the Adriatic?"

"Yes, please."

"How long would that take?"

"Ten hours, maybe longer."

Ten hours was a walk in the park. His friend Roos, of the Nobel Foundation, would have loved to trek with him through these cragged mountains, a picnic for a trained climber. As they spoke on the phone back in Dajti, Roos had suggested a fishing village south of Kavaja from a map on his computer. He had camouflaged his directions with old hiking stories. The plan was to charter a boat in Brindisi and meet up in four days. The nights were warm enough to sleep in the open. Even without food they would make it. The boots were yielding in shape. The trick was to keep clear of people.

They crossed a broad riverbed where a small tributary had resisted the summer drought. Hot and thirsty, they stopped for water. After washing and stretching, they walked for some hours, and then rested in the shade.

He probed her mind. He was getting better at that. Not that he had offered anything in return. Her father had been a laborer on a collective farm, ill-tempered when drunk, and often drunk. Her mother was browbeaten, secretly orthodox without knowing much about her chosen poison. He saw the soot-black patina on the Greek icon her mother kept wrapped up in the spare dress in the private place. In the end it had cost a ten-year sentence to a labor camp that took her life within the first year. The girl had loved her husband, but their time was brief. He recalled the boarded-up shop he visited, faded wedding photos inside a broken display case. Black and white pass photos covered with fly shit and dust.

Before that, it had been the happiest place in the world.

There was no hurry in these empty mountains. They walked, led south by the sun, moving steadily further from the roads. A couple of times they saw people in the distance; on their way to somewhere else. Finally, they sat in the shade on a far hillside overlooking a valley.

The German was the key to the riddle. He wanted to probe her memories of that man, but that part of her mind was closed to him. When he tried to see them together, his mind would not cooperate. Helmut Mayer had uttered his name as he died. Already back then, somebody knew he would be coming here. How could that be? And the girl had saved his life did it because of her love for the man who killed his mother. None of it could be a conspiracy brewed by Karl Leamas.

As they rested in the gathering dusk, gazing over this peaceful land, the girl let her curiosity free, politely asking about his family. It surprised her to learn that he was raised by a single mother, never a mark of affluence in these parts. When he told her that she had died recently, she identified with his loss. He found her mind still reeling from the loss of her brother.

"Life is unfair, Shequere, you a widow at eighteen. At eighteen I was a student in Trelleborg."

"You study what, please?"

"I was a medical student at the university in Lund."

"Medical student like doctor, yes?"

"Yes, I am a doctor of medicine." She turned to him, wide-eyed and pretty.

"You are medical doctor, please?"

When he nodded, she laughed, a small, glorious laughter, her face again engulfed in the flames of her heart. He found it pleasing; he had put to shame the inbred notion that all foreigners had nothing but money in their sights.

"Wallenbergi work in State hospital, yes?"

"Yes, in the city of Lund, Sweden."

He described the emergency ward, putting in months of overtime, sleeping on call in a cubicle with a couch. He left out the fond memories of nurses who helped remove the tension of constant duty, beeping pagers that always seemed to end these frantic encounters. His first year had the flavor of war and the footloose contacts that went with it.

The slope was growing soft with the mild evening. He found in her mind that her respect for him had grown by leaps and bounds. The two men she had loved were dead. He saw her bike rides with Emir in the countryside, the sensation of freedom, of being in control, scattering the odd flock of chickens. Sometimes in the early days, he remembered them spending time off the road in distant places, like this spot, picked to make love.

Wallenberg knew the girl was his for the asking, but she was not his to have. He sensed the deep resistance in his own mind, not in hers, and he was one with her mind. There was something bigger, he was not privy to. She often feverishly wondered about the lie told to her that Mayer had raped and killed a woman in Sweden. Wallenbergi came from Sweden.

They rested on a lonely patch of bleached grass, under a canopy of leaves. The breeze swept in from the south, and they fell asleep in the dusk.

At the first blush of dawn when the chill of early morning woke him, he felt her against him warm and close and asleep. It touched him deeply. They seemed to float on a spread of mist upon the woods below them. There was a nauseating pain in his belly, but when she woke, she laughed off the complaints of hunger. Here in the countryside, they could always find something edible.

They stood and watched a couple of women scouring the hillsides for firewood, then walked higher into the hills, steering clear of the peasants. Later they found wild berries and decided to rest. Two days had passed since he had phoned Roos at the Nobel Foundation. The cragged ranges and river gorge to the south looked unpredictable, but they had two days. If the boat didn't show, that would be it.

Wallenberg turned inwards to fight for control he must not surrender. It troubled him that he seemed to be losing his grip and caring less about it.

Chapter 14

THAT NIGHT THEY STARTED the journey down from the hills, past the town of Kavaja. It had started to rain in torrential showers. In his miserable state he followed as the girl tugged at him. In populated areas, they stumbled across collective farms, skirting the small bungalows with white pillared porches, coveted by party officials.

They passed under woefully unsafe power lines into which the locals tapped at every turn, truncating them like water hoses, siphoning off power. They lost the light. The pitch dark called for creative footwork on a slippery journey across treacherous ravines and fields.

Avxhiu, who had stolen some ears of maize, dragged him towards untended greenhouses to bunk down. They were simple constructions: a forest of concrete pillars connected by curved rods of iron to hold plastic drapery in place. With most of the plastic gone, there was no longer much inside. She found a spot where a strip of plastic provided some shelter. It was damp and forbidding and smelled of mold, but comfortable enough to huddle on a spot of dry earth. She held him close for warmth, and they nibbled at half ripe maize to restore that precious balance between starvation and hunger. The boat would slip in at three o'clock tomorrow afternoon while the locals rested.

When he woke, it was too late.

Through the forest of concrete pillars, lights of oil lanterns danced through the wet sheets as men combed the strips of plastic. There were shouts, and in moments they were surrounded.

At first the civilian clothes allowed a flicker of optimism, soon replaced by enough uniforms to make it official. Avxhiu shook him by the shoulder, as she clambered sullenly to her feet, scared out of her wits, avoiding the gloating faces. Even in the warm light from the oil lamps, the foreigner looked ashen. He did not inspire much hope. This was not his world. Avxhiu knew that he would soon find out that the rules here were neither fair nor just.

Wallenberg was baffled by his senses. He knew these men, their names, where they came from, what they wanted, where they were going. The prisoners were herded like stray cattle through the forest of concrete pillars as the bunch formed a jostling ring around the captives. The swarm of peasants and criminals, police, and army privates, laughed and chatted across the maize fields. A reward had been posted. None of them expected any part of that money, knowing the system, but it was a rare moment of success. It felt good. He was glad for them.

The rain had stopped, but the bleak grayness of dawn held little comfort. By the bungalows, a battered Mercedes awaited. The men bundled them into a backseat where most of the stopping was missing. Although the springs annoyed Wallenberg, he did not complain when Avxhiu ended up on his lap; secured with a man on each side. His mind was otherwise occupied. They drove for hours. The girl relaxed in his arms. Their chain-smoking captors kept the car windows closed against the morning chill.

They had been growling up the side of a mountain when Avxhiu saw a bulky old man on a mountain donkey up in front, the man bigger than the animal. The donkey shied into the road. There was a thud and the car lurched to a stop. The driver spent a minute examining the damage to the car. The downed animal brayed in the road with the old peasant pinned under it. A man from the front seat walked over and shot the donkey, and then shot the old man. After frisking him for valuables, the two dragged the animal to lift into the trunk. It was food. They rolled the dead peasant off the road, and the journey continued.

In a distant desolate valley, the car turned off the main road, and onto an earthen path. A horse drawn cart appeared for another bumpy ride. There were no straws in the cart. Every jolt hit home. Only the dead donkey was at peace; and for the first time. In the far distance, an abandoned barn came into view, by the tracks of an old railroad.

The barn had survived because its shrunken timbers were too rotten for recycling. Within this dark building they awaited interrogation. That evening they were served a large portion of steaming meat. Avxhiu had never tasted a more filling dinner. It was a part of a donkey, roasted whole. Dazed by food, she wanted to steal a furtive roll in the hay, but the foreigner resisted. He had barely uttered a works since they were caught

The next morning, through the wide cracks, she saw more captors loll on the grass outside. The flock moved along with the barn shadow as the sun crept across the sky, and their number grew. Soon a ragged bunch of smalltime crooks sat scattered by the dozens around the barn in the depths of boredom. Wallenberg dozed among the bales.

As Wallenberg drifted off, he had an entirely different vision.

He was in full control of his own thoughts and senses, walking into a large white room where three kindly persons welcomed him from behind a table, two men and a woman, all of them vaguely familiar. He knew this was imagination, and he knew it was real. The restructuring of his brain was on the agenda. He had been invited to meet the advance staff of Heimdallr.

"This is a bit awkward, Birger," said the young man on the right.

"We have tried to make our meeting as relaxing as possible. Would you like another setting?"

"Not at all, this is fine. Do I know you?"

"Well, we are not really human. We were fashioned in your mind. We want to look like someone you can carry on an educated discussion with, so we built a composite of several persons whom you value."

"Would you like us to be different," asked the woman in the middle. They both seemed to have the same voice.

"No, not at all, I find you all very comforting."

"Our reason for this meeting is to inform you that the preparations for the ascent of Heimdallr are complete. It is now up to you to accept his guidance."

"Thank you, I'd rather continue being myself."

"We understand," said the man on the left with the same voice. "It may be problematic in your situation. We can inform you that in his mind, General Skender Krasnigi has decided to take your life after interrogation. You are of no value to his people, and perhaps a threat. He runs powerful fraction of the Sigurimi Camorra."

"I am a wealthy man."

"Your captors have no way of transferring funds without aid of an enemy fraction within the Sigurimi. It is not in their interest to take that risk."

"How would you know this?"

"The preparations for Heimdallr are complete. It is a wonderful system. There is nothing in the world like it."

"What does it do?"

"It is a monitoring and communication system of human minds. The system has an array of specific parameters. Its main purpose is to judge if human plans, or deeds in the offing, are in conflict with intelligent design."

"I'm told Heimdallr is guarding the designs of his masters. From where I'm standing, it takes more than a few mercenaries or a private army to change the big picture."

"Our task is not micro-managing, with exception of chosen children, and nobody likes to meet Heimdallr as the opposing party. The Second World War was not fought over politics. It came about when certain parties thought they had a final say in human design."

"The Second World War?"

"Using the system is very efficient. Would you like a tour?"

"I'm not committing to anything."

"Of course not; it is more to show you the ropes than anything else. Is there anyone special that you would like to monitor to illustrate the system?"

"You mean like another person."

"Yes, and you might want to choose someone who is difficult to fake on a short notice. We are all concerned by your distrust."

"Alright, make it the General Secretary of the Soviet Communist Party, Mikhail Gorbachev. What is he doing at this moment?"

The transformation was immediate. It blew him away, so irritated was he by the drunken voice yelling at him over the phone.

"Mikhail Sergeyevich; you should be in Moscow. Are you backing out of our deal," Russian President Boris Yeltsin at the other end was his usual rude self, "why are you hiding in Crimea? Did you forget what we decided?"

Gorbachev was angry. The Foros dacha was supposed to be his retreat. He looked out at the quiet landscape. Last time he was here, Bush was on the phone because Hussein had invaded Kuwait, and the struggle for Baltic independence was getting ugly. Yeltsin had a finger in that too.

"Boris Nikolayevich; we only discussed the possibility of replacing Alexandrovich. Don't rock the boat now. The conservatives are in majority."

"He is smearing us, using bogus documents. Stand up to the man or your perestroika is dead. He will push glasnost back up your ass. Replace him as KGB chairman with Vadim Viktorovich and you better do it now."

Gorbachev sighed in resignation. "You know that Alexandrovich is eavesdropping on the line, don't you?"

There was a roar of drunken laughter on the phone.

"Yes, he's had you under surveillance all summer. How can you take it lying down? Maybe I should address you as Subject 110? That is your name now Mikhail Sergeyevich. Did you hear that Alexandrovich? I know what is in your logbooks. Never forget that. Some of your best men are Russian patriots, not Russian traitors like you."

"Boris, I'll return to Moscow on the twentieth; to sign the union treaty as planned."

"No, you won't. If you don't get off your ass, you'll have a mutiny. Why should I care if they push you out? I will remain president of Mother Russia."

Mikhail Gorbachev hung up in anger and grabbed a sheaf of tele-grams to throw in the wastebasket. They had also been forwarded by Alexandrovich, the plotting KGB chairman. Typically, Alexandrovich had selected only those messages that accused the General Secretary of betraying the Motherland, and of selling resources to cronies.

Yeltsin, his supposed ally, was in on the game, insulting him in the media at every turn, proclaiming an autonomous Russia, passing laws that challenged Soviet laws, his popularity soaring at everybody's expense. What did Yeltsin care that he needed to normalize the collapsing financial sector? The normalization program was mired in resistance. Gorbachev closed his eyes. He had not felt human in ages.

When he opened his eyes, the Foros dacha was gone, and it took a moment to gather his senses.

"It is a wonderful system, isn't it?"

Wallenberg looked at three smiling faces that were not really human.

"Are they plotting against me, I mean Gorbachev?"

"Yes, of course."

"Will they succeed?"

"We cannot tell the future. Nobody can. Not even the gods."

"So, all you can do is to spy, like Alexandrovich?"

"That is partly true. Pledging loyalty is a public tactic, and the KGB sees what people say. The mind tells the truth. Heimdallr can enter millions of minds at the same time. He does not intervene unless intelligent design is threatened."

"I want to underline that the 'he' is not gender related," said the woman in the middle with a male voice.

"I do not want this task. I am a scientist."

"You do not have to explain."

Wallenberg nodded curtly, turned, and left the white room. He woke up to straws getting up his nose. Their imprisonment turned into days. They had a bucket to relieve themselves in. It saved the girl from the shame of observation. Threats were grunted angrily for her benefit every time they brought food. The bread was recently baked, and they wolfed it down.

He had turned catatonic.

They awaited the arrival of the general in charge of the local Camorra faction. They were clearly not high on his agenda. The men grew restless, they were used to loitering outside a birrari, they needed diversions.

It came to ugly fistfights.

Book 4, Heimdallr

Chapter 15

LATE AFTERNOON, AS THE restiveness of the men started to get out of hand, the local leader brought out the two prisoners, as a means of controlling the crowd. He used English as he played with the pair, lapsing into Albanian for the benefit of his enfeebled minions. His wish to entertain showed in sexual slurs thrown at the terrified girl and in taunting of the foreigner.

Wallenberg sat on his haunches inside the large ring of raucous thugs and ignored them.

"We fuck your woman, yes, you agree?"

And all the while it kept coming on, rising from within. The molecular stain was spreading. The madness was growing.

"This is custom. We share. You agree?"

Avxhiu fought their jeers with brave thoughts averted. Life and honor were cheap among these outcasts. She held Wallenberg's wrist in an iron grip, and never relaxed it, until he spoke. Then she let go. This foolhardy foreigner had no right to give her to animals. Why did she have to suffer so?

Wallenberg felt the icy calm descend on him in the burning sun. His mind cleared, and he studied them with disinterest. They were nothing to him. The girl was in danger. She was in his care. They wanted entertainment.

"I will fight any man among you for the young woman, a fair fight without weapons."

He felt her grip on his wrist fall away. He did not look at her. The minions looked to their leader for a translation, but he was struck dumb. When at last he gave it, a cheer broke out. The men howled and shouted, some whistled and taunted the foreigner who watched them coldly from his haunches, one after the other. Their eyes met. One by one the shouts faltered and died. A tone of doubt struck all but the most imbecilic.

The local chief pondered his choices, unsure of the wisdom of his position. It was good to give the foreigner a lesson without mistreating him too badly. There would be repercussions if was killed. A strong man could take him down without much damage. If the foreigner was any good, and he seemed confident enough, it would be shameful to have him win. His trouncing would give his men something to talk about. The man he chose would get his way with the woman. She would be no worse for wear.

He called out a name sharply. There were shouts and roars of laughter from the men. Gazmir Kalushi was a giant, the butcher from Teppelena, they called him. Teppelena, where he earned his title, had been the worst extermination camp in all of Albania. Now, used as an army barracks, the butcher was out of a job. Nobody ever fought Gazmir Kalushi.

Wallenberg was past all that. He eyed the man who stepped forward. A saner man would have paused to recall his superficial training in contact sports. He found no fear within. His body was fairly well tuned but he had no intension of playing that instrument. A guest was waiting in the wings to do that. Something that was not Heimdallr had entered the secret back door. He had granted access. A detonation of arctic cold gave his core a superconducting quality. He let go of reason, and anticipated madness as if it were a woman.

He rose slowly and stripped off the shirt given to him by the child Rakipe, handing it down to a petrified Shequere. Their eyes met, but he gave no response to her anguish. The eyes were no longer his to command.

Then he turned to face the butcher from Teppelena, a big man, brown as a nut, stripped to his waste, his muscles shielded by fat, his size overwhelming. He was a hairy beast; black wildness covered his chest and arms. The giant stomped the ground and leered at the foreigner and the girl, one after the other, the victim and the prize. The crowd cheered and bets were offered. The odds went high before there were any takers.

Gazmir Kalushi stared Wallenberg down, putting the fear into him. As he waited for the signal, he found that something was wrong. There was no trace of fear in those eyes. He had never met a man this hard. To his amazement he felt wary of the foreigner who stood there with no more apprehension than a dead fish. And the appalling whiteness of him was like the belly of the same fish. The foreigner was not fit for this fight. He had the muscles of a long-distance runner, but how Gazmir Kalushi hated those merciless eyes. Nothing in this world is as debilitating as fear. Something in those eyes was not of this world.

When the signal came, the butcher from Teppelena, for the first time in his life, did not charge. Instead, he hesitated and poked at the foreigner. The men jeered and shouted, pleased that their man had decided to draw out the show.

It was the fish-belly-colored foreigner who charged.

Wallenberg had a vivid impression of what happened. He saw it and he felt it, but there was nothing he could do about it. His commands came out of his marrow, smooth and hard and without thinking.

The giant stood ready for him with his feet planted in the earth, prepared to repel any attack. The foreigner's swift advance broke into a turn, as if he had thought better of it. He was lining up for a devastating and precise kick. It went for an unexpected spot of weakness.

The small round bone on the giant's knee, known as the patella, shielded just that spot. The knee was locked in position at both ends, by the Earth at one and the lesser mass of the giant at the other. What gave way against the force of the precise kick were the ligaments of that knee.

And so it happened that the butcher from Teppelena, for the first time in his life, curtsied with his left knee: in the wrong direction.

The pain must have been devastating, and the doctor in Wallenberg knew the damage by heart. Yet the giant gave no sound other than a fuming grunt. Then he fell on his whole knee to keep his balance. His guard came briefly down as his hands went back to steady his body. As he looked up, both he and Wallenberg saw what was about to happen.

Hidden in the giant's nut-brown neck was the thyroid cartilage. As rumor has it, the piece of forbidden apple that Adam ate, and which stuck in his throat. The brute who must have sneaked that bite was about to have his bit of Adam's apple unstuck by the worn heel of a chafing army boot.

The blow caused the man drop on his side, smashing his cauliflower ear into the ground, where he rolled onto his stomach. It was over, but it was not.

Wallenberg tried to assert himself, but he was not in control. He had gone berserk. His body took two steps and bent down to grab a handful of hair and pull up the slumped head. He looked at the stunned leader, as if to make a point. Then he slammed his right knuckles into the base of the skull. The sound said that something had given way: a spinal cord in mortal shock within a broken neck. He stepped over the dead man into the empty ring.

It had happened too quickly. The display of mindless rage took seconds to run its course. Crumpled Lek notes of worthless Albanian currency were changing hands in preparation for the final humiliation.

As the jeers faded, things became deathly quiet. Hands grasped after worn knife handles. There was something uncanny that vibrated in the air. They had all heard the stories, the incident at the birrari.

But nothing came of it.

The local leader ordered the prisoners into the barn. There would be no more fights. Hi men had got what they needed. The foreigner pulled up the girl. The men stared carefully at his back in disgust. They had seen that insane face. They wanted nothing from this man, not even his life.

Killing a madman was bad luck.

Deep in the night, Wallenberg woke and felt he had regained control. He could not tell. There was laughter outside the barn. The tale of his captors gained momentum; the story of how the butcher from Teppelena met his maker. They would never know how close they came to the truth.

Wallenberg stared out through the wide cracks. He felt tears trickle into his stubble. He could not stop them if he wanted to. The words of his mother as she read to him from the Icelandic Edda came to his mind unbidden.

Hard is it on earth, | with mighty whoredom; Axe-time, sword-time, | shields are sundered, Wind-time, wolf-time, | ere the world falls; Nor ever shall men | each other spare. Fast move the sons | of Mim, and fate Is heard in the note | of the Gjallarhorn; Loud blows Heimdallr, | the horn is aloft. In fear quake all | who on Hel-roads are.

He had never been so terrified in his life; Heimdallr stood on the Bridge of Bifröst.

Book 4, Heimdallr

Chapter 16

THE FOLLOWING DAY AT NOON, the general arrived in a Mercedes. In the shadows of the barn wall, inches away, Avxhiu saw him greet the local boss in a slow embrace with warmth and kissing of cheeks. She heard them discuss the fight; the man had killed Gazmir Kalushi with less compassion than crushing a fly. The foreigner was an assassin. Not that it mattered; their faction was under threat. The reasons were unclear. They must prepare.

The prisoners were of no value to them.

General Skender Krasnigi had a chair brought into the barn, away from the afternoon sun. The prisoners were stood before him on the earthen floor. The minions, keen for another historic moment, jostled for positions within earshot, lining the rotten walls in the dusk, standing ready to shoot the foreigner if he went for the general. Avxhiu knew it was the end of the line. She braced for it. No amount of information could avert their death.

Last night she had made her peace and prayed as her mother taught her. In the night, she had the strangest dream. She was again crammed into that phone booth with Wallenberg. This time she was making the call. She pushed the disc with the numbered holes and watched it return by itself with a clicking sound. Almost immediately there came an unhurried voice on the line.

"How can I help you?"

It was the strangest thing. Avxhiu had never heard a question carry such conviction. It was hedged with no reserve. In that split second, she realized that Heaven and Earth were already moving in furious union to her rescue. She did not know what to make of it, but it imbued her with boundless courage.

Now with the morning dew outside yielding to the sun, so did the comfort of that dream. The general spoke passable English and his questions were blunt and to the point.

"Who you work for, Mister Wallenberg?" Avxhiu knew that form was necessary. He was careful about the Mister. It gave legitimacy.

"I am the Director of Asgard Park." The voice was comfortable, balanced.

"The Italian Camorra is asking about you. Why are they willing to pay ridiculous ransom for a man like you? What makes you so valuable? I told them that we can clean our own house. I turned them down."

Wallenberg shook his head slowly and the general lost interest, turning to address the girl in Albanian.

"Your brother, the traitor Spiro Shituni, I killed him at Gradishka. Have you heard?"

"My brother was no traitor!" Avxhiu spoke with slow dignity.

"Why did the German criminal let him live?"

"I told him to."

"The German criminal did what you told him?"

"Yes."

"Why?"

"He loved me."

Avxhiu was so unreasonably proud that she forgot the foreigner at her side. She was taking a last stand.

"The German traitor loved nobody."

Her defiant cheeks flushed dimly in the dark.

"May God forgive you," she added.

The general studied her calmly for a moment.

"So, now you pray to God, like your mother."

It was the moment of truth. She accepted the inevitable and spat her unbowed defiance in his face, literally. The general wiped it off. A silence fell upon them. It reached out and took charge. Death waited at its conclusion. The moment seemed to last forever. The men paid homage by allowing it to run its course.

There was nothing more to be said.

Out of nowhere, vague vibrations began to eat into the silence, allowing it to dwell with her a little longer. A train was passing down the tracks. The rails went by the barn. It felt like an earthquake coming. The power of primitive men withered in its mighty voice. The thunder embraced them and climaxed. The bursts of the steam-powered old horn seemed certain to demolish the rotten barn.

As Avxhiu stood defiant, emboldened by unexpected theatrics, the foreigner suddenly tackled her. They tumbled into the dirt. She clawed at Wallenbergi for degrading her in her moment of glory, but he pinned her down into the mud.

The rough bunch by the walls around them roared in laughter. The foreign madman was a coward after all. She saw teeth flash in the dusk and eyes glitter in contempt, but nothing rose above the rumble of the passing train. The air vibrated with its power.

Chapter 17

AND PRECISELY AT THAT moment, Hell was visited upon them. Two horizontal walls of large caliber rapid-fire projectiles of lead and steel cut through the rotten timbers, moving along with the train. In seconds, its entire length of the barn had been punctured on two levels, breast, and thighs, too swift for meaningful reaction.

Avxhiu started to raise her head. Her eyes recorded the scene in terrible slow motion. The roar of the train could not block out the bark of rapid gunfire sweeping by. The awful punches left an eerie shower of guts and blood sailing on the air. It lasted seconds, but for most of the ragged lot, it lasted forever. Avxhiu blinked in the merciless glare of day as the barn door toppled off its hinges. The maelstrom of flying guts and debris within the barn lit up from behind. The blood and the guts turned to pure gold.

The clanking of the receding train was followed by an instant attack from the grounds outside. Judging by a new growling sound, a heavily armed motorcycle contingent had moved in while noise blocked out communication. They rolled over the remaining resistance with vengeance.

Avxhiu pushed her head back into the dirt. She clung to the foreigner and bided time, waiting for the carnage to stop.

The noise died down. People were moving among them. A pistol shot rang out, then again, and she ventured a glance. A leather-jacketed man walked among the fallen. He found a wounded man and stooped to shoot him in the head, and another, carefully. It was an execution. To die defiant is a worthy thing; Avxhiu scrambled to her feet and dragged Wallenberg up with her.

The man watched them rise and take a stand. Then the strangest thing happened. The man smiled at her. It was a friendly smile.

Then he turned and continued his macabre task of wiping out the remaining vestiges of life from this earthen field. She did not wish to fathom it. Aiming for the awning of the collapsed door, dragging Wallenberg, they side-stepped bodies and stumbled over disentangled timbers into the midday sun. Avxhiu slipped on dismembered body parts in a pool of blood. Her knee came down on a soft stomach that yielded without complaint.

Waiting for the bullets to arrive, she clung to Wallenbergi. They made their way towards the blazing opening of the collapsed barn door, out into the haze of the Adriatic sun. She had one wish, to see the sky before she died. She held that miraculous voice in her head, 'How can I help you?' A trembling went through her in wild bursts.

The mayhem was familiar. She had escaped the birrari the same way. It had brought only pain and adversity. She groped across a flattened door into blinding light. The air was filled with dust and strange smells. She let go of his arm and went down on her haunches to squat against a punctured wall, unable to believe her insane luck. These men had no mercy. They spared none. Death was all around. They were killing machines, but they were men.

Her eyes adjusted. She singled out a leader barking orders; a foreigner with a tongue she did not understand.

What reason would he have to kill a good-looking woman? Should she beg for mercy? As she sought courage, she saw that Wallenbergi was aiding one of their wounded men. Another was beyond help. He was a doctor with a service to offer. Afterwards, he would only be a witness to a criminal act.

A shudder passed through her. She braced herself for it. The leader of this cold-blooded creed was kneeling by his dying man. He had his back to her. His hair was in a bun on the back of his head, like a woman's. It ruffled her confidence. He was different, unsympathetic. This was her chance. First crawling, then half cringing, she made her way to where he stood watching the doctor handle the arm of a wounded man. Wallenbergi was working fast to stop the bleeding, to set the wound. His expertise showed. It impressed the leader.

Would she do better with Wallenbergi asking for mercy than striking out on her own? She reached out and put her hand on the side of the foreign back, feeling the tough hard body beneath the brown leather.

"You let Wallenbergi and Avxhiu go, yes please?"

The man was younger than he had looked. He did not strike her. She was halfway there.

"I see nothing, yes," she stammered. Her life was on the line, but she could not bring herself to take the Kid's advice; to offer what men wanted. Again, and again.

"Shequere Avxhiu?"

How did he know her name? She had seen how he looked at the doctor. Had they come to capture him? Had they exchanged jailers?

"Yes. You know Wallenbergi, yes please?"

"Don't worry, Avxhiu, no harm will come to you."

It was cryptic. Foreigners often answered like that, but his words lifted a load of fear from her mind.

"You no harm Wallenbergi, please?"

The foreigner took her by the arm abruptly, leading her aside. She panicked. Had she annoyed him? Why barter for his life? Did she not have enough to deal with? Would he force himself on her, here among the dead? That was no better than being dead.

A fire had started inside the barn. The smoke wafted their way. The sweet roasting smell was disgusting. Soon there would be nothing but charred timbers and bodies. The smoke would arouse interest; people would appear in droves over nearby hillsides. Again, they would find only Avxhiu alive, only Avxhiu to blame.

She started to cry as he led her at a rapid pace to a large motorcycle. Dazed she allowed him to steer her. She had never seen anything like this bike, a shining monster with controls and meters, black as the devil. He let go of her arm. Out of a large saddlebag he took a small leather satchel and handed it to her.

"Keep this for Wallenberg. Tell him to take this bike." He pushed a photograph at her with an address on the back. It confused her.

"Do you know this house?"

She collected her wits, "Horxha summerhouse?"

"Can you guide Wallenberg to this house?"

"Avxhiu take Wallenbergi to Horxha house?" Confounded, she wiped her face, the tears smudging the dried flecks of blood.

"He is having some trouble with his mind; it is too risky to take you with us. We will be challenged at the border. Wait at the Horxha house."

"You no kill Wallenbergi, please?"

"We are here on his orders. He called this strike. We are all happy for him. He is angry at me for cutting it too close. Not because of him but because of you."

A realization began form in her confused mind.

"Wallenbergi leader?"

"We don't die easily, but for him we die with a smile."

Out of the fog, the truth bore down on her like an ocean liner on a puny raft. Wallenbergi had taken over after Mayer. She felt drained of energy, a piece of cloth out of the wringer, slowly starting to breathe.

The man left her standing and there, off to prepare their departure.

She had made a greater fool of herself that anybody had the right to forgive. She had wanted to give herself to Wallenberg as a passing figure, a loser she could take pleasure from. He had resisted her in the hills without a hint of promise. She looked at him on his knees, binding up a wounded man without consideration for his position.

Tears of shame clouded her vision. Standing paralyzed by the big bike, her hand played idly with the seat, banding away smoke in the heat of the sun, as a new fascination spread in her. The vice that had clamped her gut in its grip for more than a month started to loosen. She had to move fast to mend her fences.

She fingered the leather satchel and folded it open, her eyes smarting from the smoke. The pupils, contracted in glaring sunlight, widened. There were thick bundles of dollar notes. She had never seen anything like it. It was much more than Charles Grenville had had in his belt.

Wallenbergi finished binding up the wound. He walked over to where she stood smudging her watchful tears.

"They are an ugly bunch, aren't they," he said.

She laughed out loud and embraced him in unfamiliar ecstasy.

The biker gang was filing onto the railway tracks that would take them to the border, the only unwatched road in Albania. All the trains had stopped and left untouched when the government collapsed.

"Let's go the Horxha summerhouse, shall we? This is our bike."

Chapter 18

BURTON CRANE HAD PICKED up the trail of Birger Wallenberg with help of an old friend in Rome. After a boat trip to Albania, the earth had swallowed the Swedish scholar. Registered for a Psychiatry Congress in Florence, his traveling schedule made no sense. To try and learn anything of his whereabouts from outside Albania would be a waste of time.

Without Sidney holding his hand, authorized status was out of the question. The British Foreign Office had expressed its irritation, and this was apparently seconded by their colleagues at Foggy Bottom back home.

Passing himself off as a New York Times reporter with a press card to prove it, Crane arrived at Durres on the ferry from Greece as Mr. Douglas Cole with no other luggage than his hand valise. To look carefree as a lark was the only way to travel on a false passport with a fake visa. The visa had posed an unusual problem. Preparing the worn-out stamps was easy but finding cheap enough paper was not. They didn't make it like that anymore.

There were the repeated checks of papers, shipside and again in the small arrival shed. Both were a breeze. In a wooden shed through a single hole in the glass, the ten-dollar bribe went down well with the broad-faced boy who inspected his visa. Crane was out in front of the gates less than an hour after disembarking. There were two taxis outside. In shirtsleeves and drenched in sweat, he gave his destination as Tirana.

The taxi driver had a trust-inspiring gaze that made Crane instantly mistrust him. Happy to have the ear of a big-shot New York reporter, Engel Vorbsi spoke passable English and was a fountain of information. How much of it was based on fact was anybody's guess. When they arrived in Tirana, he had signed the taxi driver on as a paid assistant with a prospect of a hefty bonus in dollars if the story went big. This of course depended on his depth of inside information.

The man was doubtless a snitch for the Sigurimi. Crane queried him on the massacre committed by a foreign biker gang. The driver would have some access through his friends, and there was a lot to be said for camaraderie. He hired the taxi for three days, one day in advance. The old green Toyota was sturdy and robust despite its age. As many cars in this country, it had no rearview mirrors.

Crane's greatest problem was to convince the driver that he wanted to stay at the Hotel Europe, not the Dajti. He had to argue his way through that one; he was partial to the name Europe, being superstitious, as were all reporters.

Hotel Europe was a big, run-down dump of a place, no longer considered worth bugging by a Sigurimi on the economic ropes. After careful study on a shoddy desk, the clerk registered Mr. Cole's papers.

Next morning, he got Engel Vorbsi to take him to the morgue, keeping the small leather valise close at all times. The morgue supervisor was the same blue-tattooed one he met earlier, relaxing in the shade outside, smoking with his helpers. It was as if Crane had left five minutes ago. The old man didn't recognize him and failed to notice the different name and profession. Foreign names were hard. Crane had a story ready, but the man didn't care one way or another. That was the beauty of bribes from a repeat customer.

The scene down in the cellar was, if anything, grimmer than on his first visit. This time the corpses were all locals, and the electricity was on. The cold in the freezer had dropped below zero and started to cover the half-thawed carcasses with a new film of frosted dullness. The air had a nip in it after the oppressing heat, and the stench was less poignant.

The sturdy wooden tables in the freezer were still stacked, and with more corpses on top. It was difficult to imagine that the supervisor had any idea who was at the bottom. Perhaps files had been mislaid or forgotten in a city cabinet? To get out from under that load, they would have to await a spring-cleaning.

Evidence about the barn massacre was scarce. The crime scene investigation consisted of carting away bodies. Nobody had any interest in collecting evidence; autopsies were dispensed with; not a single bullet dug out. Crane studied some of the coup-de-grace entry wounds. This was an execution, and the police appeared none too keen on clearing it up. Most of the victims had been claimed and buried.

Back at the Europe he put Engel, his taxi driver, on a temporary retainer for inside tips. The New York Times needed background about this massacre. Engel Vorbsi, the veritable fixer, went off to haunt his contacts in the Dajti, a happy man with eighty greenbacks of expense money in his pocket.

To wait him out, Crane withdrew to a dingy room without water or electricity. Every few hours his driver, an old hand in the tourist trade, returned with information he had culled from his gossipy buddies. He was of course playing both sides of the fence. Crane uncapped a bottle of Jack Daniel's and refused to budge from his room. He was not a sociable foreigner, which suited Vorbsi fine. It gave him sole rights.

They talked in the light from an oil lamp, and Crane played reporter, carefully jotting down the tidbits brought by his driver, probing as the mystery deepened.

Book 4, Heimdallr

Chapter 19

THE FOREIGN MOTORCYCLE GANG had hijacked an old train and used it to spray a barn by the tracks with machine gun fire. The tracks indicated many bikes. The gang had attacked a splinter group from the local Camorra that held hostages in the barn. None of the group survived. Kidnapping was a common way of financing local gangs after the fall of State authority, but foreign bikers were a new development.

"What hostages?" Crane asked idly.

"One foreigner and his Albanian whore."

"Got a name?"

"Wallenbergi, I think, Mr. Cole."

Crane almost choked on the bourbon and bit his tongue to keep a straight face as he scribbled in his notebook.

"This foreigner, Wallenbergi, was he killed?"

"Sigurimi not find his body."

"And the Albanian woman?

"Woman is wanted dead or alive, like in America. She murdered a rich businessman from Canada, and she planned the birrari massacre."

"Does she have a name?" It would be wrong not to ask.

"Shequere Avxhiu; a nobody."

Jack Daniel was half empty. The pearls of sweat trickled into his eye, but Crane gulped down more bourbon.

"How do you spell that?" He wrote it carefully in his notebook. "Any thoughts on why they grabbed these two? Are they rich or of good families?"

"Avxhiu wanted for murder."

"Ok, dead or alive, so why take her hostage?"

"The Tirana Sigurimi wanted them to be freed. They ask Camorra to let the foreigner go. General Skender Krasnigi did not listen. He was killed."

"So, there is a war within the Camorra now?"

"Yes, in this you are right, there is gang war."

This was uncanny. Like in New York the dead were all criminals. Like in New York, the common thread was Birger Wallenberg.

"Who is this foreign spy?"

"I think maybe Italian."

"Why do you say that?"

"The Napoli Camorra asked the Sigurimi to help. They say America pay."

"So now everybody is looking for this spook?"

"This spy? No, no, no, nobody wants him. The Dajti Sigurimi only wants Shequere Avxhiu."

Engel Vorbsi went on to explain what he had learned. Elements within the Sigurimi wanted Avxhiu; something about a general and a broken arm. The Italians were paying good money to protect the foreign spy. There was a gang war, but nobody knew what it was about.

"Maybe the Sigurimi knows where the foreign spy hides," Vorbsi suggested. "Sigurimi very careful not to tell. I never tell state secrets."

"I'm sorry, Vorbsi, there is no meat on these bones. The New York Times cannot run hearsay. Besides, I think the folks back home have lost interest. Tell me about the explosion in the Valiasi mine. Who is responsible for sending men down there with the electrical wiring falling apart?" Burton Crane poured himself some more bourbon and made a mental note to shop for another bottle, then gratefully accepted the ensuing monologue without interruption. He had stopped listening.

Was this educated tycoon just drawn to danger? This guy controlled vast international resources. Like baron Keltenbrunner, he could summon help from the countries pouring aid into Albania, with a snap of his fingers. Why rely on the Italian Camorra to grease the wheels and bail him out? Crane knew the answer by heart; it was the method of an agent who does not want to leave an official trail. There would be no footprints here to be laid bare, no pattern that somebody like Crane could spot.

Every agent built an invisible network of underhand channels. Crane could speak on that with some authority. You rely on a network of friends and contacts. Sometimes your contacts were in plain sight, a source of pride and support. Often the threads are buried. Dig them up and somebody wished you hadn't. That was his work, being unwanted.

Mostly the buried threads led to pots of gold at the end of tainted rainbows. The world had always worked that way. But where were the threads in this case? There were no rewards to be seen. Why did old Hugh Miller, the

Bureau's ramrod man rush in to help this guy to cover his tracks? Why would the New York Mob? Why these two-bit Balkan hoodlums? Who was Birger Wallenberg? Why did the high and mighty tremble in his shadow? The smell he felt in the Vogelscheuche camp had grown exponentially. Fear and money were the catalyst, but how could a simple girl like Avxhiu be involved?

The Sigurimi Commandant had not forgotten his broken arm. He wanted to pluck that girl, which meant he did not know where they were holed up. Somebody in the Tirana Sigurimi would know, probably the Dajti faction. While Vorbsi droned on about the dire state of Albanian mines, a plan was forming at the back of his mind.

"Alright, my friend, you've been a great help. Let's call it a day. Say, Vorbsi, you wouldn't know any girls? Life should not be all work and no play."

"Mr. Cole want girl cheap?"

"Come to think of it, a colleague of mine stayed at the Dajti a while back. This guy boasted about a great kid over there, Rakipe or something."

"I know this girl, Rakipe Hallidri, the Kid. She is good. I can fix this girl for Mr. Cole, yes?"

"Can you bring her tonight?"

"It will cost. Everybody wants the Kid."

"A hundred dollars for one hour in my room; fifty for you if you bring her soon." He knew this was big money.

"I go at once. It is still early."

Vorbsi disappeared down the darkened stairwell at full sprint. He was back within the hour, knocking. He was not alone. Crane sent him away clutching his take. When he turned, the child was already out of her jeans.

"I just want to talk to you, honey."

She grimaced with a flash of anger. This was not the first time she had been tricked.

"Engel Vorbsi say fuck one hour, hundred dollars."

"I want to talk, Rakipe, for one hour. Here you are, your hundred dollars."

The Kid looked doubtfully at the trousers on the chair, then back at him. He suspected that her English was no good for talking. In the light from the oil lamp, after some hesitation, she started to put her jeans back on.

He watched her, another misused child. Tonight, he would misuse her some more. It was the way of the world.

Chapter 20

"I WANT TO TALK to you about your two friends Shequere Avxhiu and Birger Wallenberg."

The girl froze, one leg caught in the trousers. Crane relaxed. He would not put it past Vorbsi to shaft him with a false kid.

"I know you are a close friend of those two. I want to help them, but nobody will tell me where they are hiding." He watched her light a cigarette and glance at him, pulling a bored face, hands nervously hedging.

"Who is Wallenbergi?"

"A foreigner, very rich, very powerful."

"No fuck this man." He made no move to correct her.

"You and Shequere were childhood friends!"

"No longer friend!"

There was no reason for her to trust him. He had no time to win her over. The Kid was the only one Avxhiu trusted besides her brother. She told him that.

"Listen, Rakipe, the Sigurimi would love to get their hands on me. I am the one who broke the commandant's arm."

It was just as well. With his career in ruins, he had this one shot. He was out on a limb like never before.

The child took a deep drag of the lipstick-stained cigarette and flipped ashes on the floor. He pushed his point.

"The Sigurimi would love to get their hands on me. My guess is that they would torture me first and leave me for dead as a mugging victim. They are good at that." He sipped the bourbon. His eyes read her resisting him with a bored face, not too forcefully.

"Don't get the idea of reporting me to the Sigurimi, honey. That is not the easy way out for you, Rakipe. I have documents. I'll say you helped Wallenberg and Shequere. They will not forgive a traitor in their organization."

"You lie. Rakipe no hide Wallenbergi!"

Her voice had a note of resignation. She was trapped. Well, at least she would not run from the room shouting rape. Did she know a real spy when she saw one? Was she a good judge of character? She would know that he'd sacrifice her without a second thought. He wondered if he would.

"If you tell me where they are hiding, I'll burn the papers and never mention you again."

"I don't know. Sigurimi no tell!"

"But do they know?"

"Maybe." She raised her thin shoulders and made a face and threw herself backwards on the bed.

"Buy me a drink, handsome?"

"You're not old enough."

"I fuck. You pay nothing."

"The Sigurimi at the Dajti?" He watched her think and steal time by lighting another cigarette.

"Yes, he know."

"Got a name for me?"

"No name."

"Is he a friend?"

"No," she leaned over and spat at the floor, "a pig."

"I want to question this man. He will never know who told me about him."

"He tortures girls. He'll know."

"He will not after I talk to him."

"Why?"

"Dead men don't torture girls."

She went still. He saw her think about this hard. She flipped ash from her cigarette and thought some more.

"You kill Sigurimi?"

"Give this guy to me, Rakipe. He will say his piece and then he will die."

"You break commandant arm?"

"Look Kid, life is like a hard-on; if you got nowhere to put it, you take matters into your own hands."

While she tried to figure that one out, she poked out the cig in the sardine can that served as hotel ashtray. This was a big foreign spy. For the first time she studied him openly. Decisions are heavy when your life hangs in the balance, but they come, even to a child.

"Okay, handsome."

Without any more hesitation she tried her best in broken English to tell him about the Sigurimi officer at the Dajti who liked to question young women. He would know if anybody did.

To calm her, Crane kept the setup simple. Out of his valise he pulled a sheaf of documents and sat at the desk to write a letter. He then gave her an envelope to give to the Sigurimi officer on her return to the Dajti. She was to tell him that a foreigner from the British Embassy had handed her the letter at the front desk to deliver to him in person. This would cause no suspicion. Complaints about the unstaffed Dajti desk were routine. Her juvenile ass was off the hook. And Rakipe Hallidri bought her ticket for freedom by setting up a guy who was milking her for all she was worth.

Inside the envelope, an unsigned note on Embassy stationary asked the pimp by name to meet the British charge d'affaires. He would be waiting outside the Tirana morgue as he read the letter, requiring advice on a delicate private matter of the greatest urgency. Do not to contact the embassy where every call is recorded! A boy that they both knew has died in a tragic accident.

Enclosed were ten fifty-pound notes.

The Embassy note delivered by the Kid simply implied the need to dispose of a body. Greedy people are malleable. A man of certain leanings would read into it that the official in charge of the British diplomatic mission had accidentally snuffed a boy. This opened new avenues of opportunity.

The area was industrial and abandoned. The lock on the morgue door was an easy pick in the dark. The electricity was off. It dawned on Crane that this was the one place in the city he frequented; the one nobody else tried to burgle. Inside, he lit a couple of oil lamps, and stepped outside to wait in the dark, valise in hand.

With nobody to run interference, he could cope with an extra driver at best; a favorable outcome depended on it.

He need not have worried. The effeminate Sigurimi pimp saw the chance of a lifetime and went for it without a lifeline. As the right man to talk to, he came alone. His reward would be a permanent visa or even citizenship. There would be fringe benefits. Until that moment, nobody had ever thought of Burton Crane as a fringe benefit.

The half-open door to the morgue cellar signaled of presence. The warm light beckoned the visitor. Crane lent forward, using his best Oxford clip to address the flighty figure that arrived, shadows obscuring his face, the leather valise making it official.

"Please excuse this intrusion, sir. I know this is unforgivable but there has been an unfortunate accident. Our charge d'affaires is waiting inside, in quite some distress. He would be very grateful for your advice on a delicate personal matter."

"Yes, all right, who are you?"

"Thaddeus McBride, a close friend, sir. Please, if you would be so kind."

And eagerly, the head of the Dajti Sigurimi descended the steps through the heavy wooden door into the underworld where Hades the son of Zeus reigns over the dead.

And behind him stepped Hermes to collect a coin of truth as his reward for taking a man across the river that no mortal crosses twice.

Chapter 21

AVXHIU GOT HER FIRST glimpse of the famous villa as they came around a bend in the country road. The Horxha house huddled on a small island of trees that provided shade. The sole point of access to the fenced-off fields was a wire-strung metal gate that blocked the road. They slowed to a stop, and she got off to push it open.

Avxhiu was excited. This was like a wild dream. Closing the gate, she jumped up on the comfortable seat. Slowly, they sidled up a long strip of asphalt through the fields towards the main house. The men came out to meet them from a separate building, the servant's quarters, Italians, she guessed. They looked closely at Wallenbergi as they passed. Not a word was spoken. They had expected this arrival.

"Wallenbergi men, yes please?"

He shook his head, impressing on her to keep out of his business. As they entered the unlocked house, she clung to him with one hand, and the leather satchel with the other. He walked her through the villa. In a large room with a bed made up with clean linen, he opened a clothing cabinet with big mirrors on the doors to check clothing on wire hangers. Avxhiu stood in the background, keeping her wits about her, careful not to touch anything. She had just seen herself life-size for the first time. The Albanian girl in the mirror looked downbeat and dirty.

"Wallenbergi clothes, yes?"

"My sizes it seems, not my taste."

Was that an answer? There were dresses in the next cabinet. He hardly noticed, but closed the mirrored door, shutting off the sudden intimation of another woman. The presence of women clothes put Avxhiu instantly on edge. She dared not ask. Could there be another woman?

"Come", he said, "we both need a shower."

In a large, tiled room with glistening taps, Wallenberg turned on the water and let it run while he threw his clothes in a basket. He should not let the water run if he was not using it. She turned away to stand in the hall with flaming cheeks. She could not help peeking. Entering the shower, he used shampoo from a bottle on the shelf. She wondered whose it was. When he found nowhere to place it, she came and held it for him. And why not, they were almost lovers in the hills. It was apple shampoo, the same as hers from the Dajti. Then she tried the water with her hand and was startled that it was warm. This was an astounding luxury. The Kid had told her of warm water in taps at the Dajti. She had dismissed it as a tall tale.

Wallenbergi was taking too long. He would empty the tank and leave her nothing. Finally, he stepped away and the water kept coming, and she quickly conquered her shyness, slipped out of her dirty cotton dress, and jumped under the pleasant water. It was like a dream. She pointed at the apple shampoo, "Good shampoo, yes please?" Wallenbergi dispensed almost the rest of it into her cupped hands, and she screamed out in delight laced with fear. The opulence was scary but delicious. He watched her shamelessly. She pretended not to notice that his body betrayed his insistence on refusing her.

"Avxhiu first time hot shower, yes please," she explained.

Wallenbergi moved his hand in under the water to adjust a circular knob. The water became warmer. It was like magic. Afterwards he brought her a large fluffy towel, and she savored the feeling. Throwing the dirty cotton dress into the plastic basket on top of his own, he handed her a white bathrobe to wear. She had never worn anything remotely as expensive. Wallenberg continued to walk about naked.

He led her into a bedroom. Spotting him across the room in the large mirror, Avxhiu burst out laughing at his erection, then saw herself and almost choked. In the long white robe, she looked stunning and foreign. She let herself tumble into bed, relishing its softness, like snuggling on a cloud. Joining her, he kept his distance. Shyly she moved closer and blew upon the moderate body hair on his chest and under his arms.

"Your hair is so light, yes please." But there was apparently no mending the broken trust. Wallenbergi seemed unusually withdrawn.

He presented her with the dresses she had seen in the cabinet earlier. She slipped out of bed to parade in front of the large mirrors, playing to him in an unashamed display of sexuality. Judging by his smile, he took pleasure from watching her, but other than that, he would have none of it.

"You rest here while I find something to eat."

"Guards have food, yes, take money," she had taken great care to keep the valise within reach. He laughed and shook his head.

She expected him to be gone for a while and return with slim pickings. Apparently, the Hoxha kitchen was well stocked. He had made an omelet with fresh champions in butter, and he brought cheeses and fresh bread with Italian red wine. Avxhiu could not believe her eyes when he brought the overloaded tray. She realized that she would never understand a man who walked around naked in a striped apron.

The stillness of the countryside crowned the moment in her mind. She took a swallow of wine from a long-stemmed glass, like the one Mayer dropped on the floor when he died the first time. She offered her new foreigner a warm smile across their barren bed of plenty.

It was a troubled little smile. In her mind, Heimdallr knew why, and Birger Wallenberg smiled back at her.

Chapter 22

THE NEXT MORNING, BURTON Crane let the taxi driver take him for a ride that lasted hours and brought them to the black cinders of a burned-out barn.

There were large-caliber shells in droves by the track, and he slipped one into his pocket when the driver was looking elsewhere. Everything he did openly would find its way back to the Sigurimi.

His cover as a reporter was wearing thin.

Crane walked back to Engel Vorbsi and his green Toyota, pondering his options. As the diligent reporter he pretended to be, collecting atmosphere, he jotted down the letters scratched on the hood of the taxi: JA QIFSKA NANON.

The boiling Toyota rocked them slowly towards the main road with all its windows open.

"A friend of mine is staying in Hoxha's summerhouse, somewhere east of here. Do you know it?"

The driver's face lit up. In a land of pedestrians, Vorbsi was a willing driver. It was an honorable occupation.

"Yes, in valley on the way to Berat, maybe one hour."

"Alright, let's pay the guy a visit."

Crane closed his eyes. He was not in this country to uphold the law. Last night, a crying man had revealed the Horxha hideout. That was before he made the mistake of his life by implicating himself in the murder of a foreign spy. Ordering the killing of his agent Konrad was a step too far.

Now the guy rested under four stacks of frozen corpses. His presence was sure to raise an eyebrow or two, if there ever came that spring-cleaning. It was not easy to tear naked carcasses of both sexes from unyielding embraces, and to lay between them a soft warm newcomer. It would be the first time the Sigurimi pimp found himself in the company of more cold-blooded people.

And, as always, he would adjust.

A low iron gate blocked the road. Crane got out and pushed it open, studying the villa in the distance. He had noted that there was no wire between the telephone poles by the road up the hill. It was common knowledge that Sigurimi entrepreneurs were hawking miles of copper wire on the black market, with more available if needed. With no working telephones, incommunicado in this remote country house seemed to him a terrible choice for a strategic hide-out, and with the Sigurimi factions at each other's throats, the use of curriers was unsafe.

As the taxi idled on, a handful of armed guards with shotguns sidled down the sloping fields on both sides of the road. The car rolled to a stop, and they stepped out. Vorbsi was first to address the guards. Although this had been the house of Horxha, the driver was unsure on whose land they were trespassing. The men spoke no Albanian.

"I have come to see Birger Wallenberg", Crane interjected. The English worked well enough, and a glance told Crane to keep the Sigurimi turncoat on a short leash from now on. Vorbsi had realized what this was about. After frisking them and looking minutely through his valise, they led him up the asphalt path where the ground rose gently to a fringe of trees.

Left in the company of two sharp-eyed Italians, Vorbsi was not about to argue. He was just the taxi driver. A small compact Italian with a shotgun took Crane up to the house and knocked on the door. Together, they scrutinized the new Harley Davidson motorcycle out front, as they waited.

Birger Wallenberg was wearing a towel. Behind him in bare feet and a bathrobe stood the girl he had rescued from the Sigurimi weeks earlier in Tirana. Perhaps they had been having a kip, as the wife would say. Wallenberg waved him to enter, and the girl vanished.

"Come in, Burton. I've been expecting you."

Without ceremony he threw off the towel to stalk in front of him naked, same as his colleague the baron. Crane wondered what the matter was with these guys, recalling Baron Keltenbrunner.

"Can I tempt you with a glass of cool vine?"

The room opened out on a terracotta terrace. The girl was back in a fresh dress, moving to her master's voice to pour him white wine from a frosty pitcher. In that soccer stadium in Tirana, she had been dirty, and her dress soiled. Even then he had noticed her beauty. Now it was startling.

He had saved her life, but she feared him. He figured it had slipped her mind to tell this guy that she had been in bed with his mom's murderer. Crane accepted the cool glass gratefully. He looked at the paintings on the walls.

They were surrounded by workers raising the flag. There was nothing of value here. The post-impressionist originals that Horxha had been so fond of had been spirited abroad in diplomatic bags and sold by shady dealers with Swiss passports. He turned to Wallenberg who was lounging in a large Chinese chair, apparently without any interest in his visit.

"Hope you don't mind me speaking frankly, son. You got me stumped. You are the image of a sensible upright man. Given a reputation for hedonistic pursuits in med-school, with a fortune that has every blue-blooded nubile watering her raspberry bush, why hide in a crummy safe house in the Albanian countryside?

"I am happy to see you, Burton. You were my voice of reason for a while, but I have all I need here."

"After your mother's death," Crane winked at the girl, "I had the agencies check for press clippings on you. It was a lousy harvest for a billionaire tycoon, and the same goes for every major owner of the Midgard Group."

The girl must have worked out the mother bit. He saw her recoil from the connection and make herself small on the sofa. The girl was playing this guy for all he was worth, and that was plenty.

"The low-key image cultivated by your partners, the likes of Doctor Leamas and Baron Keltenbrunner. The three of you own half of Europe between you; and half of Asia on top of that. The gutter press should be making a meal of you guys, but there's barely a word. That takes skill and considerable effort."

"And your point is?"

"That is what people have been asking me. All I have is a handful of influential people, given to irrational behavior, doling out money to strangers. I am told that they are eccentric; that there is no hidden agenda. My grievance is that when it comes to national security, my superiors seem happy to ignore when you yank their chain."

"What do you want to know?"

"What is Heimdallr?"

"Heimdallr is the last god to perish at Ragnarök. He is what religious scholars call a frame god, one who exists at the beginning and is active to the end. In between, he works untiringly to guide his kinsmen though life.

"I did not mean Old Norse religion."

"The definition comes long before that in the Bible: I am the Alpha and the Omega, the beginning and the end. You must understand, Burton, that religion is an attempt to understand reality. The Viking interpretation is another in a long list of trials and errors. Midgard is the old Germanic name for a world inhabited by humans. The myths tell of all life being destroyed at Ragnarök when Jormungandr poisons land and sea with venom, causing the sea to rear up and lash against the land, with the Earth sinking into the sea."

"You should be on the United Nations Climate Panel."

To have his humor met by silence was not altogether rare.

"Look, Birger, whichever way I parse the data, it makes no sense. I was hoping to learn; what is Heimdallr today?"

"I know of no Heimdallr but this prehistoric god".

"A secret American national intelligence organization by the same name does not ring any bells?"

"Let me put it this way, in whatever measure I and you follow orders from above, they come from the Commander in Chief."

"I suspected as much. Thank you for clearing that up."

With a wineglass fogged over from cold liquid, and a blank expression, Wallenberg studied the ochre fields. Crane took a deep swig and continued.

"Look, son, thank you for making it clear to me that Heimdallr is at the heart of my government, that his orders come from inside the administration."

"But I really need to tell you that hiding out here in this godforsaken place is not any safe haven. I am here; somebody told me where to find you."

"That's because you were desperate, Thaddeus."

Crane felt the blood drop from his face. It was unthinkable. Nobody knew the name he whispered on the spur of a moment, outside the morgue last night.

"Take my advice Burton, as a friend. The surveillance of Heimdallr is more advanced and more secret than you can imagine. For example, the Sigurimi is now waiting for Douglas Cole at the Hotel Europe. Without my protection, you will not get out of Albania alive."

Crane could not bring himself to ask. It was humiliating. Looking at the girl, he forced a meaningless reply and hated it.

"I can blow my own nose, thank you."

He could tell the you man a couple of secrets that would get up his nose. He would be unaware that Avxhiu Shequere had rolled in the sack with Helmut Mayer, the German who killed his mother. The girl had clearly guessed his game, and he hesitated in her terrified gaze.

The voice that rang out in his head was immediate.

"Don't go there, Crane. Accept unreservedly that you can tell me nothing that I don't already know. Special agent Hugh Miller was being a friend when he told you not to dance with the devil."

Crane stopped short. This was impossible. This was beyond the scope. This was Heimdallr showing its teeth again.

Wallenberg studied the sunburned fields across the terracotta terrace, "all your secrets are safe with me; Burton." The young man smiled at him without speaking, and then spoke up, as if nothing had happened.

"I will be leaving here shortly Burton. I have been away from Asgard Park too long. Let me give you a ride.

"Thank you, but come to think of it, do not rely on Baron Keltenbrunner's biker gang to save your ass. The Sigurimi has secured every exit out of the country, and if Baron Keltenbrunner sends in a chopper, they will simply shoot it out of the air. NATO has been supplying the Albanians with defensive weapons."

"I know you don't like the Baron. He has no patience with people who do not follow orders. Whatever you may think, Burton, he is not your enemy. Both of you serve the same organization. Find some way to make the STASI file useful to your carrier."

"We never found that file."

"Fair enough, but there is a letter with the dossier waiting for you in Schoolbell Mews. I'm sure you can make it work for you."

Book 4, Heimdallr

Chapter 23

A DAY HAD PASSED. Avxhiu felt empty. The numbness did not loosen its grip. She did not trust the NATO spy who came in her brother's car. The car had been impounded by the Sigurimi to be used as a taxi for their informers. She slipped out to make sure that the curse the vandals had scratched into the matted green paint was still there. She wanted to plead for the car but thought better of it.

Wallenbergi seemed more stable, more serene. He had told the NATO spy to stay in his room while they waited for their escort. She knew that no armed escort could get them out of the country. They were trapped deep in the Sigurimi maze.

She watched him stand half naked in his shorts on the veranda, looking out over the fields. The Italians always made the cross: they were guarding a madman. He had been studying a few grazing cows in the distance. There was a sound in the distance.

A courier in a light blue parka and police cap arrived on a motorcycle. The guards brought Wallenbergi a large envelope. He spilled its contents on the dining table. There were two Swedish passports. Casually he handed her one. Her hand trembled. It was the first time in her life she held one. She stared at the picture, dumbfounded. It came from the card Emir had submitted to the Sigurimi when she started her work at the photo studio, except this photo was in color. How was that possible? How was her signature possible; Shequere Avxhiu; a Swedish citizen.

She sat on the sofa and cried, staring through the tears, for once allowing self-pity to engulf her. It was a luxury to let down your guard. Nonetheless, after days of lavish comfort, she felt the familiar tongues of fear. Nothing had changed, and the Sigurimi neither forgot nor forgave.

The nausea overcame her. She threw the passport on the table to run out on the veranda. To vomit by the wall the side. Wallenbergi came to stand by her, this time fully dressed, his hand supporting her forehead. It felt like the end. Avxhiu dried her mouth and wiped her hand on her dress. Her dress would smell, but there was no room for sober thoughts. Foreigners could not understand. She knew how the Sigurimi operated. Eighteen years taught you that. There would be passport controls. The checks would continue until the game was up. Avxhiu wrung her hands to wash from them her penance.

Suddenly, there was a sudden enormous roar that felled her terrified to her knees against the wall.

Burton Crane came running out on the terrace, looking after the two F-15C Eagles that had steaked overhead at low height.

"What the hell is this. What is NATO doing here."

They skyline to the east, to the west, to the south and to the north, seemed to gradually darken as immense fleets of helicopters swept in across the valley. Some were landing to disgorge soldiers into defensive positions, blocking roads to the valley. Several transport aircraft crossed the horizon.

Wallenberg smiled, "You had not heard? They gave the go-ahead for the planned joint NATO exercises. Lots of countries participating, well, mainly the closest; Italy, Greece, Turkey, Spain, and France.

"They shelved the exercises. The Albanian were no living up to their promises. They'll give us a ride out of here. I'll go and contact them."

"They got their orders days ago. It takes time to put on joint operations. You must understand that NATO is here to escort us out."

"Heimdallr?"

"You are beginning to understand. That is good. I need a floater."

"A floater?"

"A roving troubleshooter, as you explained to Dr Kirkpatrick in New York."

"You are a scary man!"

"I am only a conduit of a name you must not take in wain! You know too much, so I must take you aboard in some capacity."

"Not a ringing endorsement, but fine. Who's leading this exercise?"

"31 Fighter Wing, Aviano Airforce Base, Italy."

"The Wolf Pack."

Their conversation was drowned out as a massive airplane suddenly sunk vertically out of the sky above them towards the ground a few hundred feet below the sloping ground, its engines pointing upwards, the downstream lambasting the dancing grass on the hard ground.

Avxhiu had come over to cling to Wallenberg's arm.

"That's what I call an airplane," Crane shouted at the top of his lungs, "the V-22 Osprey." His interest was genuine, "I was told it was years from general service"

"They are testing it for special operations."

An Air Force Officer walk up the slope in combat fatigues, turning to Birger, as if they had met before.

"Your jet is waiting at Corfu airport, sir. You folks ready?"

"Yes, thank you, officer."

"We'll have you in Greece in eighteen minutes. Ignore the armed escort. The protection is part of the exercise.

"I'll be damned," said Burton Crane.

Avxhiu did not let go of Wallenberg's arm or soften her grip as he followed the soldier down towards the airplane. She was thoroughly confused. Could these soldiers be here without the consent of the Sigurimi? Guards stood with machine-guns on either side of the door into that strange windowless plane. The Sigurimi at Shqiperi airport had armed soldiers line up on either side of departing passengers because desperate people often tried to steal in among the passengers. Her every step became an exercise in determination, waiting for them to pounce.

As they approached the airplane, its size would have scared her if there had been place for that extra burden. Would they be checking papers? She clutched her new passport.

A friendly young woman with golden hair in army uniform, smiled at her and said hello. She was already inside that iron bird. It was he first rational thought.

"I want you to sit up front behind the pilots. It is so claustrophobic back here," said the golden-haired girl.

What struck her, was that the air was cool and comfortable. She breathed deeply, and broke a small private smile, as she sat down. At least she had breathed foreign air. She wanted to tell Wallenberg the joke, but young woman was back to snap a belt to constrain her, and an unexpected movement froze her. Had the time come? The immense plane fell upwards, pushing her back into her chair. In panic she squeezed the arm beside her tighter.

Her seat was like a hand that held her, quickening with unbounded reserves of power. She felt tiny in its roar, a straw in its raging wind, and she recognized the feeling: her night with Helmut Mayer.

For the first time since they entered the airplane, Shequere Avxhiu let go of Wallenbergi's arm.

Knowing why, Heimdallr smiled at her.

"They cannot touch you, Shequere, this is a US Airforce aircraft!"

Book 4, Heimdallr

Chapter 24

OUT THE WINDOW SHE saw the Hoxha's summerhouse fall away from her. She saw the Italian guards and grazing cows drop away like stones in water. Her mind reached a blinding acceptance. She was free.

It came slowly. She started to shake. She could not help it. Gently she touched her belly. She was carrying Mayer's child. That is why she had missed her period; that was the nausea every morning. Her mother had been like that. The emotions crashed over her in debilitating waves. She had no chance to soften them or sort them out. She leaned back and let it ripple through her body. Tears streaked her chin; not that she was crying; she was free.

A few minutes later, Wallenberg pointed at a vast shimmering surface below them.

"Look, Shequere: the Adriatic." And in some wonderful way, the sight of all that water closed the canals of her eyes.

Wallenberg smiled to himself. Once again, Heimdallr, on the bridge of Bifröst, stood ready to guard the designs of his masters; his mission to protect and nurture intelligent design. It was not at all what he had envisioned it to be. For the first time in months, he felt whole. His person was intact. The god was a separate system. It did not interrupt or take over his personality. Its depth of knowledge was phenomenal: it gave access to stunning information in real-time. His task was to tend a hidden empire, to pass his untraceable orders.

The Asgard Park Institute had a new director at the helm.

It had been a joy to spend time with this beautiful girl. She would never know that in her presence, a new watchman had been chosen to settle social order among humans. Thor, the trespassing designer who entered Mayer by the old back door of his default program, could never keep its hands off a lovely creature, male or female. When the god found Avxhiu to play with, his revenge for the beastly murder of Catarine Wallenberg got sidetracked for a day.

The following morning, they sipped coffee outside a bistro in sunny Paris. Wallenberg studied her transformation. The designer clothes and the gold watch on her wrist seemed to diminish her peasant beauty. It was not that her slender fingers were a touch too red, or her knuckles a trifle marked by work. The reason was that the girl was missing her natural self-assurance, the mandatory accessory of a well-bred woman. She would need time to grow into her costume, to wear it as if it were her birthright.

The girl would grasp what happened this summer in human terms. Her child would be under his protection, but she would not know that. Shequere would get guidance, but the future remained in her hands. The chosen ones were protected until they came of age; no more, and no less.

On reaching the age of eighteen, the children would stand on their own.

"Listen carefully, Avxhiu; I will honor Mayer promise to arrange a home for you, an apartment, a short walk from here, in the Latin Quarter. You will learn French. It is not easy, so we will start you off with private tutors. You like to draw, and there are schools for that. It suits your sensitive temperament."

The tears came. It was clear to him why.

She thought she had a secret. In her mind, her hope of a place in the shade was slipping away. Why did it have to happen to her, why this punishment? The secret would come between them. The girl felt the wet weakness on her face and pounded her knee to regain control. Wallenberg knew she could take any hardship; she was an expert, but the dam had cracked. this was too much. The past reached out to pluck her from the pedestal. They would send her back as her state became self-evident. Avxhiu fought to become the master of her bitter house.

"What is the matter?" He asked for the sake of form.

"Avxhiu have baby, yes please; Mayer baby."

It was said, she had come clean. He could do with her what he wanted. She braced herself to look, turning to meet his eyes in angry defiance. Wallenberg eyes met hers with the mellow look of a father appraising a favorite child. He felt how it stunned her. His eyes carried mercy to the condemned. The truth had lost her nothing. It had gained her everything.

"Your child will want for nothing," he told her with finality. "You will have the best guidance in its upbringing and education."

"Yes, please!"

"One more thing, young woman: for political reasons you are never to mention anything that happened this summer in Albania. Not a word must be spoken of what Mayer told you. You must never tell anyone about me. This here", he indicated the Paris scene around them, "will be your life. The past must remain our secret forever. A loose tongue will cost you the right to stay in the West."

He recognized in her mind that political reasons and survival were easily within her grasp.

"Avxhiu promise this, yes."

"Paris will suit you. I shall arrange a nanny who speaks perfect French. It is a beautiful language."

"A nanny, yes please." She knew this word from her books.

"Would you like me to arrange for your friend, Rakipe Hallidri, to stay with you in Paris?"

Again, she was moved to tears, this time meekly and without resistance.

"Wallenbergi can do this?"

"On one condition: that you keep the Kid off the streets and out of trouble. There are too many foreigners in Paris, and neither of you will want for money."

Shequere Avxhiu looked at him coyly, flushing red through the smudged tears.

"Okay, no more fuck foreigners."

"And never discuss me or what we went through with Rakipe."

Wallenberg brought her hand to his lips and gave her a kind farewell kiss. The slender fingers smelled vaguely of puke.

Book 4, Heimdallr

Chapter 25

BACK IN LONDON, BURTON Crane had spring in his step as he crossed Lambeth Bridge to Century House. In mid-August, the air was autumn crisp. The music of the flute floated on the breeze: a royal tune with an Irish flavor recalled British orders, a part of old England that no longer was.

Sidney had no idea what Crane was bringing to this meeting. Wallenberg had been right on the money. The STASI file had been waiting on his kitchen table in Schoolbell Mews in a Deutsche Post envelope with second class postage. The nerve of these guys, he thought.

Burned by the debacle, Sidney had been saddled with a chaperon from above. He was a colonel who Crane had met in Wiesbaden but had never got a handle on who was his daddy. Both left it to Sidney to sort out the muddle.

"You are a hard man to handle, Crane. It was reckless of me to allow your Albanian fishing expedition. I rather hoped you would take advice and wait for Central Command. I hear you went down there and left an almighty mess."

"What mess would that be?"

"There are rumors that you killed a Sigurimi Colonel in Tirana and stashed his body in a morgue."

"I can't say I'm proud of it."

Sidney lowered his pen in genuine surprise. "It's true? You realize that this means the end of your career?"

"That's the tricky bit, Sidney, knowing how far you can go to protect the realm."

"Crane, the STASI file you lost in Berlin was all the protection we coveted, not a drunken binge in Tirana."

"Thanks for holding your hand over me, old top. I had to know what Mayer was doing down there."

"Yes, well, I am a soft touch for old hands."

Crane studied the Colonel who studied the Thames.

"My doubts about Dr Birger Wallenberg did not pan out. This is a wealthy young man. It beats me, but if working as psychiatrist in a forgotten funny farm is his calling, who am I to question that."

"That is something, I guess." Sydney looked affably at Crane, and then the colonel. "We were wondering."

"This being a confession, I must admit that my suspicions about Baron Keltenbrunner have been alleviated, aside from his rudeness."

An inner calm had settled on the Colonel from above. He swiveled his chair towards Westminster.

Crane had not bothered to move his Gibraltar and Guernsey accounts. Heimdallr would know the numbers before he did. He opened the old leather briefcase, and placed a cardboard covered dossier neatly on Sidney's blameless desk.

"And this is?" asked Sidney with a different wonder as he reached for it with a well-manicured hand.

"The STASI file you sent me for, old top."

"You recovered the file in Albania?"

"Yes, Helmut Mayer had the dossier with him. After he got himself killed, his stuff remained with a widow he befriended in Tirana. She passed it to a prostitute for safe keeping. The girls had no idea what it was. They were happy to sell it for a few dollars. The Sigurimi Colonel from the Hotel Dajti was trying to retrieve the dossier. I'm guessing his friends behind the iron curtain wanted a peek. I met him at that Tirana morgue, and I thought you'd like to read it first."

The story would not withstand scrutiny, but the cracks would not show unless somebody started to dig in the muck. With the dossier in hand, it all became an accident in the line of duty. It was in nobody's interest to set up an investigation to sort it out. All things considered, he found this to be a sturdy stalemate.

"How extraordinary," Sidney flipped through the folder with a proud look, "our idea paid off. Jolly nice!"

They had him wait out in the hallway while they decided his fate. The place was all abuzz over an impending Soviet coup. General Kalinin had declared a curfew in Moscow. Crane watched folks run around with coded telexes left and right.

When they let him back into the meeting; his conciliatory attitude proved rewarding. He was forgiven. In this business, there was no point in asking for a golden parachute. The best you could hope for was one that opened.

Afterwards, the Colonel took him aside for a private chat.

"Tell me Burton, what is the definition of a floater?"

"A roving troubleshooter, I believe, sir."

"Thank you. Central Command is setting up a covert high-level taskforce. A little bird told me that you might be interested to serve."

Someone up there was smiling. "Any conditions for me?"

"Generally, enough to fill a book, all top secret, but I'm told that you have gone through all of that. The only reserve would be your acceptance."

Crane nodded assent.

Instead of being barred from that amazing operation, he had his foot in the door. If they needed an operator with hands on expertise, he would lay down his life for Heimdallr. His amazing judgement calls could be trusted.

Back in his empty bungalow, with Evelyn off working, the TV confirmed a Soviet coup. Crane poured a stiff shot of bourbon and lounged in a favorite chair to follow the news. Gorbachev had been cut off by the plotters in his Crimean dacha. Now he denounced them on television. The Evil Empire was tumbling down on their red asses.

What a whistler of a summer.

EPILOGUE

FROM A WINDOW HIGH up in the Asgard Park Institute for the Criminally Insane, Birger Wallenberg looked out over the morning meadows. Autumn was in residence with winter on its breath.

He thought about the bygone summer.

To the rational mind, nothing in that colorful tapestry showed the secret thread that held together the fabric. That is how it should be. Insanity is part of nature, a glitch in the system. How the rich spend their fortunes, or evil people earn their living, exempts none from the laws of nature.

A delivery van was parking on the gravel drive in front of the Victorian building. The delivery man hoisted a box of newly baked bread to his shoulder and gazed upwards upon the edifice.

Through the youngster's eyes, Wallenberg saw himself; a naked man at a window high up, balancing an open Bible on his head. He turned the young man's neck to smell the warm bread on his shoulder.

Wasn't this a wonderful world?

The youngster in his mind smiled and praised the Lord, thankful that the criminally insane were locked up behind these sturdy walls.

How could a young man know? How could anyone know?

That since the beginning of life, through the faltering steps of intelligent design and partial enlightenment, one entity has tirelessly watched our progress.

Always awake, listening to every thought, and every prayer; alert enough to hear grass grow and a single leaf fall.

Heimdallr.

'Say to those with fearful hearts; be strong, do not fear; your God will come, he will come with vengeance; with divine retribution he will come to save you.'

The Bible